THE LAST THIEF

LEE
LAMOTHE

THE LAST THIEF

ECW PRESS

Published by ECW PRESS
2120 Queen Street East, Suite 200, Toronto, Ontario, Canada M4E 1E2

NATIONAL LIBRARY OF CANADA CATALOGUING IN PUBLICATION DATA

Lamothe, Lee, 1948–
The last thief / Lee Lamothe.

ISBN 1-55022-599-5

I. Title.

PS8573.A42478L38 2003 C813'.6 C2003-902182-3
PR9199.4.L357L38 2003

Acquisition editor: Robert Lecker
Copy editor: Stuart Ross
Design and typesetting: Yolande Martel
Production: Emma McKay
Printing: Transcontinental
Cover design: Paul Hodgson
Cover painting: Janine White

This book is set in Minion and Argo

The publication of *The Last Thief* has been generously supported by the Canada Council, by the Government of Ontario through the Ontario Media Development Corporation's Ontario Book Initiative, by the Ontario Arts Council, and by the Government of Canada through the Book Publishing Industry Development Program. Canada

DISTRIBUTION

CANADA: Jaguar Book Group, 100 Armstrong Avenue,
Georgetown, Ontario L7G 5S4

PRINTED AND BOUND IN CANADA

ECW PRESS
ecwpress.com

For Rob Benzie, Rhonda McMichael, and Ella;
and as always Lucy White, Katy, and Michelle

"But those aren't thieves!" the connoisseurs among us explain. "These are the *bitches* — the ones who work for the prison. They are the enemies of honest thieves. The honest thieves are the ones imprisoned in their cells."

— Aleksandr I. Solzhenitsyn, *The Gulag Archipelago, Volume One, 1918-1956*

"One must suppose," he said slowly, pausing after each word, "one must suppose that there's a spark of the divine fire in you."

— Isaac Babel, *Awakening*

PART ONE

Chapter 1

ON THE DAY the weeping poet was assigned to the Thieves' barracks, Bone, in the sea of timber encasing the camp north of Irkutsk, was presiding over a circle of five inmates who approached his status. The *skhodka* was convened in a clearing full of fractured Siberian sunlight, flattened wild grass, and bright ax-cut tree stumps to adjudge punishment for a violation, the miscreant having gambled his eye on a hand of cards, and the hand of cards having been thrown down against him. He had refused to pay his debt, claiming drunkenly and loudly he'd been cheated by the dealer, a criminal of status, a *vor*. And when confronted by the dealer, the miscreant slapped him in the face. Then he soaked himself more thoroughly in wood alcohol until his mouth spoke secrets too close to the ears of the guards. The judgment was foregone.

The miscreant, now sobering and aware that the penalty was beyond the mere loss of an eye, offered to surrender the eye, even both eyes, if all would be forgiven. But Bone adjudged that while that would level the violation of barracks law — that bets lost must lead to debts paid — the accusation of cheating, the slapping of the dealer's face, and the consequent indiscretions within earshot of the guards were all violations of the *zakone*, the Code of the Thieves that governed their *mir*, their world.

The Code, the shuddering Bone quietly told the circle of princes and the miscreant, governs all. "This *zakone* guides our every step, our every breath. It bids us to train and guide young Thieves, to be married only to our Code, to provide aid in harsh times and make laughter in good. It raises a few to status, and that status is a protection, a shield from that world outside of us. If within, we have misbehavior against one of status, we have no Code, no protection.

"Fifty years ago the Code changed. Imprisoned Thieves were offered an illusion of freedom if they wore the uniform of the country, fought at the battlefront to repel the Germans. This is history, our history. Many went and many died. Those who survived were free, but soon returned to the camps for new offenses. A Thief is, after all, a Thief and must steal. And when they returned there was another war in our world, the Bitches War. True Thieves and the Bitches — the *suki* — settled this violation, and after thousands had died throughout the camps, the true Thieves lost, among them my father, who stood his sentence and died for it. The pure Code was changed and we have now a Code that contains an impurity, as a woman in pads. But we must live by it. It is only in the Code that we are free, whether we are inside the wire or outside. We are in history, each of us. We may leave this *mir* and walk alone, but we must walk alone with the Code.

"This, today, is a violation. What, after all, is an eye? What is there to see? These eyes don't look inward where we live, they look outward to where we die. A Thief looks with the eyes of his soul. This one," Bone said, nodding at the miscreant, "this one says he will pay double for his violation of the barracks law? Fine, this is just. But there's a larger violation here that must be dealt with. Is it worth his life? A worthless life? What is the value of that thing? But, then, what of the Code, our precious *zakone* that governs our conduct, our relationships, our love? You —" again he looked down at the mesmerized miscreant "— what have you to say? What can we take that will right this violation?"

The man on the ground, a middle-aged, tattooed, slightly drunken Muscovite, stared up at the wide blue sky bleached by the remote Siberian sun. He believed he smelled the scat of the tiger, always roaming but never seen, only paw prints in the after-dawn, furious blood splashes and torn carcass. I believe in this tiger, he thought, although I've never seen it. It shits, it walks, it devours prisoners and leaves the wreckage of carrion. It is as the Code. He smiled at the lulling cadence of Bone's voice — I believe too in this man with the frozen heart that makes him vibrate with a chill — as though hearing the songs of mothers, and began singing in a high soft voice:

Around the Thieves the wires grow
My brothers: my home is in my heart!
To drink and sing and pass the deck!
My life will end to start.

"Sung well, thief and cheat," one of Bone's brigade laughed. "Sung fine and with the voice of an angel."

The man looked at the faces around him, impassive — not unfriendly faces floating above the frayed collars of ragged, padded gray prison tunics. "My brothers, my punishment is yours to give. I ask little, but let my body rise full, not emptied of its blood. My life in the *mir* has been without a scab, pure as the skin of the Mother. Please, take your price, but I beg you: jump high. Take my soul."

Bone looked at the miscreant with a sad and faded tenderness. He loved this rare fat inmate and regretted the man's wet tongue, he who loved potato juice in tin cups. "Then. This we shall do, my brother. You may keep your useless eyes, the better to see all as you pass on up. This debt is forfeit." He looked at a squat blond man known as Woodcutter. "Woodman, jump high."

Woodcutter handed Bone a dagger, a twelve-inch length of pitted, sharpened tin that had been folded and hammered and folded and hammered and set in a birch-bark handle. The miscreant basked in the compassion of his peers: he wouldn't be pricked at his arteries and bled dry, sent off with his life's fluids drained into the dirt of the loamy forest floor, his white body sent up as some pale shrunken thing so unlike the reality he'd become. And, he knew — the relief palpable on his face — he wouldn't be danced to death, jumped upon from the bottom up, first the ankles, then the knees, then the groin and abdomen, then the chest, and finally and mercifully the head. A death that could take hours, with the dancers pausing to drink and gamble and even take short naps before completing their duties.

Woodcutter leaned over and kissed the miscreant's rough cheek. "Don't be afraid, my friend. Where you go, we will soon come. You'll wait and we'll be above all this. You today, we tomorrow."

"To you, my friend, my love also." The miscreant inhaled deeply, his nostrils sucking in the essences of the forest and the hot sun. Where is that tiger? "Jump true, Wooden Penis."

"Yes, if you don't dance about and squeal like some Lithuanian whore with a prick up the ass."

The miscreant laughed. In the distance the men heard a truck roughly shift gears and grind along the road to the administration office. Birds swam through the sky, and a hundred yards away, the thawing stream that fed their camp burbled. His hands bound, the miscreant rolled over and smelled again the depth of the forest. Woodcutter lifted the man's head gently and positioned a hunk of wood under his chin, a pillow to sleep upon. Then he climbed onto a stump.

Woodcutter looked at Bone and raised his eyebrows.

"Fly, Wood Testicle," said Bone.

Both heels of Woodcutter's leather workboots came down solidly on the back of the miscreant's neck. A clear snapping of bone rang through the forest. Birds wheeled out of trees, spanning a brief but dense shadow across the sky, their wings aflutter and urgent.

For the remainder of the afternoon, the men sat over the miscreant's body, toasting him with wood vodka gulped from dull tin cups, telling Thieves' tales and singing Thieves' songs. The wheeling birds had silently returned and observed the men's laughing grief with curiosity.

Fyodor Sliva — Bone — carried a Russia in his heart, a Russia uncharted by books or political structures. It was a secret history that was broken into regimes of attrition led by men of whom few had ever heard — Tank, Silvest'r, Otari, and Tomay — instead of Kruschev, Brezhnev, Gorbachev, or Yeltsin. In Bone's *mir*, his world, histories weren't told in the transient coups of ideologies or political parties, heralded by tank fire, but were whispered into cupped palms in front of bowed heads and ears touched by lips, and subtly passed on, secrets that began on the breath and ended in the blood.

Bone's *mir* had no borders or frontiers — he carried his world within him. It was a barred and barren scape littered with what, to outsiders, were slicing, glittering dangers and constant uncertain shifts of gravity. Men of the Code negotiated this vast landscape with the absolute certainty of mountain goats, and often with the instinctive luck of a drunken clown falling down a hillside, laughing. All that mattered, all that had permanence, was the *zakone*: it was law, love, mantra; it was both a mirror and a window: all was reflected, all was seen.

This secret world was an eternal calendar of days that began with a hope that rose with the sun, and closed in the black nights full of hoarse shouts and broken glass, of shattered wooden doors and pursuing uniforms. If he went to sleep under the ledge of a Berlin subway station and awoke in a park in London, Bone would see no significant difference. His pulses would beat with the firm tenets of the Code. His lungs would fill with and empty of air until their expansions and contractions ceased; then it would be the end for him and the beginning for someone else.

He'd served his prison sentences enveloped in a dull, internal chill, with the certain and indifferent expectation of experiencing his death behind bars. Where younger apprentices of the *mir* counted out the days of sentences, sometimes even the hours, looking forward to mad feasts of orgasm, gluttony, violence, and chance, Bone's concept of freedom was to walk in warm sunlight and meditate upon his precious *zakone.* Inside the wire or out, it made no matter: he walked with a persistent cold inside him that no sunlight could penetrate.

His face was as a parsimonious monk's, skull-like, wide at the temples and pointed at the chin, and his sockets were receded pits; his eyes seemed to have retreated above the black hollows of his cheeks. A serrated white scar in the shape of half a tin-can lid bisected his left eye. A deep, perfectly straight, two-inch groove ran horizontally along the left side of his head, his short hair — dry-shaved monthly by a trustee using a straight razor and a cold bar of acrid soap — indenting like a wind trough on an arid prairie. His ears were sharply pointed and flat to the skin of his skull; his nose, straight and thin, had a Roman bump from a break. Growing around his wide thin mouth was a vague beard a little longer than the shallow dust on his head. His nine fingernails were scraped clean and cut back to the quick, and liver spots were forming on the backs of both hands. His exposed arms were thin and buffed hairless by decades of rough prison tunics, but the skin was stretched taut over a network of cabled tendons and long knotted muscle. He weighed twenty-five per cent more than when he had been a slim teenager, and his shoulders had thickened out, as had his waist and chest, giving him the fit but stocky torso of a circus performer.

The camp's administration office contained bulk files of his life, but his true history was on his body. There were nine characters tattooed on his fingers — one on each of the four fingers of the right hand, two each on the index and middle fingers of the left hand, and one on his remaining finger. The first joint of the pinkie finger of the left hand was absent, the digit ending in a bulbous callus seared by fire. He had no tattoos on his thumbs, but between the knuckles of the first two fingers of his right hand was a small, elaborate skull. On the back of his right hand was a faded blue screaming eagle, its talons exposed, and several Cyrillic characters written in a semicircle beneath it. In Russian the characters were an anagram for "In Life Count Only on Your Own." As clearly as the skull identified him as one who had killed — but never for money or profit — the eagle, and the fact that it was well-faded, gave his criminal ranking as clearly as gold on the shoulders of a military uniform identified a senior officer. Hidden by his shirt and tunic were a tattooed band of barbed wire encircling his left biceps and another series of Cyrillic characters too faded to discern. His back was adorned with a cathedral with five spires; the people in his *mir* who noted such things could read the spires as accurately as if they were printed in script: five trips to the frontier. Five sentences to the gulag. Above his chest but under the collarbones were two eight-pointed stars the size of small teacups and etched in deep blue ink. These *vory v zakone* stars — the true marking of a Thief within the Code — were sacred. Those who wore them undeservedly were subject to their removal by knife and fire, pre-mortem.

Of his sixty-two years, Bone had spent thirty-five inside prisons of the gulag. He had never worked a day in his life, had never worn a uniform, and had never violated his Code. Being inside or being out was a matter of indifference to him.

The truck with the faulty gears pulled up in front of the Thieves' barracks. A political prisoner — the weeping poet — wearing a cloth hat with big flapping ears, a new gray padded tunic, striped trousers, and iron handcuffs, was taken from the open deck of the vehicle and led inside. His hands were unbound and a guard pushed him into the wide common area surrounded by iron-framed bunks with straw-filled mattresses. "Meat, for you bastards. Eat your fill and we'll be back for the bones in the morning. This one is an enemy of the State and an enemy of your *mir*. By morning he'll be dead or a lady, eh?"

The poet, a *zek* — a political prisoner — who had undergone horrors at the hands of his State captors, was, while he remained conscious, amazed at the wild carnival that ensued when the door shut behind the guard. He was stunned at the sheer whirling focus of his new barracks mates, who flowed at him with the mindless persistence of metal filings attacking a magnet.

When Bone and the others returned before the dinner hour, the poet had been passed through the barracks. His face was battered; one eye was swollen shut and some teeth broken. Tufts of curly hair had been pulled in clumps from the back of his head, leaving patches of skin as white as bone. A bite mark on his cheek was crusted in blood. He lay naked, face down on a mattress in the common area. He bled thin brownish blood from his anus and the fingers on his right hand had been bent back and snapped. A loud card game was in progress to determine who got the poet's rations and who got what was left of the poet himself.

Bone walked around the mattress to his bunk beside the stove. He sat on the edge of his bunk and watched the card game. The poet stirred periodically, moaning with every small movement. Beneath the battering, Bone saw a thin, intelligent face, the soft, curious eyes of a scholar. The unbroken fingers on the left hand were long, like a pianist's, but the nails were encrusted with filth and splinters from trying to gouge to freedom through the board flooring of the barracks.

After a few minutes, Bone got up and crossed to the poet. "Can you hear, *zek*?"

The man nodded.

"You will die here when the lamps are out, do you know that? Do you want to live?"

He nodded.

"Do you want to live in the woman's role?" This suggestion was for information only: Bone had long ago expunged his desires and was able, through his focus on the precious

Code, to internalize his liquids into harmony. That which did not make him more pure before the Code was discarded. "Do you desire the life of a woman?"

The man made an aching groan. He didn't move.

"What do you have, *zek*? Do you have tobacco or money or skills or packages to come from loved ones?"

The man shook his head.

"What is your profession?"

It took a few attempts before Bone understood his answer: "Words, ideas. I write poems, tracts. I teach languages."

Bone sat back on his heels. The card players grew raucous, slamming cards onto the wooden tabletop with shouts of triumph or anger. The table was tipped; there was a rough, laughing tussle. A thick dull bell sounded lineup for supper. The camp was isolated enough that the inmates could line up in the frozen air without fear they might bolt for the wires; outside there, all knew, the elusive tiger was the least of their worries. The trick was to gather what food they were assigned and wolf it before their plates were looted by Thieves.

Bone looked at the poet and asked if he wanted soup, or to be the bones for the soup. The man both nodded and shook his head.

"Then, *zek*, what have you to trade, that you can eat our food?"

"I have words. Many, many words. In many languages. That's all. I know nothing else."

"Can you make me warm with these words? Or should I take your clothing and your blanket, wrap your skin over mine, scalp your hair for a fur hat?"

"I can. Words."

"So, then. You'll have to walk to the food line."

In this special regime camp, as in the others throughout the gulag, the Thieves preyed upon the political prisoners and lesser criminals and, when they could, upon the guards and administrators themselves. Rare packages from loved ones were looted from the commissary. New prisoners were quickly deprived of their clothing, their meager possessions, even their hidden precious photographs and clouding memories, and in return were given horror. In the hierarchy of the camps, the *vory v zakone*, the Thieves within the Code, were above all others. Around them they kept lesser Thieves, apprentices to the Code. In many camps, the Thieves were used by the administration to terrorize political prisoners and to keep order on the work details, to ensure each *zek* met his work quota. Where Bone ruled, this was forbidden. We did not plant the trees, Bone said, so we will not assist in cutting them down; we will not ride the railway, so we will not build it. We are not policemen — *musor*, garbage — so we will not enforce upon those we haven't imprisoned. The Code, he said, did not allow for any cooperation with the administration. We will if necessary eat the *zeks*, but we will not use the knives and forks of the cunt State.

There was no shortage of *zeks* and trustees to work evil upon. Almost daily, depending on the tilt of the government in the city of spires — Moscow — dozens and sometimes hundreds of dazed victims were delivered to the camps, slight men and women, intellectuals confused behind their thick glasses and inside their defeated, tortured bodies, weakened and unable to imagine that horrors could follow upon horrors. It wasn't only the voracious Thieves who had at the *zeks*: nature's weather devoured them with its brutality. *Zeks* were found starved in the wood fields, their bodies frozen into twisted postures under wheelbarrows where they tried to find shelter from arctic winds and the battering of cudgels. Stiffened *zeks* — Jew lanterns — were found hanging by their bootlaces from trees, unable to foresee a future in which they could survive on a few ounces of bread left to them by the Thieves. On a memorable recent morning, all awoke to find a rare love sculpture: a couple kneeling in the trodden snow at the wire. He, a bearded political from the men's camp; she, his wife from the women's colony. They embraced through the tangle of barbs, frozen together where the silver sheets of tears on their faces met. Political prisoners refused to part them; Thieves merely stood and laughed, scratching themselves. A guard chipped the bleached-out, melded faces apart with the point of a bayonet.

Veins were gnawed in the night, silent liquid deaths, after fuck circuses of lust fueled by the wood alcohol that Thieves crazed themselves with before rampaging. Some died as hope leaked from their bodies and their will melted; they could actually be heard laughing to death.

But the *zeks* couldn't die off fast enough. *Zeks* were endless.

Bone's poet slept beneath his bunk. Unlike other slaves, he wasn't tied with laces to the iron pipes that framed the bed, cuddling with a Thief's boots in his crotch to make them warm for the Thief's feet on chilled mornings. The poet whispered words of warmth to Bone to still the freezing skeleton inside him. Stories of arid beaches, wheeling birds, screaming children in the sand, a sun that baked with the dry heat of an oven — all were softly sung until in sleep the innards of Bone stilled.

Four years later, outside the wires and lazy constant spotlights, the kleptocracy began to dissolve. The chaos of worms burrowed inside the body of the State; having devoured the flesh, having nibbled the joints of the skeleton, they had begun feeding on themselves.

In the final months, as the skeleton teetered before crumbling, plans were instituted to align the followers of the *zakone* with the new reality of bureaucrat-criminals — businessmen who exploited black markets, spies whose corruption had made them offshore millionaires, soldiers, militia, and connivers who had looted in secret. The new criminal reality began to impose organization onto the anarchy of collapse. Thieves and their Code were now seen as agents of chaos that could disrupt the harmony of organized theft. Emissaries from this new criminal reality visited prisons and camps to sound out the *pakhany* — the bosses of the *mir* — to entice them from the path of their Code to the new harmony. Many of the Thieves recognized the new reality, however reluctantly, and as they followed, so did their followers. Others, wary and averse to external organization, turned their backs, choosing to walk their own way. These refusers, the wild Thieves, were left in the gulags and slowly killed off as prison officials moved them into barracks populated by the adherents of the new criminal regime, then sat back to let nature take its course. The slaughter went on for months and the men of old were decimated.

Outside the wire, the effects of the cleansing were immediate in the streets of the cities: followers of the wild Thieves took revenge wherever they could, killing the traitors to the Code. They themselves were searched out and in turn assassinated. Anarchy imposed itself upon anarchy, chaos upon chaos, and finally the men of the new reality sent an emissary to visit Bone.

"In Moscow, the paving stones are red and wet. Many Thieves have gone up. It must stop."

Bone and the well-dressed, fleshy man were alone in the barracks; outside, inmates huddled against the building to eke warmth from the board walls, and to listen. "And many of the new have also gone up, eh?"

The man shrugged. "We are many, we can lose many."

"Then you've come this way for the food? The wildflowers?"

The man shrugged again. "As we win, we lose. But those of the Code lose and then lose again. It's unharmonious — a dirty finger in the wet asshole."

"I am removed. I can do nothing."

"The Circle is in Moscow. A meeting could save lives, wild Thieves, and the new reality alike. A maker of peace could become an icon to all. All could profit, all could live."

"Profit and life? They have nothing to do with me. I am here; those others are there."

"Passage could be made. Your name and voice have a weight of gold."

This was true, they both recognized. In the streets of Moscow, children played at being the legend Bone, although none had seen him. In their games, they slaughtered lesser and weaker children who had the roles of militia or the new mafia. Young gangsters, operating from rumors and legend, had named themselves Little Bone, Bone the Large, Bone the Conqueror, and affected his famous shivers. To bring Bone into the new reality would effectively settle the streets of the cities, much as the surrender of a general would calm a battlefield. To kill Bone would be a mixed blessing: he'd be eliminated once and for all, but his legend could spark a cause, like the death of a revolutionary. None would believe Bone was dead: he'd be sighted in far-off cities and invisibly command a cadre of loyal Thieves who'd never met him.

Bone stood up. “I go where I’m taken.” He thought of snapping the man’s neck. He waved his hand at a face peering in the thick, rippled-glass window. “I’m a poor Thief. In rags.”

“You will, then, come when you’re taken?”

“My journey takes me many places. I couldn’t refuse to attend the Circle of Brothers. It would be a violation.”

“Yes, then. They will be pleased. I leave you with their thanks.”

The man outside the window came in. Bone took him aside and told him to escort the emissary to the camp office. “This one is fat with the greases. He carries a happy message back to his masters. Returning, he should look less happy with himself.”

“A tasty morsel, this.”

Bone looked into his eyes. “Some days the soup is thick, other days it is thin.”

The inmate led the emissary from the barracks. A cloud of buzzing Thieves gathered outside the doorway. The inmate spoke in a low voice and the Thieves packed themselves around the emissary, pulling at his clothing until he was naked on the ground. They were relentless, persistent, blindly focused. A dark-skinned young man, all his upper teeth removed except for his incisors, which had been sharpened to points, chewed a chunk of skin and flesh from the emissary’s cheek, then sat back on his heels and howled at the white-rinsed sky. He spat out the piece of cheek and began gnawing on the man’s nose, holding the emissary’s ears in his hands as intimately as a lover. Another man, his fingernails grown into gnarly claws, began ripping at the emissary’s thighs. A dagger was produced and chunks of the man’s calves were hacked away. Guards slowly strolled to the frenzy, continuing a laughing conversation. They rescued the man indifferently, took him to the camp office, and wrapped him in a greatcoat for his trip back to Moscow.

Days later Bone's prison records were altered, magically turning him from a predator feeding on the lifeblood of the System into a rehabilitated leader who brought his fellow inmates into line with the true reality of the glory of the Soviet Union. Reports of stabbings and murders vanished and testimonials took their place. A nourishing family was invented, a wife and two sons, she a tireless worker in the agriculture that fed the country, the sons brave heroes of the Soviet Union who had given their lives selflessly in the Afghanistan conflict. From a *pakhany* of status, Bone became a shining example of the State's efforts to influence delinquents into the glories of hard work and indoctrination.

On a Sunday dawn, after the season of brief nights, before the iron stoves were lit by low bitches to warm the room, Bone crossed the common area to his bunk. Beneath it, the poet slept with the face of a baby and the guarded, curved posture of a victim. Bone stood, watching his poet, then reached under the bunk and seized his throat. When he finally released his stranglehold, he'd leaned and kissed the corner of the lips, beside the fat protruding tongue, under the crudely carved "B" under his left cheekbone: "I loved you, my child; this world not for the kind. With God, rest."

Hours later the poet was still lying on the floor of the barracks, his body rolled beside the stove, naked now as the younger men violated him in death, joking about how he responded like a Ukrainian whore: not well at all, but worth the ruble. As the guard waited, Bone stepped to the doorway of the barracks with his small canvas bag under his arm: "I salute you, my brothers; today me, tomorrow you. They can imprison your bodies unto death; your hearts are birds. I love you each and all. For you I will send a policeman to meet our dead poet."

The men in the barracks cheered and stamped their feet, and the building's supports vibrated and floorboards cracked. Across the compound, Bone could hear their whoops and yells as he stepped into the back of a black Mercedes, freshly stolen and still bearing Berlin license plates. The driver was silent and required no directions. When he heard the door softly click, he rolled out of the compound without looking back and sedately drove for four hours, depositing Bone at an airfield where a small jet — also bearing German registration markings — waited to take him three thousand miles to the city of spires. Bone boarded the aircraft, clutching his small carryall.

The driver drove off in the Mercedes, picking up speed where the roads were in good condition, and arrived at his home three hours later. His wife waited with a boiled meal of root vegetables and scraps of meat.

"And the day," she said, "was good?"

"Perhaps. I drove one who is either a dead man or a prince." He lifted his bowl to drink the vegetables' liquor. "But I think dead."

Chapter 2

THE RUINS of Moscow contracted Bone's heart. The union had been collapsed for five years and the vultures circled and fed upon each other's carrion, friend and foe alike. As the Volvo sedan carried him through the streets, he peered through the smoked windows in search of Thieves; for a long time he saw none. In front of hotels and tall cement buildings that scraped the low sky, bands of muscular young men strutted in short leather jackets, track suits, and sunglasses, holding cigarettes close to their faces and yelling into cellular phones in parodies of importance. Sunshine whores dragged purses along the sidewalk in front of the Intercontinental. Businessmen inside pods of bodyguards made rapid determined strides across busy sidewalks, sucked into the security of long, armored Mercedes. At a busy corner, four men wearing suits and T-shirts had a Western businessman crowded against a bank. Three of the men were stripping the Armani suit from the businessman's body while the fourth held a seething mastiff on a short chain leash. Two militia, their coattails flapping behind them, dashed past the robbery in pursuit of a teenaged boy running for his life with a bloody butcher's package clutched against his chest. Momentarily Bone's spirits soared at the sight. Go, Thief.

Babushka were everywhere, their mean, blemished apple faces swathed in drab scarves as they displayed broken vegetables on upturned cardboard boxes. A militia patrol made a perimeter around a pair of bloody legs in suit pants and polished shoes poking from the mouth of an alley; the patrollers smoked cigarettes and looked around for something more interesting to hold their attention. Bone had heard of the division of the dark people — those from the mountains — and the white Thieves — those of pure Russian blood — and how the Thieves' Code, which once accepted a Thief of any color or race, was now split into camps, with the authorities concentrating their efforts on the darker men. He saw a group of Chechen men, banded tightly together for protection, make their way through traffic into Dorogomilovsky Market, watchful for both the whites and the authorities.

Bone hadn't been in Moscow for fourteen years and he didn't recognize the street the Volvo carried him into. The houses were vast and walled and clusters of men with ill-hidden machine-guns lolled in the afternoon sunshine. Dogs barked, out of sight. Some of the men wore suit jackets that ballooned around them, and their square shoes scuffled on the paving stones. Others wore Western jogging suits and fat designer sneakers. Four suspicious swarthy men with thick black hair and stocky torsos stood apart, each holding an oversized briefcase as long as a machine pistol. The driver purred the Volvo at the end of a row of luxury cars, each backed in, each with a driver in sunglasses at the wheel. Bone's driver oozed the window down and chill air filled the car as he murmured into an intercom. Bone recognized the aspect of the men, former grunt soldiers now in the service of profit, gymnasium thugs, men of the mountains ill at ease with concrete under their feet. If they were going to kill me, he thought, they'd have done it between Irkutsk and here, left me to feed my brains to ravens and rats.

The Volvo's window went up and a pair of wrought-iron gates parted, allowing the vehicle to pass a hundred yards to a dacha with whitewashed wood and glowing gray stonework. Trees and shrubbery had been cut back to reduce lines of fire and infiltration. A group of ex-military idled in front of the dacha, wearing sleek suits as they had once worn uniforms: buttoned, immaculate, and uncreased. Unlike the gaggle of security at the gates, these men were deployed rather than idling. They watched as Bone, in his rag clothes, emerged with athletic economy from the back of the sedan; they parted respectfully as they gazed in bold curiosity. The Volvo silently slid away; the military-level security clearly forbade the parking of vehicles within explosion radius of the dacha.

A guardian carrying a wand stood beside Bone. "With respect." He took the carryall and gave it a finger search. He removed a dagger and handed it to a guard behind him without taking his eyes off Bone. He waved the wand around and behind Bone's body, then stepped back as the device emitted a beep of increasing loudness near Bone's armpit. Bone undid his tunic and showed a purplish scar on his left side where the front inch of a prison blade had clipped off on his ribs.

The guard nodded. "Souvenir."

A liveried footman with the mien of a prison trusty carefully descended the stone stairs leading to the entrance of the house; wordlessly he took Bone's carryall and ushered him into a vast foyer decorated with every manner of art and textile. A spidery chandelier made the entryway aglow, welcoming.

Outside, the guard holding the dagger smiled and said, "These old ones. To be truly secure, we should take their teeth and fingernails."

In the foyer, the footman told Bone, "Master Mikhailov asks that you enjoy an upper room." He pointed his chin at an effeminate young Jewish man in rimless glasses and a suit of similar livery. "Zev will be your attendant — anything you require or desire will be provided. The master regrets he is away and unable to attend dinner with you; however, he will return for breakfast in the morning and looks forward to greeting you properly. When you wish to eat or if we may be of assistance, merely pick up any telephone."

The footman left. Zev seemed to shuffle his feet, even while standing still, his posture that of a *zek*: his head stooped forward as though there wasn't enough nourishment in his body to command it upright, hands looped together behind his back, evasive eyes hoping to avoid being chosen. Chosen for anything. Ah, thought Bone, the brother of my poet, this Zev.

Bone let the slinking Zev, carrying the carryall, lead him up a broad staircase and through a wide, decorated hallway. They entered a suite of thickly carpeted rooms and Zev introduced him to the layout: the washroom to the left; the bedroom to the right, changes of clothing, nightshirts, socks in the closet; and straight ahead a living room with a wall of electronics and devices to operate them. The television set was as wide as a window; alongside it was an inlaid samovar and beside that a glittering bar service of copper and marble, of crystal glasses and ornate dispensers. A sheaf of wildflowers exploded from a silver vase beside a matching bowl containing an array of fruit. An immaculately scripted card, leaning against a silver bell, welcomed Bone: "My brother, my brother. Freedom at last; prosperity for all. We shall, together, steal this world."

"Shall I unpack, master?"

"Leave."

When Zev quietly closed the outer door, Bone wandered into the washroom — as he passed sensors, lights were activated, creating an arctic of blazing white porcelain and gleaming golden fixtures. Feeling nauseous and faint with unreality, he sucked air and mucus from his sinuses and loudly spat in disgust in the center of the tiled floor. He left the room — sensors extinguished the lights — and urinated thoroughly on the carpet behind a gold-woven drape. He lay down in front of samovar. This truly is a hell, he thought, and reflected his day in the mirror of the Code. Yes, I couldn't refuse to attend the Circle. It would be a violation. But, hijacked by connivers and sycophants of currency, is it a Circle or a perversion, a circus? Could an honest Thief live in such a way as this?

The elusive chill, a malaria of his bones, entered his body. He curled into a ball and let the rhythms of the shudders rock him to sleep.

The owner of the dacha, Simeon Mikhailov, put the telephone down without speaking. He held up his hand, making it vibrate. "The cold one has arrived."

He smiled at four members of the Circle in a sitting room on the other side of the dacha. The four sat two-by-two on facing leather couches with silver clawed feet, while Mikhailov reclined in a matching leather armchair. All took advantage of the failing milky sunlight angling through the leaded glass of the windows. They wore well-cut suits, snowy white shirts, and silken ties tacked with elegant gold devices.

The men had nicknames they'd worn since they'd entered the *mir*: Mikhailov was Madhouse, Izrailov was Ranger, Grigorev was Chinaman, Golubev was Wrecker, and Razinkin was Tomahawk. All were of the white tribe, except for Ranger, a dark Chechen. All were between fifty and sixty; again excepting Ranger, who was in his early thirties. Each had done at least a quarter of his life in harsh prison time, except again Ranger, who had served less than three years. And each wore the eight-pointed stars under his shirt, faded and worn, again except for Ranger, who came from a family made rich on contraband: his crown and bright stars were newly purchased, an act that would have led, before the collapse, to scorn and spittle. Now, in the new reality, the five Thieves had come to accommodations and aligned themselves with the criminal bureaucracy of *biznesmen*, KGB agents, military men, and masters of the decrepit State.

To the five Thieves, the Code was an ancient document written on air with invisible ink, a quaint document that had withered and yellowed and become dust before the winds of change. The wild Thieves, those stubborn practitioners of the Code, were dead, dying, or in hiding, trying to rally some coherent response to the bastardizing of their precious candle. Already in St. Petersburg, in Odessa, in the countryside, Thieves had first stood firm; then, finding themselves leaderless, had swayed; then collapsed under the blandishments of wealth and power. The hook-nosed sniper Solonik, a piper of precision, wandered Europe, meticulously weeding out the wild Thieves of old.

Razinkin smoked at a cigarette with a gold filter. "This one, why don't we just —" he held up his open hand, then closed it into a fist "— psssst?"

Mikhailov shook his head. His hair was silvered and sprayed, well barbered above the collar of his shirt. "There are Thieves who are wavering. If we can bring this Bone to us, those on the fence will fall to our side. Some others of those will come from the shadows and we can eliminate them or embrace them, at our choice. Every one we have to kill becomes a martyr to this old Code; better we bring them in. We must bring order to the *mir* for the prosperity of all. Having this cold one with us will settle unruly elements."

"And," Razinkin asked softly, "if not?"

"Then he must go. Remember, this Bone has spent a life of eating iron and drinking piss."

"As have we all." Razinkin didn't look at Ranger.

"And, like us, he is perhaps ready to go from the larva to the butterfly. To steal a country instead of a loaf of bread — the ultimate theft."

The other men were silent. All were willing to abide by Mikhailov. Under his leadership, the bastards of the new *mir* had become rich beyond their wildest hopes. Mikhailov's links to the new reality were undeniable; he was the savior who would take them even further.

Grigorev — the Chinaman — kept his reservations to himself. Of Bone's age and background, he regretted not standing for the Code. These criminal bureaucrats, he mused, they are this cancerous crab eating in my stomach. Making honest Thieves into foot soldiers. Putting honest Thieves on stipends like mistresses to be fucked and forgotten. Making honest Thieves steal to their demand instead of to opportunity. When did my life become more important than my heart? I shame myself with these clothes, these decanters, these linen walls, with these sparkling crystal baubles reflecting this sickening light. He sat silent, feeling the pointed stars engraved upon his chest burn in shame. He detected a scripted aura to the conversation and believed Mikhailov and Razinkin had rehearsed their dialogue and were laying tracks of their own.

A manservant came silently into the room, lit a roaring fire, and left.

Mikhailov crossed to a marble shelf and poured himself a glass of vodka. "I will meet with this cold one in the morning. He'll have a night of silken sheets, women if he desires — boys, if not — and meat with no maggots. I'll show him a golden path and if he chooses to walk it, things will be as they should. If not —" he made the shape of a hooked nose in front of his face: Solonik, the sniper "— and I'll plant an apple tree over his grave and its fruit will be a remembrance for us all of the greatest of time, long passed." He lifted his glass to eye level. "Yesterday, theirs. Tomorrow, ours."

The Chinaman looked at the others as they lifted their drinks. Razinkin is the one behind this, he thought. Mikhailov is in essence a cheap pimp; his accommodation with the new reality began before there *was* a new reality. His past violations of the Code were notorious and pervasive. Wearing military uniforms to invade homes of victims, his disappearing of Thieves whose power he feared, isolating the Thieves of the dark skin of faraway mountains. But this Razinkin of the hatchet, the man of the plastic bags, this Tomahawk only desires to have America with its oceans of money and clouds of power. To him the purity of the Code was merely a stepping stone. One who had ever walked the true path of the Thief would never put up a puppet like Mikhailov to carry his face: one true of the path would revel and take all, credit and blame, and show teeth. But the dunce Mikhailov, appearing as the leader, could be eliminated by Tomahawk in the blessing of success, or eliminated in the damnation of shame.

Tomahawk will eliminate Bone, the Chinaman suddenly knew with a certainty as real as the voracious crab that awoke and began tickling in his entrails. Even if the cold one were to turn his back on tradition and values and sleep in silken beds surrounded by embroidered walls, if he were to gather and tame the wild Thieves, Tomahawk would surely eliminate him, wiping out the legend, then he would wipe out the rest of the wild ones. And if suddenly the wild Thieves found strength to retaliate, Razinkin could point at Mikhailov as the architect of all horrors that ensued, Mikhailov's crime of flawed statesmanship. If the wild Thieves did capitulate, then Razinkin could easily usurp the fool Mikhailov and become the administrator of the prosperous world to come.

To save Bone and that precious Code from these whores, perhaps that is to be my legacy, perhaps that will expunge my shame and treachery. But will this unsatisfied crab allow me? As if awakened, the crab inside his guts nibbled.

Something about the bodyguards itched at Bone's mind. It was full night when the whispering scratch awoke him and he could smell his pungent piss soaked into the carpet across the room. He let his mind unravel this thought of the bodyguards. And the cars, with their various license plates. And the variance in the bodyguards' clothing. Some in tracksuits, some in suits. Four dark men from the mountains, clustered together off to the side. Cars from sectors in and around Moscow.

Bone rose silently from the thick carpet and stood, not breathing, in the ghostly moonlight, the room's air perfumed with fruits and lavenders, overpowering the reeking ghost of his urine. Like the sudden shuttling of boxcars that carried Thieves and *zeks* to the camps, a rush of thoughts and deductions clanged rhythmically in his mind and ordered themselves.

The mix of bodyguards and vehicles meant there were various *vor* — whores all, he believed — in the dacha. The ex-military men guarding the entrance to the dacha clearly belonged to Mikhailov; they had an air of proprietorship.

Mikhailov's intrigues with the black marketeers of the Red Army were notorious.

There were wild Thieves, he knew, living in holes and sewer pipes under the cities, in ditches and forests across the vast landscape. Each day, for certain, there were fewer, as this new circle of vultures feasted, seeking them out and butchering them, using assassins like Solonik to pick off the *pakhany*, the leaders, or using the soulless military men of torture to leave their torn, eyeless bodies in public to terrorize the rebellious.

I have been chosen, Bone realized, by the Code to wage a justice. And, he decided, tonight we begin the merrymaking.

He found a gold-plated antique telephone on a table beside the bed. Picking up the receiver, he waited through a single continuous ring, and when a soft voice answered he said, "Meat," and hung up. He went into the bathroom, the sensors activating at his entrance. He filled the expansive bathtub with cold water and went into the living room. In his carryall he found a package of half-smoked cigarettes and a box of wooden matches. Back in the bathroom he sat on the edge of the tub and smoked dreamily, cupping his hands around the warmth of the hot ash. When he heard a soft knock at the suite's door, he dropped the cigarette butt into the bathtub.

Zev, carrying a tray with a silver dome over a silver platter, bowed his head. "As you requested, Master." He passed into the living room and arranged the meal on a round, dark-wooded table with clawed golden feet. "You would like to drink which, sir?"

"Potato." Bone stood watching Zev move like a subservient woman. This one reminds me of my poet, he thought. Outside, a man; inside, a girl. And this place is his gulag — a gulag with iron and wood, or one of gold and linens; both are still a gulag to a *zek*.

Zev crossed to the bar and opened a small freezer. He took a bottle of vodka from the ice and poured a glass full, then stood demurely with his hands crossed in front of his genitals. "Shall I remain, sir?"

"Sit." Bone lifted the silver dome and saw a stack of rare meats cut into small pieces. A bone shaped like a T had a thick rim of filet attached to it. There was a heavy silver fork with dulled tines, but no knife. He picked at the meats, drew on the vodka.

Zev, seated on a gold lamé sofa, leaned forward expectantly.

Bone sucked at the meat juices on his fingers, plucked an apple from the fruit basket, and sat beside Zev. "Are you a prisoner, child?"

"I serve, sir."

"And are you more meat for me?" He rested his open hand on the nape of Zev's neck.

"As you wish." He placed his hand on Bone's thigh. "As you wish."

"And if I don't have these tastes, what then can you bring to me?" He closed his hand tightly around Zev's neck and pulled him close. "Come into the chamber for shitting."

"Sir —" Tears began running down Zev's cheeks.

"Silent now." With his free hand, Bone stuffed the apple into the man's mouth, forcing and twisting it in until Zev's jaws creaked and his eyes bugged. "Come." He half-dragged Zev, in a headlock, into the sudden white blizzard of the washroom. He closed the door and removed Zev's spectacles, placing them carefully on a shelf. He wrestled Zev into the cold water of the bathtub and pushed his head under, then pulled it out again. He drew the apple from Zev's mouth and replaced it with the T-shaped bone from the meat, jamming his jaws wide open, the hinges popping. Bone pinched Zev's nose closed and again submerged his head; water ran freely into Zev's gullet, into his lungs. In the gulag, hens — informants — had suffered a similar but more humiliating fate: sticks were tied into their mouths to keep the teeth apart, then much urination, defecation, or merry masturbation ensued, a leisurely poisoning by wastes and fluids.

Bone held Zev's head underwater for several seconds, himself getting soaked in the noisy thrashings, then he pulled the man's face out of the water. "There, there," he whispered. "The air, take the air. It's sweet, eh? As you speak, I will reward you with the air."

Zev took mighty heaves, alternately choking and vomiting water and chunks of apple. Bone dried his hands and lit another cigarette stub, sitting on the toilet seat as Zev recovered and tried to dislodge the steak bone from his mouth. The sharp point of the bone tore the roof of his mouth and he managed to remove it.

"We haven't much time, my friend. I must know things and I beg you to tell me."

"I know nothing."

"I will eat you."

"This . . ." Zev shook his head and spat blood into the water.

"My friend, I will eat you." Bone held up his own left hand where the small finger joint was absent. "I've eaten me, and I'll eat you. Rest a moment and then we'll speak. A cigarette?"

Zev shook his head.

"How many in the dacha?"

"Guards outside. Inside we are five keepers."

"And guests? The filthy Mikhailov?"

"All have left."

"The filthy Mikhailov?"

"Here. There was a meeting. They drank and ate and the others left."

"Tell me, child, of the others."

"There were four. One called Tomahawk. One other appearing to be of Chinese eyes. One dark mud person, Master Izrailov, of whom I know nothing. And the master Golubev."

As he reflected, Bone allowed his fingers to caress Zek's soaked hair. The one of Chinese eyes was of course Grigorev, the Chinaman, the *vor* of Vladivostok: the loss of this true friend, when the rumors reached the prisons, was met by an almost insane disbelief. The Chinaman was of Bone's stature, perhaps at times even greater. The messengers who told of Chinaman's betrayal were set upon and ripped, so impossible was the very idea of the Far Eastern *vor* engaging in treachery. It was well known that Tomahawk — Razinkin — was born of whoredom and lice sperm, a fanged vampire who had long been a stain upon the Code and had in fact become the first of the *vory v zakone* to embrace the new reality. Of this dark person Izrailov, I know not, thought Bone, but in this new reality, in a *mir* that separates the darks and the whites, his future will be brief. Golubev was a past legend himself, but was now clearly whore's mucus.

Bone looked around the room and found a silver container of talc; he spread a thin coating of it on the tile floor. "A map. The hallways, the rooms, the guards. Who sleeps in which room. Exits, windows, balconies. The grounds."

Zev climbed out of the tub. He wadded toilet paper and swabbed the inside of his mouth. "I am just a servant. Not of those others."

"A map."

"But they will kill me."

Bone pulled him to the floor. He took a thick green towel from a stack beside the bathtub and wrapped it around Zev's head, squeezing his hand where he felt the man's mouth. He picked up Zev's right hand and, struggling, put the smallest finger into his mouth and chewed through it at the first joint. The screams were muted; when they ceased in a frenzy of gulping grunts, Bone spat the fingertip onto the floor and crooned softly into the towel where Zev's ear would be, rocking his body.

He removed the towel. "Now, my friend, I beg your help. The map. And quickly."

Crying and pressing his hand to his chest, Zev sketched lines in the talc, the long wide corridors, the entrances to rooms. Staircases and windows. Bone asked about the exterior and Zev added walls, driveway, stands of trees, hedges.

"And where does the virus Mikhailov sleep?"

Zev pointed at the room farthest removed from the street.

"A wife? A woman or boy?'

"No. He has a wife in the north and a woman in the Metropole."

"And once away from this place, the streets go where?"

Zev stared at him and shook his head.

"Streets, my child. To make away." He picked up the bloody hand and stroked it gently.

Zev shook his head. "I must go, too."

"So you shall."

"Then I will show you the way as we go. If you don't kill me, they will."

"A smart rabbit. So it will be." Bone stood and helped Zev to his feet. "Come then, a change of clothing and we together will kiss the horrible Mikhailov goodnight, eh?"

When dawn leached night out of the sky, the manservant listened at the door of Mikhailov's bedroom. Hearing no snores, he listened for the shower. Silence. He went down to the kitchen and began preparing fresh rolls and spooning jams onto a silver plate. He peeled various fruits, arranging them in a crystal saucer. He took a cold cooked roast of beef from the stainless-steel refrigerator and placed it on the wooden counter to warm. When he reached into a cut-block knife holder, he noted the absence of the carving knife and fork. He noted a large chunk of meat had been ripped from the roast. Spots of blackened blood were dotted on the tile floor.

Fearing treachery, Mikhailov had forbidden guards inside the house at night. The manservant quickly walked to the front door and opened it wide. The morning shift of military men were at the foot of the steps, examining each other for stains, dust, and creases. They looked up.

"Master Mikhailov's room." He waved them inside. "And check the guest, please."

Mikhailov's bedroom suite was a riot. Blood was splashed across the bed and on the walls. Pieces of flesh — an ear here, a finger there — were strewn on the carpet. The head, separated from the body, was in a crystal bowl of melted ice, the water fuschia. A large piece of unidentifiable flesh had been forced into the mouth, and a piece of wire coathanger went into one ear and out the other. The nose was missing and the teeth had been smashed. The torso was in the bathroom, naked and ripped and scratched and bloodied. The arms were bent against the joints; bones were visible. The carving set was recovered: the knife was jammed crookedly into the chest, the fork's handle visible in the anus.

Zev was in a closet, his eyes rolled back in horror, mewing soft animal noises. Unharmed, he was unable to move any part of his body, except to slowly shake his head. His right hand was tucked into his armpit. He had chewed through his lips and wore a bib of blood.

The senior guard carefully backed out into the hallway. "A party was had," he told the others.

"And we weren't invited?"

"Not this time." The senior guard sighed and closed the door. "We must again look for work."

"Mikhailov, he is dead?"

The senior guard began laughing.

Zev was gently taken from the closet and into the three-story fortified garage above which lived the house security crew. He blubbered and answered questions without evasion, although he lisped and his diction suffered from his shredded, stuttering lips. Satisfied with his answers, the senior guard gave him a bottle of distilled water and led him between two identical dark gray Mercedes sedans. He told him to rinse his mouth and spit the blood into a drain hole, careful not to splash the cars. When Zev bent to spit, the senior guard produced a Tokarov 9mm pistol from his belt, stepped back, then leaned delicately forward, arm fully extended, and smoothly smacked a single shot into the base of Zev's skull.

The guard moved away from the body and called Razinkin on a cellular telephone. "The old man is away. The servant told him the names of those at yesterday's meeting. Mikhailov is dead." He listened to the eerie silence over the telephone, watching blood gurgle freely into the drain from the wound at the back of Zev's skull. The telephone clicked off.

Chapter 3

As a piper in war, Alexsandr Solonik believed that to assassinate a child was to murder a family. It only made sense. In Afghanistan he'd often passed on targets of military or fair civilian opportunity to seek out through his scope the skipping schoolgirl or wandering schoolboy, preferably with a parent to witness. A child sniped disabled an entire family; a male child sniped eliminated a revenge a thousand years hence.

Solonik often piped off only one shot before his position was polluted, so he became a man of hard decision, unlike his military colleagues, who nested themselves down and without thought chose the easiest target, sighted and fired, and crawled away backward, often too quickly, leaving tracks or making noise. This, Solonik believed, polluted the position, and even in vast Afghanistan, secure, cunning positions were hard to come by. He'd once fired on a bus carrying children to a mountain mosque, taking all four very quickly, leaving the exposed driver kneecapped but alive to pass on the message of horror: no second-hand tale could essay the voice and memory of a surviving witness. Then, because he feared a retributive sweep of the hill he was hiding in, Solonik, full of little pills that prevented shitting, stayed put for an entire night and day, sleeping fitfully and awaking finally to find himself covered in eight inches of snow. The cold made him laugh secretly; his giddy shivers warmed him as the Afghanis howled below. Ah, they sang to me, he remembered, those fierce, weeping, bearded men in tattered uniforms and billowing sheets. I loved those raggy old Afghanis: the slower you killed them, the more they spat. Some were like curious children — at the beginning, anyway, before they caught on — and would open any package or move any item they wondered about. After many were shredded with a thousand ball bearings or camel-hoof nails, the Afghanis allowed caution to murder their delight. Solonik had seeded many land mines, grunt work between missions, but he hated them, hated how they relied on the stupidity of the victim rather than the true human traits like giggling curiosity and childlike love of bright color. But doll bombs, book bombs, all the sly devices that sent Afghanis of all ages unto their heaven smiling, joyous at this miraculous discovery of a toy of recreation or distraction — a fine way up to the lap of Allah.

Retribution. The elimination of a threat unborn. This is where those of the Sicilian *mir* had made their mistake, was indeed why he was here now, in Palermo. A twenty-year-old murder and an infant son left behind to become the avenging son of the father, the instrument of the mother's vendetta of madness. An assassinated policeman's son who had since become a magistrate, with powers formed by the twin hands of revenge and justice. Unbuyable, unswayable. Now, at the end of complex maneuverings, the magistrate himself had become available for assassination. Whispers of his affairs with married women, of his penchant for boys the younger the better, his corruption, and the legion of cuckolded husbands

— all came together to make him available. Enemies were legion for this magistrate, it was believed, and the Mafia seemed to be the least of his problems. A murder could find root in many places. His evil personal life, his grasping for powers beyond.

In Brussels, where he'd based himself while single-mindedly decimating cunning old *vory* for the brothers of the Circle, Solonik had passed his time in a mansion leased for the around-the-clock production of adult videos. An incredibly ugly American with bad breath and an unusually large penis had explained the concept of the money shot to Solonik: "All the beautiful people jump into bed; the camera shows their beautiful faces, smooth skin, the handsome men's faces and perfect hair, their big muscular chests. Tits, asses, a little finger work. But when it comes time for the cum shot, these guys don't have the equipment. So they break the camera away and I step in, just my ass and my dick. A few minutes of close-up stuff, I squirt, and the scene's done. The money shot, get it?"

And here as there, it is all arranged, Solonik thought. The target will be here. The rifle will be here. For me, the money shot. An honor, for me, to work for these legendary Sicilians. A favor from our *mir* to theirs, a favor upon which many fine things could grow, like the forty-year-old meeting at the Grand Hotel et des Palmes when the mafias of Sicily and America met and charted a new, enduring history.

Afterward, he planned, perhaps some time back in Belgium where the movie girls had athletic talents, great capacity for vigorous sucking, and then a friendly mien.

Alexsandr Solonik thought about this in the lobby of the Grand Hotel et des Palmes, sitting on a worn sofa watching dour elderly men and their mistresses pass by, the men slumped and elegant in antique dinner suits; the women lagging behind a little, their shoulders warmed in thin chic wraps, their necks and hands asparkle. Nearby a pair of blond German men were photographing each other posed near the chair in which the famous anti-Semite Wagner composed *Parsifal*, and Solonik, who hated Germans of any stripe, tasted bitterness at this intergenerational connection. While the strobe lights on the Germans' cameras played, he kept his face averted.

While he loved the history of this old hotel, he had installed himself at the more affordable and anonymous Hotel Dante, a brisk walk away on the Bay of Palermo. Each day he wandered the cobblestones and ultimately found himself in the lobby of the Grand Hotel et des Palmes, pausing for tiny munchies and grappa at outdoor cafés and promenades, watching the parade of young and old idle their way to late dinners. In the lobby or in the cafés nearby, he invariably took a sketchpad from his carryall and, with charcoal held between his knuckles, sketched the street scapes, the roof lines of the crumbling old buildings, the closed faces of those around him. He had a dozen sketches of Wagner's famous chair and several of the streets around the hotel, the broad windows framing his efforts.

For those of the Russian *mir*, the Palmes was a touchstone in the long-ago intersection of the much admired American and much feared Sicilian Mafias. It was where the cream of the Italian underworlds had met and formed their enduring ventures. Padrones of the Sicilian *mir* still met at the hotel, enjoying vast meals in the dining lounge, their food wheeled silently and gently to tableside, the servers and maîtres d' unaware of their presence in the secret histories of old men.

Unlike Moscow, Solonik thought, where the iron template of crime had been imposed, here in Sicily the template itself had been forged — the difference between a sweet tea of leaves that had been steeped thoroughly and one of hot water splashed with haste onto a bag of dust. And that nose of the legendary architect and schemer Joe Bananas, who orchestrated the hotel meeting, gave Solonik an affinity for the history of the hotel. That great Castellamarese beak hooking, like his own, down over a thick, greedy Mafia mouth curved gently up into the mysterious smile of a private joke. Has the forensic study of the nose, a study like the phrenology of murderers, ever been done? Berezenki in Kabul had been a man of fine snout, a glorious hook sprouting from under a fox's eyes and the smooth boyish brow of the sniper; but Berezenki had dissolved in the weeps, cuddling himself closely after an operation at a schoolhouse and the subsequent games of flame with the teachers and attendants. But the hammerhead growing in Berezenki's saddened face had not been a gift of birth but the result of a slammed steel door. In the end it had been telling, this accident of life over the providence of the womb.

With this nose and these blue eyes and blond hair, thought Solonik, still I could be a Sicilian. The centuries of invasions have left blond, blue-eyed Sicilians, even blackened ones of the ancient blood mixings of Moors. I have seen the children with Chinese eyes, broad flared noses, spiky or crinkly hair of southern races. It showed up well in the women, but not so well in the men.

He'd had a whore one afternoon, then a second, then had the second again, rotating them through the lobby of the Dante, stopping at the bar for refreshments from the taciturn barman. The next day, the same. The clerks at the Dante were impressed at Solonik's parade and fairly bowed to his hooked nose as he returned from his day's wanderings, sketchings, and collectings of ass. Solonik enjoyed Palermo, a city he believed had been assembled from the best of Paris, Moscow, New York, and London.

The deskman at the Dante noted his Russian passport in the name Karpov and his loose grip on idle time; he mentioned it to his brother-in-law, the assistant manager, who in turn mentioned it to his cousin, who delivered unlabeled bottles of liquor twice a week to the barman, and the cousin commented on this admirable Russian hard-on to his zone commander, the men finally sitting with their heads together over a table at Caffé d'Oro.

"He's awaiting," the zone commander was told. "He drinks and he fucks and he vanishes into the quarter each day."

The zone commander told the cousin to have someone walk behind this Russian; the cousin said someone had three times been given the duty — in Palermo every question must be answered, every curiosity sated, every business of everyone else minded — but each time the Russian had turned a corner and disappeared, seemingly by accident. "It's difficult to follow a man who's lost," the cousin had said.

A search of the Russian's room found little: clothing bought in Spain; fat sports shoes counterfeited from an American brand; a bit of sandpaper; sketchpads and splinters of charcoals; condoms, their packaging written in French; handgrip devices; and some photographs of faces, hands, and torsos decorated with tattoos. Currencies — *paeseta* from Spain, rubles from Russia, Italian lira, German marks. All adding up to not much.

"He's some sort of military, I think," said the cousin. "The room girl said he does exercises like a soldier each morning, with the windows open. She thought he was on leave: he looks like a blond Palermitan and has a nose, but his accent is European of the east. He carries himself like a *uomo*."

"These Russians, they're untamed but ferocious," the zone commander replied. "Find out more, there may be things to know. Any details."

The cousin then mentioned that the room girl said she saw into the Russian's room one morning: cooling from his exercises, he stood with a telephone book balanced on his head and his feet apart, left to the front, right to the back, a strange balance. "He had his left arm extended, she said, like this —" the cousin took a stance, his left arm almost straight out in front with the elbow dropped, the right arm bent with the elbow folded down to touch the ribs, the right hand close to the right side of his chin "— and he had a handgrip in each, squeezing them quickly, *one two three four five six*, to a hundred, a thousand times." He looked amazed. "And the telephone book on his head?"

The zone commander, who had also been in the army, as well as being a combatant through both the visible and invisible Mafia wars of Corleone and Agrigento, stared at the cousin. "And there was, you said, sandpaper?"

The cousin nodded. "Yes, yes. Sandpaper."

The zone commander sighed. He had cultivated the rare wisdom to know there were things he didn't know. "Ah, fuck the Madonna." He went looking for a telephone. The cousin wondered what he'd said that made the dampness dew on the zone commander's forehead; he finished his own *limoncella* and then drank the zone commander's, and ordered two more and a bowl of nuts and crispies.

When the zone commander returned, looking relaxed and loose-limbed, he told the cousin he was required for a mission, immediately. He handed him a slip of paper. "Eat and drink up. Call no one. Go to this location and you'll be given a message. Return it here to me. You have done a great thing, coming to us with this Russian. It is well noticed." He clapped his hand on the cousin's shoulder.

The cousin was pleased to be of service. He drained his *limoncella* and gathered a handful of nuts. With a swagger, he left the café and walked six blocks, unknowing of the zone commander ambling along behind him. Tilting the paper in the light of a shop window, the cousin consulted his directions. Well aware of amateurism, the zone commander stepped into a doorway to avoid being seen when the cousin predictably glanced left and right and behind and edged himself around a dark blue Alfa Romeo at the opening of an alley between a *ristorante* and a hat shop. The Alfa was unoccupied and the windows down; a newspaper lay on the passenger seat and the keys were in the ignition. Palermitans notice these things: only a man of confidence would leave his vehicle unattended and unlocked; an unprotected vehicle was more dangerous than a locked and garaged one, just as unloaded guns kill more victims than loaded ones. The ground was smooth and had been recently swept out; indeed the cousin hadn't noticed the small pile of stones and detritus left neatly beside the rear wheel of the Alfa. He felt his way on the cracked walls of the alley heading toward an unshaded lamplight dangling at the far end.

The zone commander approached the Alfa and reached in, lifting the newspaper and taking up a long automatic pistol with a bulb of thick wool socks secured with elastic bands at the end of the barrel. He followed the cousin into the alley, his shoes silent on the freshly cleaned ground, and, when the cousin's head was clearly outlined against the naked bright light at the far end, the zone commander took three swift strides and just barely touched the socks to the back of the cousin's head and began squeezing the trigger, keeping the flaming socks against the skull. The cousin sank into darkness, his hair singed and acrid. Turning, the zone commander shook the pistol to extinguish the flames and made his way out of the alley and past the Alfa, which now had a man behind the wheel and the radio playing softly. Without a glance, the zone commander dropped the pistol onto the front seat. A hand flipped the newspaper onto it, and the Alfa drove away toward the Bay of Palermo, the driver whistling along to the current knockoff of a Madonna song.

The zone commander knew nothing beyond his instructions. He'd asked no questions, aware that many little things go into the creation of a big thing. A Russian with the habits of an assassin — this was of interest. An order to eliminate a chatty gossip could mean anything, and ultimately he didn't care, although he anticipated a great thing would soon emerge, and when it happened he would never speak of his small role.

Alexsandr Solonik sketched for the twentieth time the ships at harbor outside his hotel window. The sky was concrete, the water's anxious surface barely friendlier. Below, closer to his hotel, a dog barked incessantly. Solonik examined the terrain. His sniper's eyes opened and searched each shadow created by the shipping containers and fencing, and his sniper's ears subtracted echoes of the barking. Finally he located the animal beside a container sitting in deep shadow. He computed windage, angle, and distance and knew he could pipe the battered Shepherd with a single round and not have to worry about unborn pups sniffing for him later. He did an imaginary set-up, siting and breathing, looking down a long, invisible barrel and feeling his body relax into rock stillness. After the imaginary round was piped off, he sat like a whore, working his fingertips with the sandpaper, much as the whore would prepare her nails.

At eight p.m. he went down to the barroom and had the barman pour him champagne grappa. He was told the room lady, a thick mustachioed woman from a rocky village south of Palermo, had been found dead at the foot of the building, apparently having endured a mishap while cleaning windows on the sixth floor. The desk clerk, who had worked all day and was to work into the night, failed to show up. It was believed, from rumors, the clerk had been despondent over the death of the room lady and the coincident discovery in an alleyway of the assistant manager's cousin, and had gone berserk in the grief over the vale of deaths, leaving a fine, well-paying job to return to his village of Siculiana.

The barman shrugged and twitched his eyebrows. "Death," he said, "is the blackest of motives for change, no?" He poured a double glass of champagne grappa for Solonik, gratis, and asked if he was from Germany.

Solonik watched two porters disconnect small icy Christmas lights from the ceiling tiles of the lobby. He took his free drink to the ratty sofa in front of the windows and put it on the coffee table, ignoring it. At nine-thirty a tired-looking thin man with the rotating head and slip-sliding eyes of a beaten convict came into the lobby, spotted Solonik, and sat beside him. The man wore a thin sports jacket draped over his shoulders. The fill-in deskman affected not to notice the man at all; the barman went into the rear of his closet to wash clean glasses.

"Two things, my friend." The thin man indicated the grappa and Solonik nodded. The man picked up the tulip glass and drained it loudly, then spoke in textbook English: "Two things. The morning is the time, I'm told, as planned at ten a.m., and the equipment is in place as noted in your excellent sketches. Our friend is in Messina and will arrive as planned, via fast convoy on the *autostrada*. It will be a historic visit, I'm sure."

"And," Solonik asked, "the second thing?"

"Afterward, as you are removed from the zone, your masters desire to speak to you." The man burped the scent of lemons. "For such as yourself, great demand in these times, no?"

Solonik didn't ask about the payment for sniping the magistrate. It would be done for free for the men of the Sicilian *mir*, but the Circle would reimburse him his fee and expenses. For them it would be a bargain of favors, perhaps an access to the laundering facilities of Switzerland, perhaps a favored route for white powders. No matter to the hook-nosed Solonik. This shifty man was his second connection with those who required the service. Killing three to eliminate one, the arithmetic of survival. The trick, he thought, might be to avoid becoming the fourth. Unlikely because between his fearsome legend and his notorious skills, Alexsandr Solonik was an asset, like a small investment on a voracious stock exchange. But still.

"Fine, then. I will need you and the facilitator with me before the operation. You to assist my exit, the facilitator to assure the equipment is in place and functioning."

"I assure you, my friend, the equipment is fine. It's been tested and has murdered rabbits at great distance. It awaits. Myself, I have arranged your exit with the zone commander, and after tonight you have no need of my service. I bid you farewell and good fortune."

Solonik walked to the bar and ordered a glass of red wine. He returned and sat beside the shifty man. "Fine, as you wish. My last night in Palermo, and my hosts tell me you know of the finest house for the greatest of pleasures. Perhaps you can assist me in relaxing my damnable nerves?" He held up the hand with the glass of wine and made it shake, surfing the liquid. "Ooooh."

When the thin, shifty man's Fiat passed the Teatro Massimo, he fancied his way down through the gears and cut through several lanes of traffic, hung some harrowing turns, and swerved into a crowded market. "This house, of which I must admit I own a small portion, is the finest. Women who can suck the root and will refuse to spit. Black or the Chinese or the dwarf or the mother, all are available to you as a guest. If you desire a Madonna, she will appear, in robe if you wish. The cunt or ass or the mouth or the tits, all are open to you. Perhaps, like the Parisian, the pit of the arm? And the cost?" The man laughed. "For one who is a guest, there will be no cost. Perhaps for the lady a gratuity. Perhaps not." He laughed again. "For the day to come, relaxation is as important as the bullet, no?"

"Pull over at a pharmacy. I must buy the rubber domes."

"Ah, *profilattici*, the bulletproof vests of romance. Not necessary, but if your level of comfort dictates so, then it must be." He cut through a series of narrow streets and spotted the lit sign of a *farmacia* in the distance. He parked in the shadow. "The French ones with the feather —"

The edge of Solonik's hand caught him above the upper lip. Paralyzed in shock, the driver sat up straight, his hands still on the steering wheel, his throat exposed. Solonik took him by the hair and struck with the other hand three times under the chin, hearing the satisfying success of crunch and gurgle. He pulled the man's trousers below his knees and turned his pockets out. He draped the sports jacket over the man's crotch and with a serrated bladed knife reached under the jacket and hacked a frenzy of mutilation into the man's genitals, mindful of blood spatter. As Solonik slipped out of the car, he leaned back in and sliced the dead man's throat.

At dawn the facilitator was sitting in a rusted car along Via Francesco Crispi near the Dante's tiny entranceway. When he saw Solonik emerge from the hotel, he half stepped from the car and waved his hand. Solonik climbed into the back seat. The man entered traffic streaming into the city.

He was deeply tanned and spoke in Americanized English. "Where's Mario?"

"We went last night to a house of frolic," Solonik said, laughing. "The last I saw of him, he was —" Solonik positioned himself so the driver could see his face and, jamming his tongue into his cheek to mime the spasmodic head of a penis, he stroked his hand in front of his mouth "— resisting God's will."

The driver laughed. "Mario. Brains in his —" He grabbed the material at the crotch of his pants. "He was with a black?"

Solonik, who had the night before enjoyed a black woman from Ethiopia, nodded. "He said she would suck so hard he'd come downstairs in the morning and find she'd changed the oil in his Fiat without leaving the bed."

The driver laughed again. "This black, she is primo. You know primo?"

"You will facilitate me after? To the boat?"

"Yes, yes. It is arranged and there will be no hesitation. By the time the pig finishes dying, you'll be halfway to Napoli."

The car sped the wrong way up a narrow cobblestone street and swung without signal or pause into a morning fish market, the driver tapping rhythmically at the horn, moving mongers and greengrocers out of his way. He parked beside an open three-wheeled flatbed unloading squid, tuna, and a huge swordfish and led Solonik up an exterior flight of wooden stairs into an unadvertised, undecorated restaurant. They walked past women who were slicing calamari, breading tiny fish, and stirring with wooden paddles fish heads, guts, and skeletons in a stock pot. The women didn't look up; indeed a few wise ones turned away pointedly. The back of the restaurant opened onto an open roof; across the roof one flight of steps went up, the other down. Warm golden sunlight — a sweet honey for the eyes that Solonik would forever remember as being manufactured exclusively by Palermo mornings, could only pour from Sicilian skies, but eluded the black charcoal sketching sticks — climbed rough brick walls. Coos came from wire pigeon coops at the top of the steps. The men went down, then through another door and into a private apartment. A woman slept sprawled on a sofa, half-covered by a blanket, one heavy breast hanging from her blouse and one foot bare, the other shod with a sling-back high heel. A pillow obscured her face.

Solonik and the driver glanced at her, then passed through onto yet another roof. A piece of canvas was tented against the wall. Under it Solonik found a sleek hunting rifle with a scope attached, thin vinyl gloves, a two-way radio, and two plastic bags, one empty with supermarket writings on the outside and the other clear, containing brain matter, clotted blood, and shards of bone. A sack of sand lay nearby. Solonik heaved the sandbag onto the tin edge of the roof and checked his sightlines.

The tanned driver lit a cigarette and stood shuffling his feet. "Approve, and I'll take leave until after," he told Solonik.

"There's no tripod."

"But it wasn't requested."

"This sandbag, it's too stable, too firm." He straightened and looked at his companion. "I need some give, if the pig moves left instead of right, to track him. This is unacceptable. There was a pillow inside with the whore. Get it."

The man sighed and flicked his cigarette off the roof. He went inside.

Solonik heard them, the woman speaking in husky urgent tones, the driver laughing and teasing, then happily pleading. He appeared at the doorway. "I have a few moments for, ah . . ." He pumped his arm. "Then the pillow is yours, eh?"

"Be quick, but not so quick to not get your money's worth. We have time."

The man disappeared inside. The sounds of the struggle came moments later. Solonik listened carefully; the driver gurgled. The whore was smart; she'd kept the pillow over her face when Solonik passed through the apartment, and by this she implicitly promised she'd not be able to identify him. If she was insecure, he thought, it was a problem of the Sicilian *mir*, not his. The apartment door opened and closed and her unevenly shod feet clattered on steps. Solonik went inside, where the red handle of the ice pick was still vibrating in the driver's ear. He went to a closet and found a man's body bundled inside. The head was sealed in a clear plastic bag. The eyes had bulged from the pressure of the gases of a high-powered cartridge exploding in his mouth; the ears bled and what remained of the back of the head was still wet and the hair matted. Solonik dragged the man into the living room by the shoulders. He examined the walls for signs of struggle, blood, or a bullet hole and found none. The body was easy to transport onto the roof, where he covered it with the tarpaulin and sat down to wait. Again, from inside, he heard a door open and close, then moments later open again to sounds of men cursing lightly and struggling to manhandle the driver's body. There was a barking laugh and the door closed.

Moments before the magistrate was to arrive at the hotel, a voice came over the two-way radio. "Alert."

Solonik double-clicked his radio, tugged on the thin vinyl gloves, and examined the hunting rifle with professional indifference, although as a craftsman he thrilled a little at the walnut stock and the detailed hunting mosaic inlaid in silver. But a rifle, to him, was a rifle, a scope was a scope. The craft of sniping was more about the sniper than the instrument, and Solonik believed in the adage that a poor workman blamed his tools, that the careful carpenter measured twice, cut once. He'd had to use everything from a Kalashnikov to a ratty old Mossberg .22, and the result, with proper preparation of the tools, was invariably successful. He was certain the men of the Sicilian *mir* had arranged that the hunting gun belonged to the victim and there was documentation to prove it. He checked the basics: the clip in the gun, the round in the chamber, the sun still angled low enough behind the tall building at his back to put him into shadow without silhouette, and the supermarket bag nearby to carry away the radio and his vinyl gloves.

He removed the bag from the corpse's head, opened the plastic bag of human detritus, and positioned the body on its back close to the wall of the roof. Holding the bag by its bottom corners, he flung the brain matter, clots, and bone against the wall. He removed the right shoe and sock from the victim's foot and tossed them aside. The dead man's wife was rumored, through a campaign of much snide whispering, to be the mistress of the perverse magistrate who upheld the law strictly but was imperious to the natural laws of hard-working men. He used the treacherous wife, it was whispered in the cafés and bars, only as he would use a boy.

The sight line between the sniping post and the entrance to the hotel was narrow. If he looked carefully, the magistrate would see the rooftop position but nothing in the shadow; however, anyone a yard away in either direction would assume the shot came from a building directly across the street from the hotel. Solonik didn't like flash suppressers and feared the smoke from his round would pollute his position. By aiming narrowly between the two buildings in front of him, he'd be able to snipe, arrange the body and rifle to mimic suicide, and then disappear before anyone realized the shot had been fired from two streets away.

"In the zone." The voice, thick and bored, contained a hint of sneer. The transmission was getting more clear as the magistrate and those following him came closer.

Solonik clicked the radio twice and prepared himself, breathing and exercising his hands inside the gloves, positioning himself behind the rifle. The scope pulled the reality of two blocks hence up to his eye.

"In the block."

Solonik clicked twice and put the radio into the supermarket bag.

The doorman, who spent much time chasing away those who tried to park their *machina* too close to the entrance, was in front of the hotel brushing at his epaulettes, speaking from the side of his mouth to a desk clerk smoking a cigarette. To the artist in Solonik, the scene was flattened and without the depth of true life; in front of the hotel, a blue

Alfa came to a halt and expelled four men in leather jackets and casual trousers, then rolled a few feet out of his view. The four men took the grim mien of urban bodyguards, one watching for the approach of the body's vehicle, one watching rooftops, one peering into passing vehicles, and the fourth stationing himself to stop foot traffic coming from the right into the security box. They all unzipped their jackets at about the same time.

"Silver Lancia, brake lights, rolling in."

The guard watching for the Lancia's approach moved smoothly to stop pedestrian traffic. The Lancia slid into position, perfectly framed by the tunnel of buildings Solonik would fire through. The magistrate was in the rear right. Solonik waited until the escort beside the driver emerged, then waited for the rear left-side escort to get out on the traffic side of the vehicle; as that man rounded the rear of the Lancia, the magistrate exited from the rear-right seat onto the sidewalk of Via Roma. Then the Lancia moved off too quickly, before the magistrate was in a secure box, exposing his length to the street. Effectively, there were a couple of seconds when the magistrate may as well have had no protection at all. The car was stupidly gone, the front-seat escort to his left blocking nothing, the rear escort barely to the sidewalk. Solonik suspected there were many others in this conspiracy: the driver should not have moved the vehicle; he should have exited and become part of the security box until the magistrate was safely inside.

Inhaling the soft odor of the oil polished into the stock, Solonik almost played with himself, the games of Afghanistan and for a brief while Beirut: allowing a portion of his time to elapse before beginning to tighten his finely sanded fingertip on the trigger, or allowing the target to almost . . . almost . . .

exit the sniping field before snapping off a round that some might consider lucky. But the hotel was the historic site of the most famous hook-nose of all, Joe Bananas. Joe Bananas was, according to stories Solonik had read in the libraries of Europe, retired in the arid exile of Arizona, U.S.A., the George Washington of the Mafia and the Napoleon Bonaparte, too. This was no place or time for games, not at this historical spot in the landscape of the *mir*.

The fine crosshairs of the scope took the magistrate under his young but jowling chin. He'd fastened his necktie in the long thin knot favored lately by Palermitans of effete fashion. Solonik stopped his heart and pulses and moved his finger a sixteenth of an inch. The single round shredded the knot of the tie before the sound of the shot rocketed down the narrow tunnel of buildings and woke the stupid bodyguards.

Solonik gathered his traces. He laughed when he had trouble jamming the toe of the dead man behind him into the trigger guard. He'd heard of murder made to appear suicide only to be undone by a canny master sleuth who detected that the victim was left-handed while the gun was found in the right hand.

"My friend, are you left-footed? Hopefully for my sake you are not, you devil."

After passing through the apartment, over the roofs and through the restaurant Solonik was to step into the rear of a van parked and idling, the driver prepared to whisk him to the ferry docks and on to Naples. But, he thought, perhaps all these of the Sicilian *mir* don't have the gracious, hook-nosed loyalty of Mr. Joe Bananas and might seek to snip a thread between themselves and the deed.

Instead of going back the way he'd come, he clattered down the steps, casually swinging the plastic bag containing evidence of his mission. He turned to the right and immediately vanished, whistling into the crowds of the Palermo he'd come to love.

By motorcycle he'd be across the *autostrada* and in Messina by late afternoon. An espresso on the short, breezy ferry ride to Villa San Giovanni, and then to the train station in Reggio, where he'd dump the motorcycle. A train to Rome, at least, before he could contact his masters. He hoped the next engagement would be in Western Europe, not another *vor* to be slapped down in some black-polluted Eastern industrial city no one cared about.

Chapter 4

FROM MOSCOW, Bone fled east instead of west or south, quickly at first, distance his only ally. Motion, he knew, was more important than planning. Secreted in trucks or on trains as the union collapsed around him in a frenzy of insanity, rapine, and avarice, he didn't know if he was fleeing the Circle or pursuing the Code. He crossed a cannibalized landscape of ripped-up vehicles, abandoned factories blinded by shattered windows, billowing black smoke of burning fuels, butchered livestock by the side of rubble-strewn roads, vacant-eyed children, and women in head scarves, rubber boots, and drab, colorless clothing. Men roamed with ancient blunderbusses loaded with torn pieces of scrap metal; toting scythes, pitchforks, daggers, lengths of wood spiked with nails, they looted, striving pitilessly toward survival. Some invisible predator, a pack of human wolves the country people had never seen, had chewed the prime cuts from the body; only the organ meats and the skeleton remained — one for religious feasts, the other for flavoring soup of melted ice.

To flee toward Minsk would be expected; Thieves were rife there, but already many showed signs of capitulation before the corrupters of the Code. Thieves large and small had been assassinated or were only a step ahead of bounties sought by snipers, cutthroats, and informers. Bone's own brigade in Moscow had been slaughtered, and the survivors were either deep underground or had fled the city of spires in disarray. More murders and betrayals would follow as the cannibalism fed upon itself in carnivorous fission.

Bone had to avoid Kiev with its already emerging *biznesmen* Mafia, and Odessa with its growing infestation of corrupt authorities and their networks of informers, although from there he would have access to Bulgaria and on to Western Europe's teeming cities and a warm Mediterranean south. He would be expected to trek to Berlin to link up with the embattled wild Thieves there, to rest and organize and reflect.

So it was east then south, south then east. As Moscow faded behind him, he found the wild Thieves of the countryside and small cities milling in confusion, but tensile with inbred bones of iron, passing him from hand to hand as though he were a precious artifact. His name was a chant in some towns, a whisper in others. It appeared some knew he was coming, that he would follow this unlikely eastern path. He felt his heart grow near Kazan, where he lived in a leaning, abandoned barn for a week while the next leg of transport was arranged.

The peasant Thieves, who had always proclaimed themselves the true heart of the Code, supplied him with women and potato sweat and thick chunks of stringy, bloody meat or freshly slaughtered birds, treating him as a deity and not a broken Thief from the rot of urban decay. The peasant Thieves spoke of what was behind him: the stories circulated of his survival or of his death, of his escape from the poisonous whores of the Circle, his massacre of Mikhailov, his capture and evaporation in the moist fumes under Moscow sewers.

That he had met and — empty-handed — defeated the dreaded hook-nosed Solonik, disarming him of his precious sniper rifle and fucking his ass with it.

The poisonous spread misinformation, toxic slanders, told of his fall into drunkenness and of a woman with sucking fangs for teeth who had drained him of his Code and seduced him into a becoming a cabbage farmer while she cuckolded him with every passing gypsy, policeman, and cart mule. The loving told of his nighttime maraudings, harassing the crumbling State and the diseased Circle alike, and without quarter. His name was written upon walls of schools where children played *vor* and *musor*, thief and garbage, the stronger playing Bone and the weaker playing garbage — the authorities.

"You, my friend, are the ghost who all fear," a country Thief told him. "That the Code remains means hope remains. That you live means all live. I love you, and as your brother I tell you: this pestilence and plague will pass. We must measure the time in the life of a rock, not in the blooming of a flower." Awkwardly the man hugged Bone, spilling vodka from his bottle down Bone's shirt. "It was said before that you might come, and now I am blessed."

"And from who came this? That I would pass?"

"A whisper only: 'A greatness may arrive; see to his safety and pass him onward. He carries the Code as a candle.'"

"And you know not from where this whisper came?"

The country Thief shook his head sadly. Bone meditated upon whose hand was assisting him, upon who removed the stones from his path.

On the morning he was to leave Kazan, Bone stood, a gray man in a swirl of gray-blue woodsmoke, peering down a winding silver road, expecting a tractor hauling hay to pick him up. Instead, a fragile, noisy crop duster flew brightly fifty feet above his head, circled in a wide wow, and landed in a dusty swerve, hopping from wheel to wheel. An arm beckoned him to the still-running plane; inside, a weeping young pilot in a blue uniform, his ear sliced from his head and soaking black through his shirt pocket, stared straight through the windshield as he boarded.

"Ah," the country Thief laughed, waving his hand grandly, "my friend has offered transit. I'll ride with you to Uljanovsk, if I may."

At Uljanovsk the pilot spent another ear when he refused to assist in gathering fuel; holes were punched in the fuselage of abandoned airplanes and trucks, and the stuttering crop duster took off, the pilot and Bone alone on board. At Saratov the pilot was crying uncontrollably and, earless, was allowed to walk away with his tongue still in his head.

Bone headed almost due south, riding trucks, moving on foot around the edges of open land, and making subtle Thieves' signs. For days there was no recognition. For days he walked, finding luxurious leavings in garbage piles; once, while he slept on the rim of a field, a foolish bird with button eyes perched on his chest, itself seeking food, itself becoming food. At the edge of a small town, Bone read a sign and heard a Thief's song. He met a lone Thief not unlike himself, a spare man who predicted the end of the Code that would come when he himself was on his deathbed. He told of the men of the Circle scouring Europe for Bone's traces; he told of Razinkin's reward from the Circle for betraying the wild Thieves: the gift of America in the north. "The south of America is the property of another, who lives in the city of New York and has brigades of thousands. It is said he owns the president of that country and all the banks. He has many wives and his children stretch to the land of Hollywood. The north of America is a cold place, but there are many opportunities. This is the gift to Razinkin."

The men camped near a stripped-out factory and drank for three days while friends arranged the next leg of Bone's journey, a series of mercenary truck drivers who would swing him on south, around Volvograd and its dangers of betrayal, and on to the Caspian Sea.

At Asthrahan he was delivered to a hastily bulldozed airfield beside a bustling bandits' town of sagging tents, canvas lean-tos, and slat-wood shanty toilets. Stacks of wooden crates with military stencils were spread as far as the eye could see. They were loaded onto trucks and planes operated by staggering men who were clearly drunk. Clusters of men armed with military weapons monitored the transit of goods; others, bland Mongols and dour Chechens in ad hoc military outfits, stood with clipboards and pencils, checking off items. The air was thick with fuel fumes and swirling dust; the eyes stung and the throat gagged on muddy phlegm. Planes reeking of hashish landed almost hourly, off-loading skids of still-wet burlap bags and loading sturdy wooden crates of machine parts. Insect helicopters swept in low from the south end of the field shrouded in clouds of dust; men clutching briefcases jumped out and ran to other men supervising the cargo traffic. Seconds later, the men — without their briefcases — jumped back on their helicopters, rapped twice on the pilots' helmets, and were lifted away, nose down, to the north.

As the nearest airplane refueled, Bone stood shivering sixty feet away, smoking cigarettes while his escort negotiated with a pilot barely into his teens. He watched a man sink a long curved knife into a bag, scoop out a still-resinous chunk of hashish, and burn it off the point of his blade with a small torch; the man wandered through the throng of loaders, holding the sizzling chunk under their faces. Bone's escort inhaled deeply.

"The plane there is going to Taskent and then Afghanistan, master. There are stops, but the route is safe and paid for."

"He carries what? Hashish?"

"No, master. Artifacts."

"Well," Bone said, "that is what I am then, eh?"

Uncrated and secured in web netting used in place of heavier seats, the tattooed artifact sat vibrating among the other artifacts. He dozed and sang as the plane crossed the top of the Caspian Sea. He slept through refueling at Fort-Sevcenko and Novy Uzen, and awoke to watch, in a trance, as the dun ground below the plane blurred endlessly past. After a precarious landing in a field outside Urgenc, Uzbeki militia boarded the plane and ignored him as they helped themselves to boxes and sacks.

Just outside Taskent, he off-boarded, hungry and disoriented, and struck out on weakened legs toward chimney smoke on the eastern horizon. He found no trustworthy Thieves, the chain of his custody broken briefly. He foraged further, stealing bits of food from village shops, dressing himself from clotheslines and market stalls. Hiding on trucks and shuttle trains, he arrived a few miles from the border of China, where a small band of riotous wild Thieves waited to escort him. He forbade them to spend from the *obschak* to celebrate him — the fund, he said, was for Thieves in peril or despair, and he was neither, merely a traveler appreciative of the help of friends.

They had a conclave to adjudge a violation, but were only five among themselves. Bone's status exulted them and they held a brief, solemn trial for a Thief who had robbed another Thief. The malfeasant Thief was quickly judged to death; he wept and begged, and the faces of the circle of six grew cold and distant; there could be no love here in the face of such behavior. Pleading for a quick death on merit was acceptable, and so also to laugh, but to beg for no death at all was as futile and infantile as petitioning the rain to stop. Showing a fatal weakness of the spirit, it was also an insult to the halting flicker of the Code. The Thief was nailed to a door and bled casually through arteries. The men drank and gave him none; they gambled and yelled bets louder than his cries; they left the room singly or in twos and shared women in the barn, opening the door to exit and enter as the malfeasant Thief swung, as indifferent to them as a counterweight.

After a month they turned Bone over to slim, silent Shan men who hid him in a truck returning over the border; his passage had again been arranged. His life became impressions of light and dark, morning and night, cold thin air and warm thin air. He spoke no words, except to himself, the rhythmic music and chants of the Code. As he was passed from clan to clan, he followed the gestures and grunts delivered to him. The Shan bandits were uniformly direct and unsmiling. There was curiosity over Bone's tattoos and exhibitions of their own: letterings, parrots, birds — many placed in the most painful locations: the shins, the tender insides of the thighs. One morning a Shan shaved his head, and underneath, he showed Bone, was a blue and red jungle scene of whirling birds above writhing serpents. Whether out of need or curiosity, an anonymous woman came to him in the dark some nights, and a rearranging of warm clothing ensued, her small hands stilling his shivers as they massaged his back. To his grunts she replied with a soft singing mantra; when he completed she was gone, and he studied the women in the caravan the next day, wondering: which?

His beard grew out, white with streaks of gray, giving him a wisdom that drew the respect of the Shan children, and also made him the object of screeching mock fear. Small hands touched his pale, shaking skin; wide eyes studied his every move. He slept with unconcern: under a canvas on the ground, in an opium broker's apartment, or in a hut far above the world. When he was hungry, someone would feed him. When the temperatures dropped as his path rose, he was swathed in smelly skins and boots. His legendary chill, he knew, came from within: the elements were of no concern to him and he radiated an indifference to life and death that was instantly recognized by the Shan. As they climbed, he grew cold. As they descended, he grew warm, shedding the skins and furs and baring his face to the faraway bleached sky.

At Menglian in Hunan Province, he spent four weeks. He had a tooth pulled by a barber as a crowd of shoppers gathered in a market square. His reaction was one of joy and laughter and this pleased the shoppers — he was applauded. To much mirth he took the rubber-tipped pliers, reached them to the back of his mouth, and danced comically, bent at the waist and throwing his face to the sky while extracting another tooth. He had the barber remove his bloodstained beard and cut his matted hair to the scalp; women gathered the hair to take to their necromancers, witches, and foretellers. He was fed pork in leaves and tea at an outdoor restaurant as soups boiled away in forty-five-gallon oil drums over wood fires. Menglian was crowded with cars and bicycles and merchants and opportunities for thievery. He knew a Thief should never be a guest, but restrained himself from harvesting the markets.

An addicted United Nations Development Program agronomist, whose clothing smelled of opium smoke, was paid American cash to carry Bone out of China into Burma. A Burmese bodyguard in a leather jacket, tight blue jeans, a black Fukengroovi T-shirt, and white running shoes climbed onto the deck of the truck, a wooden-handled .32 revolver in his pocket. The guard wore aviator sunglasses and affected the loose-hipped walk of Hollywood film heroes. Bone sat in the back seat of the white Mitsubishi truck as the marked vehicle was piloted through the border north of Ho Tao. The immaculately uniformed, rigid Chinese guards at the gate executed perfect sharp maneuvers, allowing the truck to cross as though it were invisible. Instantly the roads deteriorated; poppy fields grew on all sides, attended by bright butterflies of women cutting bulbs and gathering sap.

The UN truck followed the Menglian River for a few miles and stopped at a United Shan States Army military intelligence checkpoint where it was leisurely searched. As they waited, Bone, the UNDP man, and the bodyguard were given scented tea and dumplings full of organ meats. The bodyguard slipped a wad of yuan to the MI team, and the Mitsubishi continued south.

They sped past the edge of Ho Tao, where the local opium addicts lounged and rotted in the deep shadows of collapsed sheds among packs of mangy dogs. The addicts watched with detachment as the truck roared past in a cloud of dust and continued through town to a squat hotel with a slat-board casino set up in the center of the parking lot.

The UNDP man took Bone inside, checked him into a room with a glassless barred window overlooking a swamp of gaseous brown water, and left with the bodyguard in tow. Mosquitoes filled the room with a cloud of song and Bone lit coils to combat them, then covered himself with a tent of sheets. Fully dressed, he slept a rare deep sleep, undisturbed by the constant traffic of high heels and military boots on the metal walkway outside his door.

He awoke when a fat rat, caught between the warped floor and the bottom of the loose-fitting door, struggled to enter. He rose in the dim dawn light, opened the door, and nursed the rat out with his shoe. "Flee, Thief."

The air was cold and gray. A square man in a brown military uniform with no insignia and a fatigue cap was smoking a filtered Hangtoshan cigarette on the catwalk. The soldier reached out and lifted Bone's hand, studying the markings and consulting a slip of paper. He nodded and handed Bone a Hangtoshan, lighting it with a slim gold butane lighter. They smoked as the last of the gamblers stumbled out into the smoky morning air, the music from a boom box continuing unabated. Two whores were sprawled unconscious beside a Nissan truck, one of them bleeding bright blood from under her wig.

The soldier showed Bone a gold Rolex with diamond crust and touched numbers. Both above and below the watchband were thick bracelets of linked gold. The soldier held up eight fingers. Bone nodded. The man mimed taking a shower, holding one hand over his head, fingers pointed down, and rubbing his armpit with the other hand. Again Bone nodded. The man led him down the metal steps, across the parking lot, through the guarded gates, and across the road to a squat cinderblock building. Inside, the man put his hand on his sidearm and a sleepy young woman handed Bone a thick towel and a small square bar of used soap. The soldier pointed down a hallway, lit another cigarette, and leaned against the wall.

The public shower was empty except for a young man with Shan tattoos on his legs and chest. Bone picked a stall and turned on the stainless-steel taps, filling the tiled room with steam. He scrubbed until the soldier whistled out, then dried himself thoroughly, doing some vague exercises he'd seen performed in southern China. The soldier came into the stalls and handed him a pair of bleached-out khaki pants and a blue Calvin Klein T-shirt. They smoked more Hangtoshans in front of the building until a black Pajero 4x4 with smoked windows pulled up. Bone was courteously handed into the front passenger seat beside a sullen driver whose lips foamed red with betel-nut juice.

Time became measured by distance, and when he found himself riding in a mule train across wide gyres in the Shan states of eastern Burma, he was startled at the thinness of the light, the dryness of the air, and the shock of color of the women stripping poppies in the opium fields under a rinse-water sky. For the first time in his life — except for trips to the frontier of prisons and camps, he'd never been outside the city of spires — he felt he'd reached an unimaginable paradise of dreams. If he weren't a Thief carrying a Code, he could live in these high, thin mountains with men carrying homemade, single-barreled shotguns, braces of birds slung over their shoulders, their women in camps by the side of the scratches of road, children playing with toys made from branches and sticks, woodfires always burning. He could live among the men in traditional *longji* shopping in markets, hand in hand, Russian rifles slung upside down across their shoulders. He could endure the suspicious squatting Akha women in their black turbans woven with silver decorations, who watched him sideways, as they puffed on fat bamboo tubes and let the smoke ease from their mouths.

As the convoy edged into a valley, it stopped for food and supplies at a wide point in the road where wooden buildings had been arranged around a dusty square. Bone wandered, trailed closely by a young boy with the wide happy face of an idiot. On the wall of one building were a handful of posters showing the beheadings of two men. The idiot pointed at the posters, laughed, and made fucking motions with his hips, shaking his head. Dead rapists. From inside the building came the sounds of machinery. Bone wandered in — a Thief must never be a guest — and found a family operating an ancient, cast-iron cigarette-rolling machine, all smoking bright new cigarettes. A printing press across the room was almost covered with teetering stacks of flattened red-and-white Marlboro boxes and blue Players cigarette packages. Under high windows, wooden crates of tobaccos were piled against walls. The idiot took a handful of cigarettes, tugged Bone's elbow, and they returned to the mule train where the men of the wild Wa waited to take control of his transit. To the tiny Wa, a tribe of animists who took heads to decorate their crop fields, Bone was, in spite of his fine almond-shaped skull, just another sack of opium paste to be balanced on a compliant mule. He was of a value unknown to them, as unknown as the ultimate value of the paste they transported. They were silent with him, and he, like a hefty sack of opium, said nothing. They traveled in a sometimes circuitous meander for three nights, each evening tethering the mules, setting guards, and then sleeping on the ground, covered with huge fronds hacked from the canopy of trees.

The mule train was met on the outskirts of a small village of decrepit huts by a man in a mismatched camouflage; the man beckoned Bone from his mule and indicated a black Pajero parked nearby. The men got in, and after the driver threw a handful of white pills into his mouth, sped down a half-completed road of small stones and potholes full of rainwater.

Burmese officials accepted a thick wad of American currency to permit Bone out of the Shan military zone north of Kentung, and like a vague ghost covered in the rich red clay dust of the road, he was driven south into the city and delivered to the airport. The amphetamine-addled driver pointed at the low terminal and made a palm-down gesture: wait.

For four days Bone slept behind the airport terminal, wrapped in a tattered rug. A Burmese soldier passed by each mid-afternoon with a lacquer box containing greasy rice dishes with strings of meat woven through them, and plastic bottles of water. Bone waited for a twice-weekly flight to carry him to the capital, Rangoon. But the Tuesday plane never came. When the Thursday plane also failed to materialize, his invisible hosts became impatient and he was put into another Pajero and driven toward the Thai border. Men of the Karen met him and took his custody until night; then, under a confusing whistle of mortar shells, he ran with them, crouched and breathing the war scents of freshly unearthed soil and molten metal. Urgent whispering men met him in the darkness near the Thai side, where he was pushed into another truck full of canvas sacks of methamphetamine pills and taken through the jungle, past the rebels' liberation lines, into Thailand.

Now he was moved quickly with purpose, although he thought not of the purpose itself, just that he had a mission — to keep the light of the Code. Another truck, and then a train ticket, was provided to him in Chiang Rai by a furtive, fearful man with the mixed features of a Japanese and a Slav.

To Bangkok he slept upright overnight and was met at the railway station by a crippled Muscovite who took him into the *sois*, the crooked side streets around Sukhumvit, and into the rear door of an elegant three-story brothel run by and for the Japanese.

He spent a week on the tame first floor of the building, straying out in the evenings for Heineken beer and food from street vendors. The streets thronged with vanilla men in vanilla clothing, accompanied by childlike women. These men, Bone adjudged, followed the code of the prick. There were Russian women working on the brothel's second floor; they had battered bodies, but their faces were unmarked and bland with the smoke of opium. The brothel didn't allow Arabs or uninvited Japanese tourists. Their violence was a matter of fear in both Sukhumvit and Soi Cowboy. A Russian woman tapped at his door one night and counted his fingertips. Finding nine, she nodded distractedly and passed silently into his room. She arranged herself on the musty bedcover, and when he finished she described herself as a consort, homesick and running along a wire of powerful heroin. Bone gave her no money, but she visited the room each night. Some nights he slept with his back against the front of her body. On others he summarily had her at his convenience, without request or invitation. She was grateful to speak Russian and not be beaten, and she told him of the third floor, which she described as a paradise for men where nothing was recorded or remembered, but from which shattered girls were removed every dawn. Many were found floating in the *klongs*.

After a month the crippled man returned with a sack of clothing and food in plastic bags. At the port of Bangkok the man gave Bone a dagger and he was spirited aboard a rusty freighter, along with three hundred and fifty emaciated

Fujianese migrants, mostly men, but with a few women and children, all bound for America. Descending into the dank darkness of the hold, Bone staked out his space and for three nights remained awake with the dagger in his hand, fighting off the desperate young men who coveted his food, his clothing, his leg room, and the very air he breathed. Three fellow passengers, one a twelve-year-old boy, were dead by the dawn of the third day, their blood dried and cracked on Bone's hands. The jockeys who shepherded the shipment were grim as they ordered the bodies removed. They never became friendly or outwardly respectful toward Bone, but his gruel of watery rice was scooped thick from the bottom of the pots, brought to his remote corner, and set in front of him, while the mass of migrants had to throng around battered tin pots. He was unbothered by the din and the smells and the moaning of his fellow passengers; he was focused on his Code, holding up each tenet and examining it as he had thousands of other nights. He had done it for days at a time on transit trains and in labor camps, in a trance that some Thieves feared was a coma.

One night the ship's engines cut and the ship drifted. There was yelling from the deck as the hatch opened and the passengers were ordered topside by the jockeys. The Taiwanese captain and his Korean crew forced the entire shipment, including the jockeys, overboard at gunpoint into the six-foot-deep warm waters of a bay. The night was fragrant with untreated wastes and heavy with the sinister; the lights of the boat receded and dozens of migrants died finding their way to the lights of the coast. One of the jockeys who couldn't swim repeatedly forced passengers underwater, drowning them so he could use their bodies to keep afloat until he found a sandbar under his feet. Bone made his own way, wide of the churning, panicked waters, and finally lay on a sandy beach of garbage and rocks. Thick, dark shadows emerged from the black bracken along the shoreline and attacked those who had made it to shore, ripping at their clothing and tussling them for their few packages and bags. Officials in dark uniforms waded in with clubs and protected the survivors: the officials would be paid a bounty for the surviving migrants who were picked up later by another migrant mothership. Bone waited through the night, his exposed skin caked with salty mud to screen the flying insects. When the sun came up, the chaos on the beach had ended and only a few bodies remained, undulating in the lacy surf.

Bone washed himself clean in the bay, ate a piece of raw fish, chewed some kelp, and, carrying nothing except the dagger in his belt, passed through the bracken and then the itinerant camps with their greasy fires in tins. He began walking south on a cracked, baked road. Farmworkers on a jolting, three-wheeled truck made room for him; he sat in the rear by a load of fetid fruit with children running their fingers over the decorations on his face and hands. A woman in a bright *khanga* fashioned a bonnet from a burlap bag and fitted it over Bone's head, pointing at the fast-rising run and shaking her head while making an addled face of slack jaw and googly eyes. She laughed, showing him black teeth and a healthy fat pink tongue.

A man with tribal scars grooved into his cheeks reached over and touched the tattoos on Bone's hands. He spoke in religious-school English: "Master, these I have in M'b'sa, you see?"

Bone stared into the man's happy black eyes and shook his head.

The man repeated himself in Swahili. Bone shook his head.

The man tapped the series of tattoos on Bone's knuckles. He said in English, "These decorations are of men in M'b'sa, you see?"

Again Bone shook his head. He spoke back in Russian, pieces of German and Japanese; he tried his few words of English. The man shook his head, seemingly pleased at this linguistic challenge.

"Permit," he said, gently reaching to open Bone's worn shirt, his long hands moving slowly, his eyes cautiously on Bone's. With his finger he traced the pointed stars tattooed on Bone's chest. "M'b'sa." He nodded his head, touched the stars, and pointed to a cloud of pollution far ahead on horizon of the road. "M'b'sa, you see?"

Bone touched his stars and pointed with the same hand, south. "M'b'sa?"

The man nodded vigorously, pleased. "M'b'sa."

Bone pointed at the truck and then at Mombassa and raised his eyebrows.

The man laughed and touched him lightly on the knee. He nodded. "Yas, yas, you see."

In Mombassa, Bone and the man left the truck and hitched a ride together on an open-bed vehicle crammed with singing day workers. The sullen driver listened as Bone's companion sang a chant, then allowed them to climb on. In front of a ramshackle building they disembarked, and Bone silently followed the man through the still air crowded with flies and heavy with the rotten air of a fish market. They crossed an open, dusty area of tiny children in school uniforms and into another closed market, through it and past mosques, until they came to a major intersection crammed with cars. A modern-looking bleached building with walls of barred windows stood in front of them. Inside, a black security guard in a mismatched uniform and sandals, armed with a truncheon and pistol, his belt white, waved the club threateningly in the chill air conditioning. Bone's companion bowed his head and spoke rapidly in Swahili; the guard nodded and went to a telephone. Moments later a tall, bent, elderly man, wearing an untucked white shirt, black pleated trousers, and wing-tip shoes, emerged from a door beside the security desk.

The man instantly took in Bone's tattoos and spoke Russian with an elegant formality. "A friend blesses me."

"I traveled far to meet one such as you."

"This one of the mud kingdom, he is your slave?"

"A savior. I beg he be compensated fairly. A working man, I admit, but a beacon in this darkness of the ass of God."

The Russian man was in his seventies and had a faint prisoner's stoop and shuffle, a bald head, and knuckles of discolored flesh where he was missing an ear. He had bands of barbed wire inked around both wrists, partially covering slit marks. He had a skull engraved on the web of his right hand, and a tattoo of a black bullet hole leaking red blood over his heart, visible through the thin white shirt. The stars on his clavicles were faint traces where the fabric of the shirt stretched across his chest. He gave Bone's companion a shilling.

"With respect," Bone said. "This man has delivered me."

The Russian plucked another shilling from his pants pocket and gave it to the man. The man bowed to both of them and left under the watchful eye of the security guard. The Russian man led Bone through the door by the security desk, up two flights of stairs, and into an office furnished with a cot, a desk, a lamp, and a stack of boxes against the wall. Above, a ceiling fan rotated slowly.

"I am Razor. This is my office."

Bone stared at him. "You? A worker? But the Code . . . ?"

"Old friend, fear not. The Code prevails. This is poached space. An accommodation: I steal, but not too much. Here there are capitalist Thieves, those who would harm you."

"And you know me?"

"Do I know the taste of my blood?" Razor bowed slightly. "It was said a keeper was in journey, but wasn't expected to pass here."

"A ship, then water, then here. Unplanned, I think, but . . ." Bone shrugged and looked around the office. "This arrangement, it is a violation."

"No, no. It is survival. As in Moscow and Kiev, so is it here."

"No. I must leave."

"Please, *dyed*. You are a younger man. The world has spun like a whore with an itch in the ass. We cannot survive — the Code cannot survive — unless measures are taken."

"I cannot take anything which is bought, only what is taken."

"And so it is and shall be. You are the keeper of the Code and you must be protected and held as close as a mother's locket. If this I do offends you, I will walk the streets and markets and steal at your side. We will make all as it should be. I beg you."

Bone looked into Razor's eyes and recognized his own. "I must reflect."

"I will leave you, then. If when I return . . ."

Razor returned at dark to find Bone. The men said nothing. They slipped from the building, through streets paved and broken, pausing around corners to check for followers, then moving on. After an hour Razor pushed open a door with faint streaks of light showing between the rough wood slats. The smell of food drifted out. Inside, lit by torches, a dozen men sprawled on chairs around a pair of tables as far from the stove as possible. Several pots of food were warming on the elements and a wooden barrel gave off the odor of fermenting fruit. The room was tall and warm and windowless. Razor greeted each man in turn, in order of their position in the brigade. All looked at Bone with curiosity, but none spoke.

"The dark ones call this *nyama choma*," Razor told Bone as a young apprentice Thief ladled beans and stringy meat from an aluminum pot. The apprentice offered the bowl to Razor, who shook his head and indicated he should give it to Bone. Taking the second bowl, he led Bone to a corner, where they ate with their heads together. A card game began and liquors in cola bottles were passed around. The apprentice brought Bone and Razor a bottle each, then went back to the table to observe the card game and receive wisdom.

"This place is the port used by the Chinese pig train, to transit their cargoes," Razor told Bone. "They come here or they use the island." He pointed his thumb southeast, toward Comoro. "The dark tribes have their tradition and code; they are many and we are few. There are Chinese who have waited lifetimes for the next ship, but they wait forever. They are lost people, but they too have their tradition and code."

"And," Bone said, raising his eyebrows, "all can flourish?"

"The potatoes are small. But better a thousand small potatoes than ten big ones." Razor finished his *nyama choma* and picked up his bottle. He drank, wiped his mouth, and took a deep breath. "We of the Code are a dozen. Before the pus began leaking out, we were forty. Many went back and died. Some stayed and vanished. Some — the younger ones who know no better — made accommodation with the new reality." He shrugged. "We find them, we kill them. But they too kill us. Our *obschak* depletes. We endure. We've heard of your death and your survival, but never expected your appearance. If this is to be your home, we must realign. A Thief eats stones and drinks air — plenty of both here, and room for all."

Bone drank his liquor, the taste reminiscent of the fumes of the deteriorating fruits on the three-wheeled truck. "I must be a traveler, though I envy you your —" he tapped his chest "— riches. I have been a dory in a river of many currents, but my river continues."

"And your destination?"

"Unknown to God or myself. Further on, in any case. I will stop only to plant the flower of the Code."

Razor drank. "Rocky soil."

Bone nodded. "Rocky soil indeed. But in catastrophe, whether fire or flood, the roots remain beneath the ground and grow strong."

Bone remained in Mombassa for five months while Razor negotiated his transit. The wild Thieves and the apprentices pestered him with questions of Russia and the battles against the new reality. He told them the history of the Code was as long as the history of a rock: to a rock, human lifetimes lasted less than one second. The cannibalism would end when the last mouth ate its own asshole. The rich new reality and the coopting of weak Thieves were the fires that made the Code tensile. He told them of assassinations and disappearances, and of Mikhailov's dacha where he was to be converted to give blessing to the foul Circle. He told them tales of the Shan and the Wa, of opium trains and hashish planes, and the pilot with no ears. They listened closely, laughed loudly, and absorbed an oral history that once spoken would long outlive them all.

One apprentice went out to forage and never returned. The Thieves said he had been killed, and a three-day party for his passing-up was held. Another became ill and feverish; Thieves comforted him and sang filthy, funny songs until he died.

When Bone went out, he wore long sleeves and a thick shirt. He mostly kept his hands in his pockets except to steal small. He ate a muddy goat stew and was sick for three days. "Ah, the inside comes out," the Thieves laughed. "Make quicker the shit: the more room inside for the precious." They fed him bowls of boiled rice and sweet tea. Apprentices sang Thieves' songs and read his tattoos with awe.

On what was to be Bone's last night with them, Razor appeared with a plastic bag containing seventy wrinkled American one-dollar-bills, an aluminum cigar tube, a large plastic bag, a new dagger, a pair of trousers and a thick sweater, and dry soup noodles in cellophane packages stamped Made in Chicago, Illinois, U.S.A. He told Bone a freighter was leaving the following day with a shipment of Chinese, bound for America.

"It is arranged; the journey will take many weeks, but the captain has been enticed to carry you as a precious thing," Razor said. "This pig train is always successful, arranged by the men of China. Here, now, you are to say nothing. Our missing apprentice has gone over to the new reality and I fear for the safety of all. Back there —" he made a zigzag series of hand motions in the shape of church spires, Moscow "— they are aware of the traveling Thief. In spite of their testimony of your death or falling, they surely know you are alive and well and among friends. Point south, go north."

"As always."

"You carry our hearts."

The next day before dawn, Bone was taken on foot through the now-familiar markets and bends of the city. A truck carried him to the harbor, where a fearful apprentice waited by a flat wooden boat with a sputtering motor. The bay was a gelatinous warmed stew of sewage, rotting fish, and fuel oil simmered to fragrance through days of pounding sunlight. Bone and the apprentice boarded and puttered out among the rusted hulls of boats of all sizes until they came to a caked black hull covered with pits and scrapes. A ladder of thick rope and wood slats dangled down the hull, and the apprentice steadied himself and the boat. He kissed the back of Bone's right hand. Bone slung his bag over his shoulder and ascended.

An Asian man with a single eye awaited at the top. Wordlessly, he grabbed Bone's hand and studied the tattoos. He nodded and began a casual body search. Finding no money or valuables, he examined the dagger, then shrugged and handed it back. He turned to Bone's carryall, stared at the packaged soup noodles and a box containing matches and half-smoked cigarettes. He shrugged again and handed them back, then escorted him to an open hatch where a jockey stood with a long knife at his waist. He bowed and Bone ascended into a bowel of soft, furtive sounds and the odors of shit, food, and sweat.

"Our first-class passenger," the one-eyed Asian said in Tagalog to the jockey. "A lord."

"He's in his kingdom now."

"The kingdom of the pig." Both men laughed. A whistle sounded. The ship's screw began rumbling and the deck vibrated. Chain scattled against metal. The hum of conversation from below halted. A woman screamed briefly and a baby wailed.

The one-eyed man glanced down into the hold. "Close it up now, we make way."

"The *guilo*, he had no money?"

"This one came wet on the last train. He killed a few and has traveled raw before. Perhaps a tube of money or stones up his ass, perhaps not."

"We should have checked."

The one-eyed man laughed bitterly. "And how far would you put your nose up a *guilo*'s brown eye, even for diamonds or American dollars?"

Chapter 5

THE SHIP was twelve weeks at sea, stopping twice to offload specific passengers, once to pick up stranded pigs who had been unaccountably marooned by previous captains. The hatch to the hold was opened most days for about an hour, but no one was allowed on deck; the migrants crowded for a glimpse of blue sky or free birds. On good days the scent of ocean salts drifted into the hold, replacing fetid damp air and causing homesickness among the pigs who, mainly, were from the Fujian province, a place awash at dawn and dusk with the heavy saline breezes of the sea. Two men had a knife fight over something Bone couldn't understand. The violence was quick to heat and the fatal stabbing was, as always, an unexpected conclusion: a shout, another shout, a tussle, then a jumping apart of the two men as they oriented themselves before closing again; the sidearm staccato stab-stab-stab-stab of a knife and one man collapsed, grunting, his breath squeaking from his punctured lungs as he died. One night there was a rape at the darkest reach of the hold, four men and one woman, each man in turn gently holding the woman's baby, the spectators averting their eyes as each took his turn. When the hatch opened and thick Caribbean air fell into the hold, the woman had paired herself with one of her attackers, holding the baby in her arms, leaning against her new mate's body, his arm encircling her shoulders. Another suitor's body was lifted out of the hold and given a bath in the salt ocean.

Bone sat in his corner, unaware he was to have received a special handling, that an indifferent betrayal had befallen him, but himself indifferent. He slept sitting and, there being passengers from the first ship who had witnessed his ferocity, was unbothered — in fact, he was deferred to when the buckets of watery, salty rice sometimes containing flakes of fish or tinned meat were lowered down at mealtimes. An older migrant sitting near him began a complicated game of hand signals, silently throwing fingers to make a series of even numbers. Bone's missing finger joint made the game more complex, but he enjoyed the man's company.

The Code was his clock and his compass, and for hours he could search it for anomalies; there were none, and, in an array of complicated circumstances, there were many. When he arrived where he was to arrive, would he walk his own way, a solitary keeper of the Code? But what of the Code's tenet that said he must find, teach, and train young Thieves? What if there were no young Thieves where he finally found land? And what of Razinkin? The *mir* had its own secret voice and he knew the testicle Razinkin was now in the north of America, living a fabulous life fueled by the bones of betrayed Thieves. Bone knew his escape path had been orchestrated from Moscow and the only hand that could have guided him was that of Grigorev, the Chinaman. The most reluctant of those who had flipped themselves into the new reality, the Chinaman had remained the closest to the true Thieves; it would be the Chinaman who diverted pursuit and made dust to the west when Bone fled east.

Indeed, the hand of the Chinaman appeared through the final portion of Bone's journey. When the ship from Africa arrived in America, it was a hundred miles from the anticipated landing spot near New York, farther south in black night, and, as in the first pig train, the survivors were shown a light onshore. The lucky and quick were herded overboard into small boats, shoved by screaming crew members. The unlucky grabbed the gunwales of the little motorized dinghies and hung on. Several men and women had to swim, a baby slipped away, then another. Bone felt a little body bump his legs and grabbed down, pulling a gasping infant above the water. He threw it into a dinghy. The light onshore went out and there were screams from the frightened and prayers from the faithful. There was a struggle on one boat and then a body was in the water, and then another. The light went back on as the mothership backed frantically out of the inlet; Bone felt its waves coming up behind him and struck out alone for a darker shadow just to the left of the light. His bag was tightly sealed inside the plastic bag Razor had provided; loosely tied to his waist, it provided some buoyancy.

The night was warm and the water greasy and cold, and Bone took his time, smoothly stroking, then floating on his back and examining the ceiling of black night and blazing stars above. Stroke. Float. Check direction. A shooting star scratched a brief arc in the sky: an omen. The third time he checked for bottom with his feet, he found it. He walked through the surfing water two hundred yards from the landing light. There were gunshots at sea, then the coastline seemed to blaze with red and blue strobe lights and deep voices yelled through bullhorns. A pair of helicopters appeared over the trees at the rim of the inlet, seemingly balanced on cones of light that ran like liquid silver on the water. Spotlighted, the scene seemed insane: some tried to swim toward the diminishing mothership, itself now surrounded by lit patrol boats, while others swam diagonally. Some who'd found footing raised their hands in the air and hung their heads. Now there was more wailing of grief than screams of fear. The sharp rip of a heavy machine gun, every third round a tracer, erupted near the invisible mothership and another pair of helicopters headed in that direction. More bullhorns, and then the mothership, huge and sinister, was lit up with the jerking cones of light.

Bone found sand, then grass, then low scrub. He heard sirens race along the highway. He wondered if he were still in Africa, if the mothership had merely sailed in a month-long circle, the captain laughing and counting his money, the pigs below unaware of the joke. But, he knew, the water was too cold to be that of Africa, and the cones of light and the helicopters and the bullhorns had the aspect of a rescue. Where he felt the scrub was thickest, he untied his plastic bag, stripped out of his soaked clothing, and dried himself as best he could. He dressed in dirty but dry clothes and spread the plastic on the ground. As the sound of helicopters and screams diminished, he slept.

Throughout the next day he nourished himself with his Code, and hunger itself filled him. The shivering went away as the sun rose over the inlet. Men in uniforms made their way along the shoreline; they found some bodies and marked them with long poles bearing triangular flags. Two officials came up into the scrub, but didn't penetrate deeply enough. A helicopter raced low over the brush and sand and essayed a circle around a group of large rocks a hundred yards further along, hovering there until a Jeep with a badge on its doors sped along the shore. Men encircled the rocks and Bone watched three dejected young Chinese men being brought out, their hands cuffed in lengths of plastic, then a man and two women, one of them carrying a baby. Later in the day television vans drove onto the beach and reporters stood with their backs to the water, pointing and speaking into cameras and microphones. When darkness came, Bone told the stars of his admiration. Exhausted by his delirium, he slept ignoring the sharp bites of small invisible things that lived in the sandy grass in the scrub. As Thieves must steal, so must these mites eat. Just before dawn he foraged, finding a garbage bin that yielded a half-eaten hamburger and a tin of sweet soda with an inch left in the bottom. By the end of that day, the beach was quiet, and Bone slept fully until dawn.

As the sun reached ten o'clock, he began moving toward where the light had been two nights before. In a paved turnaround, two men sat on the hood of a station wagon, drinking beer. Bone trudged past them, his bag over his shoulder, singing softly in Thieves' music a song of lengthy prison sentence, dead brothers, and the Code. The men watched him without interest, threw their empties into the tall grass, and drove away. In the parking area, Bone found a pair of portable toilets, a pay phone, and some picnic benches. A middle-aged man in blue jeans and an open workshirt over a T-shirt sat reading a newspaper, smoking American cigarettes, his sunglasses up to keep his long gray hair off his sad, heavily creased face. A white paper bag with an M inscribed on it swayed in the breeze. The man reached in and took out a french fry, popped it into his mouth, and looked around. Bone saw blurred tattoos on the back of the man's hand.

The man stood and bowed. He had very short legs and a fat, massive upper body. He put one finger to the outside edge of his right eye and pulled the corner sharply down. Bone walked unsteadily toward the man, dropped his bag, collapsed on the wooden bench, and began shivering.

On the drive to New York, the man fed him french fries and bottled water and was solicitous and respectful. He draped Bone in the workshirt and operated the heater in his van, easing Bone's vibrations but causing himself to sweat profusely.

"We were fortunate the television is so quick, master," said the man, who'd introduced himself as Cowboy. "We were awaiting you on the beach near Rockaway when a friend called about the operation down here. Some deaths, he said, and we feared our hearts had broken. The Chinese became agitated for reasons known to none and passed too far south. Razor had sent a message through true friends to alert us of our blessing, and of your mission. My master said to go here and wait until hope fled: 'It will be done for all time, if the *dyed* is perished. We will kill as many as we can and leave on each the legacy of betrayal. The spoken history will survive and it will be known we battled.' I was to await one more day, when you appeared."

They entered New York across a vast iron bridge and made their way to Brooklyn, to an apartment a safe distance from the Russian enclaves of Brighton Beach and Coney Island. Few knew of Bone's presence, and he rested up for several days. The news from Moscow was grim. He'd been reported dead under a myriad of shameful circumstances — murdered by a woman, by a boy, fucked to death by a screaming homosexual policeman. Sniped in the street by Solonik in Berlin, his carcass torn and eaten by wild city dogs; castrated by a transvestite in Prague. A suicide under a subway train in London. Battered to death after confessing all to the police in Bonn, his drug-addicted and festering, diseased lips speaking names of all, sins of many. Mikhailov — Madhouse — had been killed because he had tried to stop Bone's betrayals and had gloriously died for it. Ranger had returned to his mountains, washing his hands of white brothers and spitting vindictive blood at Bone's crusade of treachery.

Razinkin, Andropov, and Grigorev — Tomahawk, Wrecker, and Chinaman — had formed a triumvirate, erased their markings of the *mir*, and aligned themselves with the new reality. Wrecker had Berlin, where he stamped out the legends of fallen Thieves and operated drug networks; the Chinaman remained in Moscow, more a hostage than a principal, carefully watched and given the task of bringing recalcitrant Thieves into the new reality; Razinkin had been given the north half of America, where he created financial ties that encircled the globe and made the dirty coin into the shiny. The powerful *vor* Zakon, who had come to America many years earlier, sat in Manhattan, a prince admired and feared by all, his brigades in many of the east coast states. Zakon and his brigades had to be avoided, Cowboy told Bone, and plans were made to move Bone into the north of America, to a land of snow and vast frozen fields of few trees but many wolves.

On his last night in Brooklyn, Bone — fed and rested and having discovered an unending appetite for the women brought to the apartment blinded by masks with eyeholes covered in black tape — found Cowboy and a slim old man in the living room. The man's eyes mirrored Bone's, and he had patchy white hair clipped short and deep grooves carved in his cheeks by determination and prison. Cowboy poured tall glasses of vodka and put a platter of fried succulents on a tippy coffee table. He excused himself, bowing to both men. The old man pulled his shirt from his shoulders and showed faded stars, then pulled up the cuffs of his baggy trousers and showed smaller stars engraved in his knees: I bow to none. Straightening his clothing, he sat beside Bone on a sagging sofa and took his hand.

"We have a friend who may appear to be not," the man said in Russian. "It was he who, after the slaughter of the pig Mikhailov, pointed west when he knew you went east. It was he who made safe for you when he could, and directed both the Razor and us to do you a fine bidding. His confusion is around us. He made you dead in a subway station; he made you invisible and elusive. He sat the hook-nosed Solonik in Spain for a month, then in the north of Africa for another. This friend sends a message that he fears he cannot tell you himself, and he fears that in his sickness and treachery his time shortens."

The old man sat with his back against the cushions, tossing back icy vodka, and recited his words as he'd been told them: "In Moscow we knew not if you perished, whether by misadventure or through the deceit of the men of China, sunken into a watery cell. The whore of spires has betrayed us all, and Mikhailov was never the man he revealed himself to be. The Tomahawk is the architect of our destruction. Now that I have you in safety, I bid that you destroy this betrayer, a small weight on the scale to bring some balance. I ask this and may not know of your success or failure; however, as long as one Thief carries the Code, our *mir* will survive for others." The old man opened his eyes and looked around the stark room. "Since you left, there have been many events. In Africa, a slaughter of Razor's brigade. Thieves — Argent in France, Wrench, also in France, and Belltower in Belgium — are dead. In Thailand there have been events as well, but we don't know who is dead and who has fled." He waved his tattooed fingers at the window. "Out there is . . ." He made a hook of his thumb and touched his nose: Solonik.

"And this friend?"

The old man tugged the corner of his eye downward: Chinaman, as Bone had thought. A fallen Thief's redemption.

"And here, in this place?"

"This place is over. Trading companies, private banks, brigades of lawyers instead of Thieves. Zakon is a businessman who purchases politicians. He has hundreds of men, some women too, and they loot and steal invisibly inside the towers. All are allowed to steal, but forbidden to act alone, without permission. Here there are many: Italians, the men of China, blacks, even Chechens and Albanians. Zakon makes accommodation, sells services, to all who require them."

"But," Bone said, aghast, "but you fought, surely?"

The old man shrugged. "But we are alone here. The spires tower to the sun; we cringe in a low, cold shadow. No one has the Code, except you and perhaps I, perhaps a few scattered Thieves living silent lives. Zakon's spies abound — a conclave cannot be held without him knowing; he must be invited to send a representative. He travels with the fellows of sports, lifters of weight and throwers of iron. In the north you will find the same, with the bowel Razinkin. We must bury deep now in this winter, grow strong in the springtime. It is the only path."

Arrangements were made for Bone to be taken overnight by van to the Canadian border near Buffalo. Only Cowboy accompanied him. At dawn, just south of the border, Cowboy stopped the van in a train yard and told Bone to keep out of sight in the back. Cowboy walked across the stitches of railway tracks and cheerfully greeted an enormously fat man who kept looking over Cowboy's shoulder at the van, as if trying to gauge the value of the contraband within. The fat man held a piece of yellow chalk and made three vertical lines in the air, then pointed at a jumble of trains. Cowboy gave the fat man a wad of money; the man put it into his blue overalls, then continued talking, arguing now. Cowboy found more money and gave it to the man. Together they walked among the trains and out of Bone's sight. A few seconds later the fat man, blood spouting from a bright wide slash under his chin, ran from between the trains and skidded in his own blood. Leisurely, Cowboy walked across the tracks to where the fat man had collapsed. He retrieved his money with one hand while wiping a straight razor clean in the man's bib with the other.

"Three yellow marks like this . . ." Cowboy made slashes in the air with the razor. "It is the train with the two engines, through there and to the left. Erase the marks as you board, hide well, and give this —" he handed Bone the razor "— my love to the cunt Razinkin."

Alexsandr Solonik spent a spring and summer shuttling between Berlin and Prague, searching for a decent cup of coffee that would put the flavor of Palermo into his mouth. False rumors kept him shuffling his passports: Bone was with the Thieves of Berlin, organizing a coup against the Circle of Brothers. No, he wasn't, he was in Prague, hiding, biding his time. No, no, not Berlin or Prague, but Morocco, hiding among African bandits, operating a slave trade of labor into southern Europe. Perhaps Albania, that's it: young Thieves under a mysterious new master were bringing arms and cigarettes by fast boat to the east coast of Italy, returning with hard currency and dry goods. Two *vor*, one old and one young, were found hiding in Budapest, and he played his magic pipe for both. The older was found one misty morning fishing from a bank of the Danube at the base of the Chain Bridge, dispatched by an offhand snipe as challenging as a handshake. The younger was sent up with a masterful series of shots through the kitchen window of an apartment in a neighborhood near the Keleti train station, the first hornet-like .22 slug boring a hole in the glass, the second passing almost exactly through the hole left by the first, crossing the kitchen and into the living room where the young Thief was sprawled on a sofa looking with confusion at the blood in the middle of his shirtfront, experiencing the sudden sting in his chest. The little rifle was all that could be provided for Solonik; it was like a toy and he had some fun with it. That second shot shocked and paralyzed the young *vor*, while Solonik kept pumping the mean little cartridges into the chamber and squeezing them off, sending them zinging down the same narrow channel, through that kitchen, into that living room, and through that shirt.

Through the doldrums in the war of the *vor*, he contemplated finding Bone, kept an eye out for him, gently nudged his whores and contacts. It was only logical, only efficient, that he'd go west: to go east was folly, a thicket of slant-eyed bandits and cutthroats, poisonous food that polluted the bowels, and insects that brought death with a single grinning sting. Once out of the old Soviet, a *vor* would find no help in crossing the land of China, he'd just be another white man to turn into a skeleton to flavor the delicate meat of simmered dogs. But to the west: friends, even if only friends like himself, under death warrant, hiding beneath the streets and emerging only to rob garbage cans of rotting cabbage leaves. In any case, Solonik wasn't a tracker. Others would do that task, and when the target was found, the man of the money shot would appear, do his specialty, and exit.

It took months before the reports of Bone's journey filtered back to Moscow, how he'd converted the slant-eyed pirates into *vory*, how they'd kissed his dagger and were held in his sway of revenge, were now lovers of the Mother. The whore in Bangkok let slip the tired, slender, trembling bum had ravaged her and several young boys and paid nothing; in Mombassa an apprentice had told of a cold-eyed *vor* who'd appeared and stayed and disappeared onto a ship of slaves, nailing the disloyal to doors, shredding flesh for the delight of the rats that overran the harbor.

To Solonik it was paid overtime. The Circle had him on a retainer that more than met his needs; when necessary he supplemented it extorting the migrant prostitutes of several European cities. He was a roving, indifferent pimp, appearing when he was nearby and collecting his profit, even from whores he'd never met, but who he could convince of the seriousness of his demands. For months he didn't think about Bone at all, until word came from Moscow that a new rumor had been heard, a new sighting had been sworn in Spain. A *vor* who had elected to walk alone was found in Barcelona, living in a train yard in a discarded Basque beret and threadbare sweater. Solonik took an overnight flight to Spain, found it was the wrong *vor*, but dispatched him anyway, and had himself a night of sport in Las Ramblas before flying back to Berlin.

Joe Bananas was taken ill in Arizona. Solonik read of it in the *International Herald Tribune* and grieved and actually prayed one drunken night. So few, he thought, with this nose of hook. But the newspaper didn't do a follow-up announcing the death or recovery of the great Bananas, and Solonik had a whore with an internet connection search for updates. There it was: the elderly Mafioso was recovering, prognosis good. Solonik celebrated with the whore and marveled at the power of his own prayer and the endurance of her muscles.

Throughout the search for Bone and other wild Thieves, Dmitri Razinkin had been personally directing Solonik. When Solonik checked in one evening, his call was directed to Andropov — Wrecker — who told him Razinkin had gone to the West, to the north of America. There'd been many reports but no confirmed sightings of Bone; intelligence from a defecting apprentice in Africa told of a similar old *vor*, but that was one report of many. With Razinkin in the north of America, Wrecker told Solonik, he should be prepared to head on short notice to that continent's eastern coast.

"This eastern coast," Solonik asked, "is near Arizona, U.S.A.?"

PART TWO

Chapter 6

Dmitri Razinkin sat as erect as a king in the passenger seat of a southbound dark blue Jeep Grand Cherokee approaching the gridlock of Bloor and Yonge in downtown Toronto.

His driver, Jam, clutched the steering wheel tightly with both hands, joyously practicing his English by shouting fractured curses at the rush-hour traffic. The windows were up and the air conditioning blasted cold air through the vehicle. In front of the Cherokee, which was in the left-hand lane, were two solid lanes of stopped traffic in each direction.

In the seat behind Razinkin, his bodyguard, a jowly former Olympic weightlifter named Little Novak, reclined sideways, his thick legs sprawled and his face in a downward sneer, looking like a stroke victim receiving indifferent pleasure. He wore a red track outfit with white piping over a red sweatshirt that was stretched across his massive stomach. He had crinkly blond hair that looked like a carpet remnant, the thick, patient gaze of a meathead, and no discernible neck. A strong chemical odor blended with perspiration emanating from his pores. He occasionally turned his head to check the position of a white Dodge van with Martins Plumbing Supplies written in large red letters on the sides and in smaller letters in reverse across the hood. There were two men in the van, both bearded, both wearing sunglasses, both drinking from paper cups.

Little Novak hadn't found the location of the other police surveillance vehicles, but he had strong suspicions about a silver Ford Taurus with smoked windows two cars ahead, and minor suspicions about a ratty-looking brunette with sunglasses up in her hair, erratically driving an open Mazda sports car four vehicles back, now in the curb lane, riding the line to keep the tail of the Jeep in view.

Razinkin stirred to take a cigarette from a white gold case and lit it with a matching lighter. He wore a dark blue suit with a faint chalk stripe — the jacket worn over his narrow shoulders, cape-like — a gaudy wide tie patterned with gold and blue geometric diamonds and stuck down with an oval gold tie tack, a crisp white shirt, and black wing-tip shoes. A Patek Philippe Calatrava watch was fastened to his left wrist by a thin brown crocodile-skin strap; otherwise his only jewelry was a gold wedding band on the ring finger of his left hand. Razinkin's hair was black with dipped pewter tips, well-barbered, and he was cleanly shaven. He had no visible marks or scars, but under the shirt the eight-pointed *vor* stars still glowed: once earned, they could never be removed, even if the wearer left the Code. But in his mind Razinkin had never left the Code. He had in essence hijacked it, and with the men of the new reality in the majority, the Code was now whatever he and the Circle wanted it to be. He had, however, had a tattoo of a church with three spires removed from his right shoulder by drunken application of fire: the tattoo spoke too much of prison sentences — three, one per spire — and in the new reality it was what you were doing that mattered, not what you'd been; it was what you earned, not how many times you'd been captured. Only olden men and dreamers lived in history.

When he spoke, his voice was soft and his English almost perfect, except for a mangling of misplaced syllables. "This one of the old way, is it a waste of my time to continue this charade? Should he be given a banquet?"

Jam, a slim, muscular man with huge moist eyes and an unruly rag of lank, boyish hair, was smart enough to shrug. "Ushki, he is well liked, and where we require his service, he is always successful. He is faithful to his *mir* and has played the piano many times." Jam held up the fingers of his right hand and mimed being fingerprinted.

Jam and Little Novak had once been in Ushki's brigade and had been seduced away from their devotion to the Code by Razinkin's whisperings of wealth and harmony. Neither had licked the dagger or wore the stars: Novak because he had accepted State funds for his Olympic training; Jam because he'd briefly been the smallest policeman in Moscow.

Jam maintained a fondness for the olden Thief Ushki who was as the tattooed Princes told of in the fables of orphanages, detention homes, and taverns.

Jam and Little Novak had been among the deranged émigrés who hid among politicals and peasants struggling out of the Union when the swamp began draining. They'd met in New York while each was conducting, unbeknown to the other, extortions of migrants huddled under the chilly noir shadows of the elevated subway line. Their differences — one petite and of laughter; the other massive and grim — interacted and the pair became inseparable. Jam, whose true first name was Jerzy, and Little Novak, whose first name was also Jerzy, gained nicknames upon their nicknames: one the Laughing Lad and the other the Truck Transmission. Unable to make their mark in the *mir* controlled by Zakon, they'd together gone to the north, foraging stores at night and mauling shopkeepers. The *mir* in the north of America — Canada — was loose then and unformed, and in Toronto they quickly connected with a local bandit named Cabbage, who in turn introduced them to the Dumpling — Ushki.

And now, a year later, there was this Razinkin with his tales of the deaths of the olden men, the coming of a new dawn of prosperity. The time of Thieves and old bums, he said, is passed. With me you'll steal entire banks instead of robbing old ladies at bank machines. With me, instead of stealing silver from a house, you'll steal the house, the neighborhood. With me, you won't sleep with fleas in haylofts and waste your loyalty on the extinct Code of dying olden men. A new reality, my friends, in which the entire globe becomes your village market to plunder. Jam had idled in indecision as olden men were vanished, stuffed, and choked upon their wastes. The wandering dead. Not of the true world of the Thieves, he and Novak could shift their allegiance without betrayal, and did, Jam first undergoing a debriefing by the vampire Razinkin.

"Can you trust this Novak?"

"Yes, master, with my life."

"And this Cabbage? This Mikhail? And this Dmitri? And this . . ." On and on until Razinkin nodded, giving them their lives. Some, where Jam hesitated, were doomed.

"And what of this Dumpling?"

"A true Thief of quality, loved by many, feared by all."

And in that, Jam knew, he'd stupidly signed off on the old man's life. But when?

Little Novak, for his part, cared for none of it, for these infights and subtleties of the Code; when the wall crashed down, along with it went his dreams of Olympic greatness. He followed where Jam led.

The Jeep Grand Cherokee slipped forward a half car-length. Razinkin asked again, tapping ashes into the Jeep's tray. "Jerzy? The olden man. A banquet, you think?"

"Except for shopping, Ushki has been true." Jam checked his mirrors and shrugged. "A great man in perhaps not so great times."

These Thieves, Razinkin reflected. Wherever I go, there are these fucking Thieves. The olden one — Ushki, the Dumpling — was too much like that pus Bone, now hopefully dead in a whore's wet pit, but most likely not. Most likely spreading the poison of his ancient Code, rallying dreamers.

When the Circle had given Canada to Razinkin after the massacre of Mikhailov, he had been surprised and pleased to find riches and opportunities for lucrative plunder. The true America belonged to Zakon, who had made accommodation with the Italian *mir* and extorted assistance from the weaklings in the business markets of golden New York. It was said that he made millions in a single month, through offshore banks, ventures with Asians, and trophy politicians. Zakon had weeded out most of the olden men through murders and the ruthless mayhem of electricity and fire, and had cowed the remaining Thieves, putting them on a stipend. When Razinkin had visited Brooklyn, Zakon had welcomed him and advised him to allow Thieves in the north to steal small and quietly and, if necessary, to give them allowances as children. "Kill all the olden men but one, the one whose followers are the most loyal. Entice his adherents meanwhile and make them your own. Eventually he will have to steal — what Thief can resist? — and you can eliminate him for treachery and greed and at the same time make his brigade your own."

"Why not," Razinkin asked, "kill the powerful one first?"

"A strong man needs a strong enemy," Zakon told him. "A weak enemy will make you weak."

Zakon had sent musclemen to support Razinkin. There had been four Thieves of stature when Razinkin arrived; now there was one, this olden one, this Ushki. The three who perished were dispatched within a week, each in a way that bore Razinkin's signature: a huge meal liberally sprinkled with flaming Hungarian paprika and then a broomstick handle used to stuff the anus full with plastic bags, melted with a butane hand torch. And then each was tethered to a tree in the woods north of the city until he was poisoned on the backup of his own fiery wastes. As a message it was effective — at the end of the first month, the Dumpling had petitioned and Zakon's men went back to New York.

Already Razinkin had coopted many of the remaining olden man's brigade. And the Dumpling was slipping, the addiction of taking for free and selling for profit twisting in his bones as he fought to not drink from the water well of his heritage. Soon, Razinkin knew, the olden man would go. From the market stall to the pocket, as with the bottle to the mouth: irresistable and destined. Disgusted by Razinkin's weekly stipend — five hundred dollars per worker to forestall loud thefts and outrages that would bring heat and light onto Razinkin's massive, quiet crimes — the Dumpling divided his own share among the men and continued his old ways. But Razinkin admitted admiration for some of the old man's tricks.

"This fuck here. Oh my Jesus, this fuck." Jam pounded on the steering wheel and glared at an ancient VW Beetle spewing blue smoke back at the grille of the Cherokee. "Fucking Nazi suckcock car."

Little Novak laughed from the back seat. "I said, not this street. This street is a parking lot. I said it. But —"

"Steroid whore, go and lift this piece of shit off the road, and that one and that one." Jam sat back exhausted, as though the thought of Little Novak lifting cars had tired him out. "We're fucked. The Garden Ring is heaven compared to this."

"I told you, faggot driver. There's too much organization here, even in the lanes on the road. These drivers sit like sheep, beep beep beep; in Moscow just push them aside or go on the sidewalks. Who would care?"

"Or shoot them."

"That too is acceptable. Here, too many people have cars and not enough have guns, eh?"

Razinkin glanced at his watch and flicked ashes. "Hush. Novak, where are the *musor*?" He spat the word — garbage — in Russian.

"Three, I think. The vaginas in the van, there, for certain. The vaginas in the silver one with blackened windows, probably, and perhaps the vagina in the sports car."

Jam laughed. "So many cunts, so little time, eh?" He turned his elbow onto the back of the front seat and spoke around the headrest. "But with the animal genes you inject, I heard all the muscles get big and strong except one." He held up a stiff pinkie finger, then let it droop. "Oops, sorry, Ireni, perhaps you'd better find a little driver to park in your garage tonight."

Razinkin stubbed out his cigarette. Traffic moved and the Cherokee made the Bloor-Yonge intersection, four vehicles back, with the silver Taurus still two ahead and the plumbing van directly behind them. Jam put on his signal to turn left.

Little Novak leaned forward to touch his shoulder. "No left turn here, blind driver. No turns at all — the signs."

"Fuck it. Too many signs, too much obedience. Here we turn."

Razinkin adjusted the side-view mirror. The Mazda had drifted out and back into the right-hand lane. "The meeting is four streets away yet. Don't make this light — let those in front pass through. I'll get out and walk."

Behind him Little Novak straightened up and slid to the center of the seat, his bulk blocking the rear view. "We go together, on the red light. Both out on the right and into the building, there. We can use the tunnels to cross back. Driver faggot, we'll meet you at the Latvian's café after you lose these footprints."

"Okay. But I think I will meet these policemen very soon. If I don't appear in one hour, I'll see you at the apartment." He securely fastened his seat belt; then, racking the seat back so his feet barely reached the foot pedals, he emptied his pockets of his house keys, wallet, change, folded dollar bills, a package of gum, a disposable lighter, a subway token, a small fishing knife, and six foil-wrapped condoms. He took his driver's license from his wallet, the car ownership and insurance documents from the box between the seats, and put them into his shirt pocket. He handed everything else back to Little Novak. Removing two gold rings from his fingers and a Bulova watch from his left wrist, he handed these, too, to Little Novak. He ran his hands over his pockets and found nothing else. "There's a thing under the seat, you should take it. And the bag of lemons. And, steroid pig, the apartment has no food or beer."

Little Novak distributed Jam's possessions into the pockets of his warm-up jacket and reached under the back of Razinkin's seat, removed a .38 caliber revolver, and dropped it onto bundles of currency stacked in the bag. He put his hand on the back of Jam's neck and squeezed. "Don't hurt yourself, eh, driving faggot? I kiss you goodbye."

"As I do you, but without the tongue."

The traffic signal was red when the Cherokee reached the thick white pedestrian line at Bloor Street. Razinkin and Little Novak, with a Gap Kids bag secure under his arm, swung open the right-hand doors and stepped out. Leaving the doors open, they strode to the side entrance of a skyscraper on the west side of Yonge Street.

Jam slipped the Cherokee into reverse and floored it back into the plumbing van. By the time the elegantly draped Razinkin and hulking Little Novak had passed through the revolving doors of the skyscraper and disappeared down an escalator, the whooping, laughing Jam had thrown open the driver's door of the Cherokee, jumped out, and was fighting four policemen and a policewoman on the street.

In the catacombs beneath the intersection where they'd dumped the surveillance, Razinkin and Little Novak made their way through the mounting rush-hour throngs. Razinkin was completely lost, but Novak seemed to know the maze of corners and shops. With the broad back a few inches ahead moving with authority, Razinkin walked quickly, hearing Novak's harsh nasal breathing as he bulled into the crowds. There were doors to enter and escalators to ride, and suddenly they were standing on the street two blocks from the intersection. Novak took a deep breath, as if he'd only surfaced for air, then led the way across Bloor Street, through the jam of cars, and down into another underground warren. Razinkin rode in his wake, the men moving a little slower now, as they paused to sweep the path behind them. At an underground coffee shop, Novak led the way in and the men sat at a rear table, Razinkin facing the door: spotting foot surveillance required a subtlety Little Novak lacked.

Little Novak ordered Italian coffees for both of them, and they sat in silence until the gargling machine loudly began manufacturing foam.

"A moment only, then we move."

"Master, is there to be an action at the café?"

Razinkin nodded. He'd let his mind free-flow during the underground trek and decided the Dumpling's time had come for a *pravilki* — a court — before the old *vor*, God, the judge. Difficult, he'd decided, to take Ushki to the country for a picnic. He maintained much contact with the big-headed one, Cabbage, and Cabbage was a dog of loyalty — he'd sniff the scent of betrayal and, like the best of dogs, would bite first. Razinkin meditated on the problem and decided to let the solution find him.

"This Cabbage, has he a brain?"

Little Novak, while steroid-addled and stupid, had a liking, as had most people, for Ushki's man, Cabbage, who was boisterous and played fine tricks of mischief. After an adventure, he threw huge parties decorated with blood and semen and potato juice, gave money uncounted and without condition, and was always prepared to help steal the silver buttons from a dead man's vest.

Jam had told Novak to be careful, that when Razinkin asked a casual question, the answer could lead to disappearance and death for those near or far. Little Novak made his head into creases of thought while the coffee was served, then said, "He is of the new way, he has been fooled by this filthy old *vor*, with legends of past golden times. If he becomes alone, he will look for a friend." Little Novak watched Razinkin process this information. He added, "He came before, not after, like us. He knows of the Italians and the blacks and even some of the Chinese. When one needed a carrot —" Novak made a pistol of his fingers "— the Cabbage could make one appear in an hour."

"Trusted, then?"

Little Novak nodded. "He has a brigade of six who are loyal. A bandit, not a Thief." He affected indifference about Razinkin's final decision.

"And will he assist?"

"Never. But if destiny passes and is done, he will make an accommodation."

"A fair man, then." Razinkin drained his foamy coffee and stood. He considered importing the hook-nosed Solonik, but finding him would take time, as would transiting him here safely. "So, one but not the other. But if necessary: both."

On the way out of the underground cavern, they passed a hardware store. Novak loomed outside as Razinkin went in.

Chapter 7

WAITING at the café for the vile Razinkin, Igor Dimitrov reflected that he had indeed once been an *ushki*, a dumpling, until a deranged Bitch had tickled his round stomach with a dagger made of a piece of shovel blade and encrusted with shit. With the swamp outside the wires draining and the watchtowers tilting, those who lived in the muck at the murky bottom took shape, breathed air and light, believed they'd become strong for all time. The creepers of the new reality weren't waiting for imprisoned *vory* to be freed before eliminating them. Instead, inside the prisons and camps, *vory* were separated from their barracks-mates and brigades and confined to isolation cells, making them ideal targets of opportunity for the mad and the vengeful.

The ensuing slaughter had none of the joy of a Thieves' party: the murders were grim if creative affairs. Knives affixed to long poles and jabbed through food slots in the iron doors. Homemade bottles of potato poured into the cells and set alight. Some were given the spicy broth: mouths were pegged open and inflammables poured in and lit. Axes from the forest camps, hammers from the mines — all became tools of change. Screams and grunts echoed through the smoke of searing flesh. The guards laughed and turned up their tiny radios, and the *zeks* whimpered and, as always, waited their turn.

First the Bitches tried to entice Ushki from the barricaded cell: Do you want company, *vor*? We'll send the Casket to keep you company.

And in through the slot of the door came the Casket, an old Muscovite *vor* who had first brought Ushki forward to kiss the dagger, to become a Prince of the *zakone* — "Look upon him," Casket had said, all those years ago, "for he is sentenced to us for life, as we are to him." Such a round boy was I then, Ushki remembered, and the Casket was a human mountain.

First through the slot came the hands with their ancient, faded blue inscriptions, as the Casket screamed obscenities, then came his tongue to keep him quiet, although Ushki could hear the music of his drumming heels on the stone floor as they fought to hold him down, to control him. Then after the hacked hands came the cabbage, a hairy mess of genitalia, sawn vigorously, in labor, not love.

And Ushki sang:

A glorious way
To die today
He lived of potato and sorrow
A Prince's death
So few left
You today, me tomorrow.

Then, from outside, a day of silence. And then a pole. There was nothing new about the pole coming through the slot of Ushki's door, poking at him as he danced and laughed, dodging. Ooooh, you pustules, he sang, camping about like a faggot matador on a poster. *Olé*, you whores of the dollar. But the invisible axle grease that had been smeared on the wooden pole was new to him; he reacted with shock when he grabbed it with both hands, intending to pull it inside so he could poke the knife outward and perhaps pierce an eye, and it slid through his fingers and that shitty blade went into his stomach. Well, he thought, at least it's secure and mine, and he twisted sideways and indeed took the pole into the cell and lay down to sing Thieves' songs and wait to die.

Sang Ushki:

I stole the blade that killed me
Mother, love my heart
A stab of pain
To live again
My life will end and start.

But he didn't die. He gagged and writhed, listening to the whispers outside the iron door. He imagined he could taste the shit from the blade in the back of his throat and he made Thieves' songs of shit in the mouth and blood on the shoes. He embraced the pain as it changed the rhythms and tenses of his throbbing blood entering and leaving his heart. With a twist of his body, he removed the blade from his abdomen, aimed the knifepoint at the door, and continued to wait to die. He sang a song of his life, one who was imprisoned at fifteen and had been free over the next forty years a total of ninety-six days. I'll die here at home, he thought, for this is my home.

When he passed out, footsteps crept into his cell and he was lifted away to the politicals' barracks. A *zek* he'd long forgotten — a life he could have taken but didn't, for some reason

— cleansed the wound as best as he could. Kindness repaid, although Dumpling hated kindness, hated *zeks*, hated debt and repayment. He showed no gratitude to the *zek*, a Leningrad surgeon who believed in his absent god, an aesthete with wide, moist eyes who worked a minor magic with rudimentary tools and bartered supplies.

The prison camp was all but abandoned except for decapitated bodies tacked to door frames, and five wheelbarrows — five Thieves' heads on a board table, each with a window bar through one ear and out the other. There were signs of frenzy. Fires large and small had burned walls and ceilings black, ripped clothing, organs, small body parts torn, clotting. There were odors of burning meats and bloody vomit in puddles. A *zek* who had long ago been made a woman hung by his neck, a finely detailed female torso of breasts and a navel tattooed on his back, a V of hyperrealistic pubic hair tattooed lovingly at the top of his buttocks. On the back of his shaven skull the face of Lenin, mouth agape, eyes insane. Icy winds blew through the windows absent of glass.

A few guards remained, knowing that eventually their services would again be required, even in the golden glow of the bright face of democracy. Women — the guards' wives — operating horse-drawn carts that squeaked up the cracked black winter road from the village; they helped their mates load up pieces of furniture, rags of clothing, and meats hacked from the dead animals in their stalls. The horses at the fore of the carts had the eyes of *zeks*, big and wet and — like *zeks* — awaiting butchery, awaiting as ever their turn.

With satisfaction Ushki recollected his slow recovery among this festivity, remembered his fierce gnashing at the soft *zeks* when they tended him, he in delirium warning them of things to come: after all, whether first or last, the *zeks* always get it. That's why they were *zeks*. If you're not dead, he told them, it's because you aren't worth death.

A delegation of Christians came through the rapidly emptying prison and the indebted *zek* urged him to say magic words: I am a political Jew and want to go to Israel to die. And with that liberal *abracadabra*, a world emerged, a path was lit, and he took what remained of his stomach and followed that path, which so far ended here, at this café, waiting for the abscess Razinkin.

The patio of the café where the Dumpling waited was owned by an old Latvian forger who saw with her ears and listened with her eyes: heard not and saw less. Dazzled by splashed paint and chipped stone, she maintained the black clothing and noir makeup that convinced her customers she was a true artiste in the acquisition of lost treasures. Her gallery was on the second floor above the café; in the basement she kept a studio where she created new ancient treasures, as well as providing documents and licenses for Razinkin. Her lover, a young Chinese art student of photographic memory and social hesitancy, operated the café and floated among customers with a sad smile on her painted lips, her eyes downcast.

The café, aflutter with banners for dark ales and beers, was out of sight from most passersby, shaded from the sun on these late, still-hot afternoons. Through painted oblong flower boxes of spilling color, the Dumpling could see his man, Cabbage, standing at the curb, peering down the block, watching for the approach.

The sad floating girl put down a fifth cup of espresso and was gone, leaving a scent of lavender, a scent that took Dumpling back to a forest glen, a conclave held during one of the less-than-one-hundred days he was outside the wire, where he met briefly the legendary Bone of whom all were now talking. The long-ago conclave had been convened to decide whether the Thieves inside the watchtowers would be permitted to take trustee jobs. Bone and the Chinaman were adamant against this violation. Others, including Razinkin — then he was still called Tomahawk — had lobbied for it. We could steal, he bragged, imagine how much we could steal, from the *zeks* and the camps. We could control the flow of contraband in, much as we do now, but we could increase it, make a river of plants to smoke, even fuckable women and potato juice that comes in bottles with paper labels. We could control the labor: who must work and who may watch. We could rule the linkages of camps and prisons. And the soulless Razinkin, with his hyperbole and bluster, then claimed: We could *become* the State!

And upon this, both Bone and the Chinaman stood firm: it would require cooperation, doing the work of keepers of men, of guards and hens — informants. It was, in even a loose reading of the Code, a violation to assist in your captivity. And to become the State. A thought no true Thief would entertain.

In the end, Bone and the Chinaman had won. But the victory wasn't to be forgiven — when the walls began to collapse, they were left within its deterioration. The Chinaman, with the crab eating his entrails, raved insanity, petitioned, and was freed, a new and reluctant advocate of the new reality. But Bone remained, standing his sentence, and the Circle made a mistake. They brought him to freedom where he had a final, bloody laugh in a dacha surrounded by military bodyguards. A head in a punchbowl, Ushki thought, a fork up the ass. Indeed, a party was had.

Now this Bone was either alive or dead. In the *mir*, word often traveled slowly and the exploits or atrocities — depending upon the sayer — were rampant. In Moscow, Ushki knew, there were slogans painted in white on walls: Bone Lives; Fuck the Dripping New Reality; or in red: Resist My Brothers and Die; You Today . . . You Tomorrow.

In spite of the legends and slanders, Ushki knew bits of the path of Bone, the wander across the landscape of Asian eyes, the boat that abandoned him in Africa, the boat that delivered him to the true America. The Chinaman who couldn't shit out the crab kept many aware, but only those he trusted. Scratchy telephone messages, the Chinaman's voice weakened to that of an exhausted girl, planned and plotted Bone's true path to safety. A pickup in the east of Europe, a donkey ride through the mountains, a brigade in Africa. The death of the fat man at the train yards, a greasy pig gushing blood, and then the inexorable forward motion of Bone to his destiny. But what destiny?

In the long-ago forest meeting to reflect upon the Code and the trusteeships, Ushki remembered, Bone had fairly glowed, as though a cold light alit him from within, burning ice within a shadow. Even that famous shimmering of his flesh had subsided then, briefly — Bone didn't even blink, noted Ushki, who was carefully watching for it — and he awaited his turn to speak against Razinkin's treacherous schemes. He appeared to be the distillation of the Code's very essence. And then, as though Razinkin hadn't spoken, Bone stepped forward and told a brisk, melodious tale, how the Code had been fragmented in olden days; how all were paying now, generations later, for changes made; how many had been murdered and many exiled.

"A Thief can have no power," Bone had said, "if the power is bestowed by an authority. As is given, can be taken away. Birds fly in the air, fish swim in water, Thieves steal in all. We will not and must not become the radish nor the hen — the weakling nor the informant. Within each is the Code; to alter it is to alter our very bones and never will we walk the same. No Thief can be given; all he has must be taken. A trustee? A trustee is the truncheon at the arm of the State. If this is permitted, there will be a red splash that can only weaken all, and I promise you, my brothers, the first red dagger will be mine. Our past is stained enough with this blood, the monthly drippings of a whore."

Ushki recalled the red splash only in the stories of old Thieves who had survived the Bitches' War long ago, when the *mir* was divided by a similar conundrum: whether to wear the uniform of the State and fight the Germans, or remain in prison and follow the path. Many had reflected on this and many had carried rifles to shoot the Nazis. And when they were returned to the prisons, there was a red splash that left thousands butchered across the iron chain of the gulag. In the end, the turncoat Thieves had won and the Code was altered forever, the olden ways being passed only from the lips of the old to the ears of the young.

Ushki mused: Is Bone coming? Or is he hugging the knees of a policeman, begging for mercy? And if this prince comes, will I be alive to greet him? Should I wait for him to kill me for walking with the scabrous Razinkin? Or should I entice this Cabbage of mine to assassinate Razinkin and make his sleek head a gift to the cold one? There was no question that the Dumpling would never engage in a preemptive strike against Bone: to kill him, even in defense of one's own shame, would be like drinking the last flask of water on earth: all would then die.

At the curb, Cabbage touched his hip and pulled a cellphone from the waistband of his suit pants; he listened and nodded as though the caller could see him, and walked back into the patio. He tugged down the corner of his eye: "A friend," and handed the phone to Ushki.

"Watch for them," Ushki said, then spoke into the phone. "The voice of a friend. Sunlight, in this cold wind."

"I greet you, brother. Kisses, felicitations." The voice was weak and haggish, but the transmission was as clear as if the Chinaman were across the street.

"As I do you."

"An old friend requires a service. A *patsan* might be found."

Although both men were disgraced by their abandonment of the pure Code, they maintained the habit that a *vor* never asked a direct question of another *vor*.

Ushki looked out to the street side at the puzzled Cabbage peering both ways up the block. The boil Razinkin was late, although it was politic with this pig to comment that you yourself were early and he was on time. "I have but one whom I trust. The Cabbage. He is unqualified as a *patsan*, but he has the devotion of a dog that is not to be eaten."

"Good, good. There are few apprentices in these times — if your man cannot apprentice to a Crown, he can still aspire to greatness."

Ushki had had long talks with Cabbage about his disqualification as a *patsan* — a Thief under probation — and although he had sympathized, he was firm: Cabbage had once married before the State, and had swung a hammer — had worked — and by the Code could never reach the world of true Thieves. "He is all that remains of my trust, but he is of outside."

"So, then. I will make arrangements. He will be visited and must obey."

"This will be done; more information would nurture success."

There was silence on the telephone; for a moment Ushki could hear the underwater waves or the penetration of the stratosphere by beams. "It is delicate. I must speak as the world is a circle."

"The roundabout way is most often the quickest."

"A friend will appear needing warmth, yes? His plans are unknown, as are his desires. He has traveled much. His love is a beacon to all, yes?"

"I see."

"He may come and he may pass; he may come and he may remain. It must be as he wishes; his intention is only his to divine."

"I see. A friend is always welcome."

The Chinaman went into an extensive wave of hacking coughs; he left the telephonic device and returned a moment later, breathing hard. "One as yourself once was, as was I, before our hearts were diseased, so is he."

"I see."

There was another pause; this time Ushki heard measured, reflective thinking, the Chinaman tapping his tongue against the roof of his mouth. "Imagine one beside who fire freezes."

"Yes, yes."

"To one who knows all, I will pass on the name of your outsider. Then she will appear."

"I see." Ushki dragged this out. "Ah . . ."

"She is of a code, but of another code. A code of . . . bracelets."

This was too circular for Ushki, but he made a sound of assent and understanding. "My friend, our lives falter; faith flees."

"Ah. We should have remained, eh? I believed the crab was stronger than the Code. A mistake, as it came to pass. But who knew? And you? I know not. But wherever, you have my love and kisses."

"As you have mine."

"I will meet you in a place. We will maul that old God and fuck his ass."

"The angels."

"The angels too. Our *zeks*." Laughter made the Chinaman's voice weak. "We will sleep beside God's woodstove." The voice dissolved into coughs and gasps and the line was vacant.

At the curb, Cabbage made a signal behind his back — the thumb between the first and second fingers: the cunt — and reentered the patio. "They come."

"Before then, I must tell you, you will be approached and must accede. A woman of bracelets. It's a matter of history, not of the mere now. This favor I beg."

"Done, my master. And —" Cabbage hooked his thumb at the entryway "—these?"

Ushki shrugged. "As will be, will be." Then, his mouth curling into a crooked smile, he essayed a wave of good humor. "But, my friend?"

"Master?"

"If the defiled Razinkin puts paprika on my coffee, you will as my guest please drink it."

Razinkin, wearing his coat caped, and Novak visibly sweating chemical compounds, entered the patio. The sloth Razinkin glared suspiciously at the laughing men; Novak looked sad, clutching his Gap bag.

Cabbage, as a boy on his first turn in prison, had the nickname Bitchfucker because of his nightly prowls among the iron cots, his unerring alertness for the scent of the weak, even in darkness, and his persistent, tireless grapplings. It wasn't a bad name, but it wasn't one he preferred once he left prison. As he passed through his late teens, an old Thief amazed at the size of his head gave him the name Cabbage. Cabbage was an acceptable name: it might mean a bunch of money, it might mean the cluster of testicles.

He was a forty-three-year-old gallery of art ranging from naif images created by saliva, urine, and dye — sucked from prison clothing and tattooed by pins and pieces of ballpoint pens — to majestic panoramas of vast lives and violent times. There were meticulous skin canvases of religious heraldry, and angry, self-abusive, colored gougings convicts traditionally marked themselves with: barred windows and numerics and characters, daggers dripping and eyeballs weeping blood and granite tombstones and bolts of lightning. Covering his chest was a professional-quality mural of a woman with her hair in flames, swinging a sword at cowering uniformed men, droplets of blood spattering from the woman's efficiency; the background was a yellow and red stained-glass window with three spires above it. A tattoo on his right shoulder showed a skull with a lightning bolt through it and the words, in shaky English letters, "Killer Kommando" inked beneath in a semicircle by a frightened *zek* who hadn't yet come to enjoy the prick up the ass. Across the top of his left wrist, not visible under a gold Rolex watch, were the letters "B-A-R-S," a prison anagram for "Beat the Party Activists; Knife the Bitches."

The absence of pointed stars on his chest said more about him than the presence of the skull and the angel and the daggers and the red, weeping eyeballs. Those absent stars — the most prized markings of his world — would forever set him apart from the dreamy heroes like Bone and Tank and

Hardware, and even, here beside him, old Ushki. And, he knew he'd never wear the rank or wield the prestige the stars brought: as a young man he'd worked with a trowel, laying bricks and smoothing mortar, had drifted into the criminal world and then out, until finally serving a sentence for rape — What is sex without rape? he thought — when he gave himself over to the hierarchy of the prison regime. But those years of work had forbidden his admittance to the Circle, that and a vodka marriage before the State, to a woman he had long forgotten.

He had no visible neck, tiny lobeless ears, and black hair growing almost down to his eyebrows, in a sharp thinning widow's peak. His eyes, nose, and mouth were crowded by heavy jowls into the center of his face, giving him a look of either bland stupidity or dumb cruelty. On his left cheek were six tiny scars that looked like the result of fine buckshot; a half-moon scar was almost invisible beneath the right eye; under his chin, a poorly healed scar ran from the center of his throat to his left ear, the surprise gift of a desirable but well-nourished and reluctant *zek*.

Unable to raise himself to the acetic and stark life of a true *vor*, to the ethereal plane of mystics like Bone and the few remaining Thieves who maintained the purity of the Code, Cabbage had consoled himself in the trappings of wealth, being well positioned to serve those who came after the Union disintegrated. Cabbage had arrived five years before the swamp drained; before the dripping Razinkin and the others came, he already knew the men of the Italian *mir*, the boys on the loud motorcycles, and the blacks of the African tribes. He knew how to rent an apartment, purchase a car, get licenses and permissions; he could say which lawyer facilitated immigration assistance, could identify the *musor* — policemen, garbage — as well as their cars and habits. He had respect for all the *vory* and apprentices, but with Ushki it was the devotional love of a son finding a lost father.

Once, before Razinkin had come dangling his sugar plums of bundled currency, old Ushki had had Cabbage drive him around the city, stopping at jewelry stores and waiting outside while he went in. Cabbage, expecting the old bandit to come running out with a bag of stones and a pistol in his hand, had kept the engine running on the slapped-up banger Ushki somehow maintained in working condition. But instead, the besuited Dumpling idled back outside, chatting with the owners of the shops, and climbed back into the car, directing Cabbage to the next location, while he himself sat doodling on a little notepad.

"We will return, master, perhaps after darkness? With some brigade, for looting?"

"Exit this highway southward, go two blocks on the left."

At the end of the day they'd visited five jewelry stores. Ushki doodled and spoke in non sequiturs.

A few days later, Ushki contacted Cabbage to pick him up at the wood-slat shack he lived in north of the city. Cabbage waited while in the warmth of the black-iron woodstove Ushki stripped off his patched workshirt and corduroy pants. He admired the pile of skulls engraved meticulously upon the old *vor*'s narrow back; atop the skulls stood the proud figure of a big-busted Valkyrie with snakes for hair and blooded swords for arms. Ushki had hilarious tattoos: hinges inked at each of his joints, and near his hipbones large eyes focused downward where his penis hung like an elephant's trunk.

Ushki had Cabbage trim at his hair with scissors, then he shaved and put on the suit he'd worn earlier in the week. On the way back to the first jewelry store, they went on a spree through a Sears men's department, looting small — for colognes, aftershaves, wallets, even a revolving rack of cheap watches — then continued their mission. At the shops, Cabbage again awaited, watching the old man chat with each owner who took rings from display cases for Ushki to examine. Each time Ushki carefully handed them back, nodding and shrugging, before leaving. After revisiting the last shop, Ushki emptied small pockets sewn into the sleeves of his suit: sparkling rings of gold with diamonds, rubies, emeralds.

"But . . ." Cabbage, flabbergasted, checked his mirrors for pursuit. "An alarm?"

"Here." The Dumpling handed a wad of notebook pages to Cabbage: on each was a carefully detailed picture of rings. "In the first visit I stole with my eyes; in the second with my fingers. After the first visit our Jewish friends made up some-of-the-same-but-not. In the shops they gave me the real; I returned not so real."

The Dumpling was a canny Thief, aware of the dictum against bargaining prices. He sent Cabbage into the old Jews' warehouse with instructions to sell. Cabbage wasn't constrained by the Code and would surely fetch a superior price, the Jews knowing all the while the source of the booty. When Cabbage returned, he handed a plastic bag full of lemons — fifteen pounds, he said — to old Ushki, and the pair walked down the alley behind the Jews' warehouse, the old man looking into car windows, through rear windows of shops, peering into spilling garbage cans. Music played nearby; Ushki paused and sniffed the air to follow the sound. Ahead, a cracked plastic radio was balanced on a window ledge, and workers could be heard inside running faulty machinery.

"Ah, an adventure." Ushki handed the fifteen thousand

dollars to Cabbage and said they'd meet up at the shack. Then he was off at a run, his eyes focused sharply on the radio. Like a man a quarter his age, he went up off his toes and snatched the radio from the ledge, ripping the plug from the outlet. He was gone like wind through the red brick walls of the alley, dragging the cord behind him, leaving Cabbage standing with the bag of lemons as he made good his escape, like a schoolboy in an old man's flapping suit. My first glimpse of a true Thief's soul in action, Cabbage remembered, fifteen thousand dollars in hand and he steals a busted radio because it was there to be stolen.

Cabbage brooded: Many gone now, prisoners of the woods, enswollen and choked upon their shit and bubbling gases, and only Ushki remains of the old, a man as my father, a beacon and a hope. But for how long — who knew?

Now, at the meeting, Dmitri Razinkin thought old Ushki looked like a grim, laughing shadow lurking inside his clothing, a man made of gray snow, a child's melting snowman around whom the clothes would slowly slide off and ultimately be just a pile of wet rags around a pool of dirty water.

The two men sat together at a table, a bum and a duke. Cabbage and Little Novak greeted each other with crushing competitive handshakes. Cabbage glanced down into the Gap Kids bag, saw the lemons and the gun, and with his foot nudged it away from Little Novak. Both began speaking of health clubs, the women they knew, tamed doctors who scripted steroids, watching each other and glancing through the flower boxes at the narrow view of street life.

As Cabbage watched the men speak, he felt alarm growing. The four, at two tables, were alone on the patio. Razinkin was ebullient and ordering cognac for all. He produced a box of cigarettes and lit himself and Ushki with the white gold lighter. He called for more cognac. After the third visit by the Chinese waif, Cabbage was alarmed enough to stop drinking. Little Novak looked at him sadly and spoke more quickly, signaling his distraction with useless comments and information. Cabbage heard Razinkin laugh and say, Ah my brother, ah my brother. Do you remember when?

And Razinkin got up and said loudly he had to piss.

Little Novak reached across the table and grasped both of Cabbage's wrists, pinning them to the table, tugging him forward. His face was broad and sad, but impassive. "It is above us, the things of olden times, of their Code."

Cabbage saw Razinkin pull a long piece of plastic from his jacket pocket and loop it around Ushki's thin neck from behind. The cord was sharply ratcheted, a securing toothed device that, once pulled tight, could not be undone. Razinkin made it tight, the cord's teeth making a sharp rip, like a zipper closing. Then, with a mighty yank, he reefed it again before stepping away, his arms flung wide as if he'd completed a complex and dangerous magical trick and was now basking in the applause of his audience.

Old Ushki tried to find the cord buried in the flesh of his throat, digging through his own skin with his blunt old man's yellowed fingernails; he stood, toppling his chair, and his head began to expand before Cabbage's eyes. As he tried to pull at the end of the strap, he only ratcheted it tighter. The head reddened and angry engorged purple blood snakes began writhing under the skin. The eyeballs made to leave and the mouth gaped a tongue. A smell, then, of shit. Ushki bulled and thrashed, his head appearing to be that of the stout man he'd been as a youth before his stomach was tickled by an encrusted piece of shovel blade. Furniture crashed; a blurred face with Chinese eyes at the window of the café turned away and the curtains closed.

"As it is, it is," Little Novak said, squeezing harder upon Cabbage's wrists, pulling his torso closer across the tabletop. "My friend, as it is, it is, yes?"

"Novak, we go." Razinkin came daintily around the edge of the patio, watching with satisfaction as Ushki's athleticism began to subside. The face was an unbelievable crimson and the snakes were now deep black and intent on escape.

Novak let go of Cabbage's wrists. He wondered at the tears in the big-headed man's eyes, the horrible look of loss. "Please be of good behavior in this."

Cabbage took his eyes from Ushki, now on his knees, fading except for the fingers prying beneath the bleeding flesh in which the cord was now invisible. "Yes, yes, go."

Novak stared into his eyes, sending a message: "I leave for you the bag, eh?" Novak stood and checked the street for suspicion, then led Razinkin out.

As they made their way briskly toward an intersection with taxis, Cabbage took the .38 from the bag of lemons and fired six times, exploding the inflated dying head of the fine olden man who, in devotion to his faith, would steal a cracked radio.

At Yonge Street, a few blocks south of where the Cherokee had rammed the grille of the surveillance van, Razinkin told Little Novak to go home and await word from Jam. "A good day, a fine adventure. I must report Ushki's treachery and our solution." He laughed. "Once again, we have saved the Circle from an old man's betrayal."

Little Novak nodded. "The Cabbage?"

Razinkin shrugged. "He can do nothing. His brigade will become ours." He waited while Little Novak attracted the attention of a passing taxi driver, then flagged one for himself. He directed the driver to a midtown office building where he could make secure long-distance calls from a Russian–North American investment office, run by ex-KGB officers who laundered money for organizations in Moscow and Leningrad. They used state-of-the-art equipment to keep huge amounts in constant motion. Money is the shark that can never rest, they believed, money must make money or die.

Indicating to a blond man outside the glass room that he wanted to make a secure call, Razinkin used a satellite telephone headset that ran through several computers and traps before the signal even left the building, hidden in a high-speed stutter of numerals and impulses that raced invisible to a satellite before rebounding to a similar device in an investment office in downtown Moscow.

"Ah," a voice said immediately after picking up the receiver, "a friend from afar."

"A day of adventures; an olden man's treachery, a thinning of the herd ensued."

"And the cow was whom?"

"A dumpling."

"Ah." There was a genderless sigh of sad resignation, then: "The tough bough requires the sharp ax."

"Always he showed me his feet. Today, one time too many this insult."

"There may be another olden one, one of the chill, always with snow on his head and ice on his feet."

"Here?" Razinkin immediately remembered Bone's redecorating of the dacha, the head in the bowl, the fork handle in the anus. "No . . . How?"

"Our friend in the true America has heard rumors he is there. Perhaps he has left. You know who I mean, where?"

Zakon, New York City. "Can this be true?"

"Await. If the cold indeed appears, first: the accommodation; then: love."

"And if not?"

"Love all, trust none. First, the kiss."

"And if not?"

"Here it is preferred a time of harmony. We make strides in the suppression of the old. But for each that goes on up, a legend grows. The old will pass, but slowly. Few remain, some hide. The balance is delicate. Bits of grit must be removed from the watchworks with care, or time stops for all."

Razinkin drummed his fingertips on the desktop. "And if not the kiss?"

After a few seconds he realized he was speaking into dead air. "Oh, dirty God, fuck this childless mother," he hissed, turning to a computer where numbers and percentages scrolled endlessly. He saw a whack of funds backing up in Cyprus and began dealing with the problem, his anger and frustration evaporating, until the backlog was cleared and his throbbing temples smoothed.

He finished sending coded emails, then sat back and looked at the night lights of the city outside the windows. He thought about old Ushki dancing a jig and, realizing he had a persistent erection, he laughed: a fine monument here, as swollen and veined as the purple dancing head of an old *vor*. I must visit the Italian *vor* Ricci's club and share my burden with one of his fine African women, one who won't be missed if my passion is too great.

Little Novak went to a supermarket where he bought food for the barely furnished apartment he shared with Jam, then passed by a store where he bought cases of beer and several bottles of inferior vodka. He drove to the apartment, loaded the refrigerator with the beer, put the vodka in the freezer, then sat by the window watching the parking lot. When the phone rang four hours later, Jam, in a thick voice through split lips, told the steroid whore he was on his way and to get some *blyad*, young ones with big tits, because the *musor* faggots at the police station kicked his nuts gently, like *sdelat kozyol* — slavish homosexuals — and it was time for much fuckery while his scrotum and penis were of such an impressive size.

Little Novak couldn't make a joke about this. He said, "I must tell you, there was an event as you relaxed with your friends."

"A dumpling?"

"Gone up."

Over the phone, Jam sighed. "And the big head? He too?"

"He remains. For now."

"For now," Jam repeated.

Chapter 8

WHEN the gypsy woman visited, Cabbage was in one of his stash houses in a high-rise building in the north central part of the city, an anonymous nest of unfurnished rooms with cracking paint on the walls, chipped stippled ceilings, and neglected parquet flooring. The apartment had been chosen for its proximity to highways, the balcony that overlooked the parking lot — an easy single-floor jump to the grass below — and the extorted generosity and acquiescence of the building's superintendent, a meek bookkeeper from Kiev.

The stash house was part of a rotating network of dumps and storage for swag — gifts, the brigade called it. Cardboard boxes of dry goods were stacked, almost blocking out the windows of the living room and bedroom. Electronics equipment filled another room; the dining area had four refrigerators with meats, photographic film, and other perishable plunder. The bedroom closets were full of high-dollar men's suits, still price-tagged, and boxes of Capezio shoes.

In the days since Razinkin had tied Ushki's necktie for him and the Cabbage had liberated the worms — for this was the joke being told — Cabbage had gone to ground, awaiting word of his own fate. It was beaten and battered Jam, appearing at a nightclub Cabbage maintained for the grinding of laps, who came into the back office carrying a round tray containing several water glasses of vodka and a dozen beers, a platter of fish pieces, radishes, and pickles.

Before they got down to the purpose of Jam's visit, they toasted each other twice and drained two glasses of vodka. They discussed Jam's still-spectacular injuries at the hands of the policemen and policewoman he'd crashed the Cherokee into.

"They all wanted to dance with me, the men faggots and the woman who washes her face in other women. The fuckers of butts gave me a massage; the woman attempted to sit on my face. It was, my friend, the truest of love." He laughed and shook his head, his big wet eyes glistening. "What police they are. No pliers, no torches, no bucket of water. But —" he shrugged "— one must take romance and kisses where one finds them, eh?"

"And they freed you?"

"The automobile went backward. Who was to know? This automatic shifting device confused me and my foot jumped in fright. In this amazing democracy that saved me from torture and shame, I must learn to adjust and control my relief and excitement at freedom."

They laughed and Jam sat at the desk, across from Cabbage. "My friend, this other adventure. This was an old men's bitterness," he said, "and to you and me it is of no concern. The strangling was done now, but the choking began before we were born. As you, I loved the slim Dumpling, but what is gone is gone. The master learned the old man had a dream of treachery, of rebirthing his Code, of revenge and likely an adventure of depravity."

"I accept the first, but disbelieve the second. It was of an old days' times, yes, but the loved Ushki had no plans of treachery. As his son, I would know of this and would gladly have been his hand. But Ushki had respect for the Circle and would never have acted."

The two men rammed vodka and chased it with beer. Jam nodded: "As you say, so do I, so do all. But in any case, the done has been done, for whatever reason. You cannot remove the yellow fear from the pale *zek*. My mission is to know your intentions, your future. You know this, and you must know why." He allowed Cabbage to sit in silence. "All who know you respect you. Many, when we came, those of us who had shoes, couldn't correctly tie the laces. You assisted. Those who came to collect donations from the shopkeepers, they remember you finding the materials to make boxes that laugh — boom! — and those who needed a bed or a whore, they all recall you were there." He laughed. "And, I might add, finding the doctors who grew rich afterward destroying little diseases that made the cock green and sneezing. This, this with Razinkin, it is the new way. The olden men have passed their time, and if they choose not to wear new clothes, they must find another way and not interfere with those who see the clock's hands moving forward. I must know."

Cabbage maintained his silence. As he took a glass of vodka and chased it with beer, so did Jam. He did it again, as did Jam, then he laughed and stood up. "Ah, Ushki, a prison dumpling: all flour, no meat."

The men embraced.

Jam said, "I may tell the master?"

"One doesn't use a whip on an obedient horse."

"After the storm, then: calm; after the sorrow: joy."

"So, then. Farewell, Ushki. A true Thief." Each drank again.

"By now God sleeps by the toilet and Ushki by the stove."

Jam opened the door; outside Little Novak stood with a sawed-off shotgun in his hands and an expectant look on his face. Jam said, "No ducks here, thick-headed one, only true friends. We must hunt elsewhere."

The gypsy woman's name was Dagg. She arrived knocking two-one-three at noon as Cabbage stood in the living room in socks and underwear, half-moon reading glasses perched on the end of his nose, inventorying. She was in her forties and wore a summer dress that came down over her knees. She had long narrow feet in flat slippers and wore a thin silver bracelet on each of her ankles. On her left wrist was a faded tattoo that Cabbage couldn't make out. But he knew the significance of its location — if on the left wrist, an insect with angelic wings: the parasite; if on the right wrist, an angel with pincers: the political. In any case, she was, he'd heard, a Fairie; thus the two tattoos meant nothing, or meant she was both. But he, in any case, interpreted this dual tattooing to mean she was a survivor of a strict regime camp. From her age, accent, and fair coloring, Cabbage was certain the woman was the result of the Kiev purge in the 1950s, when the authorities had freely loosed the criminal prisoners among the politicals, allowing four days and nights of orgiastic violence as *vor* devoured *zek*. She, then, would have been born of the camps, the spawn of the insane periodic rape rampages inside the walls or on transit trains of slatted wood, or perhaps a seed spilled in a magic moment when the moon was full above the wires and soft words urged hasty completion. Or a bargain of bread crust.

The woman's face was surprisingly youthful, either cared for by oils or wiped clean of lines by persistent horror. She had the charismatic eyes of a changeling constantly seeking. Her hair was short and black, shot with silver, chopped to the nape of her neck. On each finger she wore a silver ring and on her wrists were the secret bejeweled bracelets of gypsy-like powers. Her body was slim and her waist long and willowy. Her eyes were still and clearly insane; she read the tattoos on his naked torso to determine if she had the right man. She looked around at the chrome racks of women's clothing, the boxes of VCRs, ghetto blasters, microwave ovens, computer screens, and Tampax cases stacked to the ceiling of the undecorated apartment. She walked to the Tampax cases. "I'll take these."

"All?"

"Of course. At ten o'clock you have them at the garbage door; Avi will bring my shop van. Of course, you'll help with the loading."

"And the price?" Cabbage felt vaguely intimidated. He looked at her body, her breasts and hips, and her lips, with exaggerated hint. These Fairies, he knew, could croon love songs as they gnawed your ear off, could hold you in enduring grips while they shredded your neck, mindless of your arterial blood tickling their throat or streaming down their thighs. The tales told that they secreted shards of razor blades in the vagina, hid horseshoe nails in their tresses. One-eyed rapists were a class of their own in the camps across the Siberian frontier, subject to either mirth or scorn.

"Thief, it will be as you say. It will be fair. This I know. If you want to negotiate a discount, you must be quick and not like a lover of leisure." She stared at him without blinking, and with a glint of wickedness that gave her a sudden beauty that stuttered his heart and lifted his undershorts. "But, of course, even pleasures are fraught."

Cabbage nodded, impressed. She was of a code, he knew: not a Thief, but one nonetheless who orbited the Code, never bargaining. The offering price would be met, and if it was later determined the price was too low, the seller would never receive Thieves' business; in fact, he might become a victim of their intentions.

The woman handed Cabbage a slip of paper with the word "Thursday" written on it above a map of two intersecting lines showing the location of the railway station.

"You are to be there Thursday. Wait in front for a man."

"And," Cabbage said, "the time?"

"Thursday, it says."

"But when?"

Her laugh was surprisingly full; the cords at her throat stood out. There were pale blue veins under there, and a faint pattern of white pinpricks. Cabbage began regretting not negotiating his discount. This one, he thought . . . what, after all, is an ear or an eye or a shredded prick? She stopped laughing, but her smile remained: "Thursday. But, Thief, if not, maybe Friday? And you are to say nothing of this."

"But, my master?"

"Your new master, you mean." Now even the smile had fled and the insane eyes were back. "Your new master is of another world, not of this one. Silence is your master, not the leper Razinkin."

"How will I know this man?"

She stopped at the door and looked through the peephole before disengaging the chain. "You have eyes? You can find the tiger among the rabbits?"

On the appointed day, Cabbage appeared early at Union Station. He wore huge white track shoes — laced upside down

— that looked like they'd been inflated by an air pump, white workout socks slouched down to expose the blue and red bands around the tops, and a white T-shirt under a Nike warm-up jacket. He had a gold bracelet fitted loosely on his left wrist above the gold Rolex with a diamond inset over each number and a crust of jewels around the bezel, a double strand of gold chain around his right wrist, a thick linking of gold around his neck, and three crusted gold rings, all on his right hand. Together the rings made a legal but effective knuckle-duster.

Prepared to present himself to a new reality *vor* of the status of the werewolf Razinkin, Cabbage spent the day at Union Station, eating hot dogs from a vendor, dashing into the cavernous building to relieve himself, finding positions that allowed him to inspect many exits at once. Seeking one of Razinkin's status and style, Cabbage had brushed off the derelict who'd approached him in mid-afternoon, shuffling on two left-footed, mismatched shoes — an easy acquisition for an outdoor market thief — out of the sunshine from between taxicabs, muttering a phrase from behind a cupped palm.

"Beg your mother, dead one." Cabbage looked over the man's head, trying to watch both of the north sets of doors of the station. "Away now."

Bone stepped closer and spoke louder, in a rasping voice, thick English with emphasis on odd syllables, shifting his carryall from his right hand to his left. "My mother? When I kissed the dagger, it became my mother; *zakone* became my heart. I bid you assist me. A long way I've come to beg you this favor."

His cadence and diction were the same as Ushki's: carefully selected words muttered as if learned from a page rather than a voice. Cabbage stepped back, his neck swollen in red embarrassment. He was a shallow and rough man, given to the explosive violence he and his brigade learned from American movies. This hollow but solid man with the spare features and ragged clothing seemed to glow with a power. Cabbage quickly took in the missing finger joint on the left hand, read the lettering on the fingers, was sucked into the impenetrable yellow depth of the eyes; but it was the almost invisible shivering, the shimmering, of this man that froze words in his throat. He marveled that he actually felt a vertigo at the presence of Bone.

This, he knew, was the dead one of whom all spoke and whispered. Two years he'd been buried alive: the stories had made their way variously of the defeat or vanquishing of the hook-nosed sniper, Solonik, the slave ships from China that disgorged him half-dead in Africa, the sightings from everywhere, all dust in the eyes of his pursuers. Buried alive, Cabbage thought, buried alive. But now, here.

"My true apologies. I — I — This misunderstanding is surely no fault of yours, but of mine. Too long I've been here, away from the world, sentenced to this place in between. How could I fail to recognize the mother of my birth? Forgive me."

The man put his palms on Cabbage's shoulders, leaned in and up, and kissed his cheekbones. "I am —"

"No, no, *dyed*." The term — grandfather — came instantly into his mind; his demeanor had become that of a young boy, the acolyte he'd been, standing in Ushki's magnetic shadow. "I know you. I haven't been far from the world long enough to forget the heart of my mother."

Even though it was now Razinkin's city, Cabbage offered all to Bone. But the old bum just told him to lead, trudged behind him into the car park, and silently got into the Cadillac STS showing neither disdain nor admiration.

"A meal, *dyed*? A woman, a bed? To desire is to have."

"A park." Bone sat forward in his seat, the seat belt unlinked, and peered around in wonder. When the few remaining true Thieves of Brooklyn had directed him to Canada, they'd told him it was a frozen north, a Siberia of bears and wolves, squat Indians, and towers of snow. He'd believed them, though he had doubts that Razinkin would allow himself to be an exile in such a place. But in *this* he could see Razinkin making his home. It was summer, to be sure, but there was no snow, no elk, no pug-nosed people chewing blubber. This was an open treasure box reminding him of the luxuries of Manhattan, but without the thousands of policemen and the security officials at every doorway. He saw a building that seemed made of gold, one building in a field of a million, many taller, many more sculpted, many surely crammed with worker bees. Here the testicle Razinkin could feast while Thieves nibbled.

Cabbage piloted the Cadillac with two fingers of his right hand, reclining in the leather seat, thinking: A park? A parking lot perhaps, to raid cars? Or a real park, where *dyed* could . . . do what? Find children playing on swings and jungle gyms, distracted enough that he could steal their schoolbags? Loot their strollers and perambulators? Or was "park" a new slang of the *mir*, for a faraway place of Thieves whence he'd never been? Perhaps a park was a bordello, a casino. Perhaps, with *dyed*'s weak but serviceable English, he meant another word. "Ah," he said. "A park, *dyed*. A particular park? A size, a type?"

Bone shrugged. "With many trees, few people, perhaps water inside it, a stream, a pond?"

Cabbage hadn't spent much time visiting parks. He thought of the lake, but the shorelines were either beaches or condominiums, much visited by tourists and cyclists. He headed toward the lake anyway, remembering a park to the west that seemed like a forest; he'd seen it from the highway only, but it was vast and had both streams and ponds. There was, off the eastern edge of the park, a long street of Eastern European shops selling sausages of Poland, meat cuts of Czechoslovakia, braided breads crusted with sesame seeds. He and his crew had requested gifts among the hundreds of immigrants there, a fine and tasty operation that netted a fair wage, even allowing for the overhead expense of music boxes. However, the remnants of earlier émigré armies had announced the turf long theirs and appealed to Razinkin. The poxed Razinkin, who craved calm waters in which to fish, had banned Cabbage's poachings.

In High Park, Cabbage was confronted by a chain across the roadway. "*Dyed*, I will try another way."

"No, this is fine. Your duty is done. I will be gone now."

"To where?"

"Inside, in the trees." Bone got out of the STS and pulled his sack after him. This close to the road there were children playing in a playground, mothers on blankets, a man and boy flying a single red-and-white-striped kite. There were dogs, perhaps too big to catch, but there would be small dogs, little foragers with tasty, rat-like bodies; the waters would hold fish and frogs. And nearby, an avenue with its European writings, restaurants, and groceries. The bonanza unseen by most.

"But, your safety?"

To Bone, Cabbage was the boy, the wide-eyed dog, the expectant smile and the urge to do good. Or was he a spy, this big head full of competing loyalties, of greeds and desires? Was the final handoff a delicate strand in the clot Razinkin's web? "Where friends abound, danger flees." He shivered.

Cabbage got out of the car, at loss as to what to do. He

looked around the park, wondering what Bone saw here that would make it his home. A secret apartment was ready for him, the refrigerator stocked, the evil Dagg available, perhaps even eager. He shook his head and took off his warm-up jacket, putting it over Bone's shimmering shoulders. "Then, *dyed*, a gift upon your safe arrival." He shuffled. "May I give you a number, a telephone that is safe, in case you require me?"

"I will make a message here, as may you." Bone pulled the huge jacket about himself and led Cabbage to the edge of the roadway. He found three rocks and stacked them, with the smallest at the bottom. "When the sun is straight up, on the following day we will meet, whoever puts this message. Failure — then on the next day, and so on." He walked a short distance in the opposite direction of the playground and turned. "I know not of your master; however, in a dark world a silence can be as valuable as bright gold."

He turned and was gone almost instantly from Cabbage's sight.

After an indifferent wander, Bone checked the sky for shadows of coming rain, saw none, and found a small place where the ground was indented and well-covered. He tucked himself into a ball and made a pillow of his canvas sack, then rode the rhythms of his trembling into sleep through to the morning chill of a late summer dawn. Then a pure yellow sun arose and awoke him twelve hours later.

He spent three days in the vast park, learning the trails and the places where small animals ran, where shelter in rain would be the most effective. The pond water tasted fetid and contained the detritus of carelessness: floating unraveled condoms, sunken beer and soda cans, destroyed toy boats, some green plastic bags containing household waste. There were dull gold fish, most dead, a few gasping in the muck. He watched children and parents playing and having picnics. One afternoon he watched an Asian man, who reminded him of the slant-eyed Shan, spend hours manipulating a kite above the trees, the swooping and dashing in the sunlight attracting children and adults alike.

Each day Bone checked several times for the signal from Cabbage, but the stones remained scattered. In New York he'd been told of a *vor* — one who had come to some accommodation with Razinkin, but who might have maintained fealty to the Code. Or perhaps not. In any case, Bone would find this man Ushki and, through him, notify Razinkin of his arrival, and of his plans to walk alone.

On the third day he recognized his growing hunger, assuaged only by raids on garbage cans after picnickers left, as illness. His clothing was deteriorated and soiled, and he smelled on himself the odoriferous rankness of a ship's hold. His famous shivers became violent, signaling illness, unlike the friendly waves that told him the Code was alive in him.

He left the signal for Cabbage.

That night, when darkness filled the hollows in the trees and the ambient glow of the city became apparent, Bone, in Cabbage's flapping jacket, vacated materials from his stomach and left the park, following the sounds of squealing streetcar wheels and traffic to a wide avenue. He recognized delirium and wandered the street, keeping to the shadows, inspecting doorways and testing doorknobs. It had grown much colder since the afternoon and a fever within confused his body. His eyes felt so hot he feared they'd glow.

At a café he reached over the railing and from a table grabbed a handful of sugar packages and the salt and pepper shakers, and made away with barely a pause. In a doorway, pouring bags of sugar into his mouth, he watched as a couple at another café drank glass cups of coffee and spoke intimately, their heads close together. When the couple arose, the man put some coins on a plastic tray and led the woman out to the sidewalk. Bone crossed the avenue and, moving quickly, feeling the sugar ignite his engine, scooped up both the coins and the tray, and a half-eaten sweet roll. A hawk watching for small movements of mindless mice, he hid himself in a doorway and ate half of the piece of the roll and another bag of sugar.

Satisfied for the moment, he foraged. From a Dumpster behind a garish fast-food outlet, he found a take-out bag containing a half-eaten hamburger with a two-inch chunk of meat between the buns. He ate the pieces of bun and put the meat into his pocket. He found a wrecked abandoned shopping cart, dragged it under a streetlight, and ripped at the chromium sides. He stepped inside a busy, noisy restaurant and took a leather jacket with a coat hanger from near the door; outside he tried on the coat — it obviously belonged to a much larger man, perhaps of Cabbage's size; it was big enough to be a sleeping bag — took it off, and rolled it into a bundle under his arm with the coat hanger inside. He pulled a wooden crate into a lane and stomped it apart, gathering large and small splinters and rolling them, too, into the giant leather coat. His exhaustion manifested itself with another evacuation of the innards and he rested before moving on.

At a dollar store, he stopped and read Cyrillic and Hebrew characters on a sign and went in. The owner was Jewish, almost to the point of caricature: an old man with a hawk's face, heavy black glasses, a pencil angled up behind his ear, pants pulled up almost to his chest. Bone walked to where he leaned on the counter beside an old brass cash register, his elbows on a spread newspaper. He stared into the man's eyes, watching them emit an instinctive fear as they read the visible tattoos. When the man's eyes dropped, Bone turned and wandered down the store's aisles.

The proprietor watched him put items into his pockets — string and lighter fluid — but did nothing. As Bone moved toward the exit, the shopkeeper sighed and punched keys on the register, took out a wad of bills and passively offered them, his palm up, his eyes down.

Bone ignored the money, stepping close: "You cannot give to a Thief. Too long in paradise, too far away from the past. You forget yourself, *zek*." He left with his small items. Outside he leaned his vibrating body against a pole and oriented himself, determining the direction to the park, somewhere under a sky now glowing with fever.

In the night, Bone was in a dizzy half-state when he felt the nibble on the piece of hamburger meat wedged between his bare toes. He reacted like a fisherman: he waited, drawing in his breath, then pulled the string, one end looped around his finger, dropping the cage he'd made of shopping-cart parts over the rodent, at the same time pulling his foot free. He threw off his dew-weighted coats. With the end of the straightened-out coat hanger, he stabbed the fatty cleanly through the body, just above the shoulder where a hunter would take a buck with a heavy-grain bullet. Its heart pierced, the squirrel died inside a scream; Bone could see its exposed teeth and bulging, surrendering eyes in the strong light of the moon.

The gulag stove he had prepared in the dark was ready: a shallow pit with tightly wadded newspaper and splintered pieces of packing-case wood atop a floor of stones. He pulled the coat hanger out of the squirrel, then kicked away the cage. He skewered through the mouth and out the rectum, sprayed lighter fluid onto the newspapers and kindling, and made a hot, fast, almost smokeless fire he fanned with his hands. A few minutes later he smothered the flames and pushed earth over the stones in the little pit, baking the rodent. When his nose told him dinner was cooked, he unearthed the squirrel and used the straight razor to skin the charred fur from the meat, sprinkled the flesh with salt and pepper, and stripped off long filets with his fingers, digging around bones for delicacies. For dessert he finished the sweet roll and another bag of sugar, then wrapped himself back up in the coats and passed, dizzied, into a shivery state, a long piece of packing wood never far from his right hand.

The delirium, when it came, felt like the entryway to death, which Bone believed was worse than death itself: a true Thief, he knew, lived always in good times and bad in this anteroom. The Code almost left him: he was devoid of mantra or reflection and the mirror of his life was in shards. He'd heard of a *zek*'s teeth freezing until they shattered, and he now believed. He put the handle of the straight razor between his teeth and kept his dry tongue lodged to the roof of his mouth to prevent shredding. Almost fatally hot and speaking softly in no language at all, he slept and woke, slept and woke, through the next day, stirring to near consciousness, but unable to do more than burrow deeper into the soil at the bottom of his grave, under his heavy coats, trying to leach heat from the molten core of the world.

He dreamed of children laughing, and actually might have heard them; he dreamed of rain and awoke, briefly, wet, but didn't know if it was rain or his leaking, feverish pores. He dreamed that a bird landed on him, and indeed one might have. Small insects might have climbed into his foul mouth and he might have spat them out or swallowed them. He dreamed he was a stove, radiating heat, radiating life, and indeed he was ablaze, a fire that couldn't be doused by the dark wet of night. Other times he was so cold he cramped his muscles against it. His true mother was the Code, but he found himself speaking to a saddened woman through a dense wire mesh, uniforms lurking in the background, and she called him Boy and he called her Mother; a noisy van ride then, and barracks of children with shaved heads and gaunt insanity for complexion. His first tattoo, painted with finely sifted ashes from a burned boot heel, mixed with his own saliva, jabbed and jabbed and jabbed with a silver needle from the orphanage workshop. He rode a donkey through howling mountains, surrounded by grim Shan men; he sawed a head from a neck, grinning his own grin at the rictus; he rode a boat and swam and hid and was fed upon by bugs — Indeed the same bugs feeding upon me now, stowaways carried this far? — and there was a small baby bundle underwater, bouncing against his leg.

Why did I save that baby? he wondered. A rough *vor*, a friend of my father, roughly presenting me: He is sentenced to us now; and — oh help us all! — us to him. Laughter. And he told me of my father, standing his sentence and fighting to keep the pollution of the Code by the *suki*, the Bitches. "Your father and I were the last ones; he's gone and soon I will go too," the rough *vor* said. "This new Code must be fought and defeated; you must find those who will follow you as you carry the true Code and hand it to them as a burning ember. Or you must walk alone and accept that with your death, so dies the Code."

Within, Bone felt the waves of wet fever break and resurge, break and resurge. There was a sudden spark of power, a small fission of warmth as the instincts of survival and will — the same will that had once enabled him to chew off his own finger — joined battle with the frantic bugs that invaded his system in the pond water he'd drunk. It was, he recognized, the Code, aglow, and he observed with detachment the battlefield within his body.

The wet fever was replaced, slowly, slowly, with the familiarity of his chills. The sun came up — again? twice in one day? thrice? — through the trees, and he dragged himself from the tomb of his sleeping pit, resurrected his exhausted self before the towering shadow that was the frantic, searching Cabbage.

Chapter 9

Dagg was fashioned from Magda. She was a *fairinik*, a Fairie, closer to fifty than to forty, and had spent almost all her life in a *mir* of indistinct lines, a life opposite that of a Thief, a life based on one's survival above any code, and a life that often intersected with the underworld of the *vory*. The Fairies were a woman prisoner network that provided its own nourishment, whether inside the wire or out, allowing her to accept all of life without a thought to anything except her own survivalist art of breathing in and out. This fractured network reached unto itself wherever a Fairie was in need, whether in mental wards, prison cells, or in the captivity of other above- or below-world forces. By wearing both tattoos — the feeder off society and the political angel equipped with pincers — one *fairinik* could recognize another and know she wasn't alone. Unlike Thieves, who were forbidden to marry, Fairies could and did, and often married each other in ceremonies of survival that lasted as long as protection was given or received, or the duration of a sentence. Outside the prison systems of Eastern Europe and as far away as South America, where many Fairies fled after the Nazi pogroms, the Soviet washings, and the cleansings of darker races through central

Europe, Fairies worked as prostitutes, beggars, pickpockets, and enticers. No matter their immediate circumstance, Fairies held at their core the value of their own destiny and no amount of beating or torture or disfiguration could make this value waver. Only in death, and that was a circumstance all Fairies fought to avoid.

Before Cabbage appeared with this Bone, Dagg had met many Thieves. In the camps and prisons of the *mir* she'd had many Thieves, had always been taken by Thieves, for a Thief could only take, never ask, never bargain. At her throat were faint tracks made by barbed wire looped around her neck to control her for the pleasures of others, of guards or inmates or both. Yoked by cold wire with sharp twists, Dagg had focused her eyes and her core on distant stars, on far horizons and softer, impossible love. Humiliation had long been alien to her. She had been beaten to the point of fouling herself, fore and aft, she had been made to bark like an animal, to lick wastes. She had been frozen and baked and stretched and torn, and the woman of herself remained a wrapped gift of which only she knew the within.

She'd come to this north of America several years earlier — like Thieves, Fairies had no measurement of time, no appreciation or knowledge of its passing, beyond the rise and fall of the sun or the moon, but it had been significant: she'd grown veins of silver in her hair and God's claws had marked the fair skin around her eyes. The instant the Union collapsed and joint ventures were made between those of the *mir* who had left through Israel a decade earlier and the new criminal structure, she had been taken from a cell in a city prison — who knew what city, in that carousel of degradation, capricious midnight transfers, laughter and howling? — where she'd spent much time. Who knew how long the unraveling loop of flickering horrors? The warden of the prison, watching his lucrative kickbacks and black-market initiatives dissolve before the fangs in the twisted face of democracy, had enacted his exit strategy, selecting her to accompany him as mother to a herd of young women to the West, where they'd been promised careers as domestics. But instead, their passports and travel documents were sold to strip-club owners, the women forced to earn them back by grinding themselves into the crotches of drunken men. Too old to play these nighttime games, and insistent on the warden's promise of freedom, Dagg had gnawed his throat and fled, reincarnating herself into a purveyor of things acquired for little and sold for much.

At the door of her shop she asked Cabbage nothing. She glanced at the rag man he held in his arms, stood aside, and indicated the stairs to the basement, then followed Cabbage down. The basement was full of boxed and cartoned goods, furniture, hubcaps, automobile parts, and cases of liquor. Chrome racks of dresses and men's clothing lined one wall; the opposite wall held shelving containing cameras, radios, small kitchen appliances, boxed cereals, cases of juice.

"In the back: a sofa; in the closet: blankets."

Cabbage gently placed Bone on a sofa still wrapped in transparent showroom plastic, and Dagg covered him with quilts and a duvet. Bone's eyes were open, but he saw nothing; his lips moved, but he said nothing. His body suddenly began a series of spasmodic vibrations until it seemed his entire torso left the bed, as if in an electrified seizure of demonics. Dagg found more blankets, some draperies, and a brown fur coat and covered him, the sheer weight of the fabrics securing him to the sofa. She placed her hand on his cheek and her magic bracelets collided at her wrist. Leaning her face close to his ear, she sang a little song. Instantly his eyes widened, then became void, and he stopped moving. His eyes closed.

Cabbage was alarmed. "Is he gone up?"

"Fool." She looked at him with contempt. "I touched him with the hand of a mother and sang with her voice. He will sleep. For how long, who knows?"

"This is the one from the railway station."

Again, the contemptuous twist faced him. "As if there were another such as this."

"We must be of small voice — my master knows of him now."

"You spoke, fool?"

"No. On the avenue a merchant was the recipient of a small adventure. He told one, and one told two, and so on. The merchant was of a camp and he recognized the written history."

"So, your master, the insect Razinkin, knows. And what of you, slave?"

Cabbage faltered in the face of her unblinking insanity. "I, I . . ." He gathered breath and strength. "He was delivered to us in safety; he remains in safety. As Ushki said."

Dagg stared fiercely at his indecision, then looked down at Bone with a critical eye, weighing as she had the tampons Cabbage had sold her. She sighed. "I will keep this one, but he is an old one, this bum. Perhaps with a little cleaning up, an antique of a little value."

The diminishing ghost of tradition within Dmitri Razinkin crowded his head with the furies and laughter of gleeful evil children. His sleek head was also crowded with worries —

these reports of the emergence of Bone, and then his vanishing. The *mir* was abuzz with legends old and new, that one had come who might change the world.

Most of the steady flow of visitors into Razinkin's Baby Point Road mansion never met with him: he remained in a far wing, brooding. The visitors were diverted to various quiet rooms where they conferred with accountants, joint-venture specialists, and computer wizards. These rooms were furnished in embassy-modern, with soft but not too comfortable couches and chairs, digital clocks on the walls showing time zones of the world's banking capitals, and an LED ticker ceaselessly running stock markets in real time. Subdued, uninteresting paintings broke up the creamy expanse of the walls. Gaunt, silent secretaries sat just inside of the visitors' field of vision, constantly taking notes, the rustle of their notebooks reminding that everything promised or proposed was documented. The windows were sealed three times against radar eavesdropping and the shouts of Razinkin's children splashing in the heated swimming pool were inaudible. In an atrium behind the house, Razinkin's wife, Olga, played bad bridge with other Russian women. Colorful wind socks were affixed to a half-dozen antennae and small satellite dishes on the roof to keep birds from landing.

Razinkin's secretary, a slim Swiss with an old man's face and the body of a boy, slid into his room and spoke softly. "The call is early, sir. Shall I tell them to call later, or . . . ?"

Razinkin stirred and waved his hand at the Swiss. The man came to the edge of the desk and put down a bulky telephone device with a key lock on the body. Razinkin took a double-bladed key from a ring on his desk and rotated the lock a quarter turn. The Swiss took a thick red wire and connected the phone's power cord to a wall outlet. Razinkin demanded brandy and sat watching as the Swiss poured a measure. When the Swiss was gone, Razinkin slid up a metal guard on the phone and punched in a series of numbers. He completed the turning of the key, punched more numbers, and removed the key.

The voice of the man in Moscow was hoarse, as though he'd been shouting. The body of the conversation regarded offshore accounting, the flowing of money through a daisy chain of interlocked corporations, brass-plate companies that existed as square plaques on Caribbean office buildings. A joint U.S.-Canadian venture based in Vancouver and New York City was discussed and the details of an initial public offering were explained, while the twin benefits of both a money-washing scheme and a planned pump-and-dump of the venture's stocks were arranged.

Finances out of the way, Razinkin — who knew the communications were secure, but still spoke in vague circles — told of the rumored appearance here of the cold one.

"This is confirmed?"

"Not yet. The children are abuzz, but no one speaks out loud. Already he seems to have a following of protectors."

"Perhaps he walks alone."

"Perhaps. But perhaps not. Much is at stake; the children are cheeky and want to grab the sky. Keeping them quiet so grown-ups may prosper is difficult."

"Have they . . . an allowance? That they may eat and doze?"

Razinkin explained that the local Thieves were receiving a stipend a week and were allowed to forage small inside the city; outside the city, in other cities, they could forage to their hearts' content. "I can't have disruption here, not now. We have great things to do, and we have great times ahead. This cold one could be a disruption."

The men listened to each other's silences on the secure link. He's afraid of making an error, Razinkin thought. He's afraid of creating a new legend of the stubborn Bone, undoing all the efforts to suppress the wild Thieves. On the other hand, he fears attention and official examination of the financial channels we've created, a stunning flow of currency that dwarfs the budgets of nations. Razinkin questioned himself for even reporting the rumors of the cold Bone back to Moscow: I should just locate him and make him vanish. In time, the shuffling old bum would be forgotten, would become at best an exciting dream in the late nights in taverns and around the campfire by the rivers of Europe, old toothless men reading their own tattoos and recalling a buried history. Perhaps a legend for children. In any case, Razinkin was positive, he didn't want to wind up like Mikhailov, dissected into hunks of flesh that never quite added up to a total man.

Finally the man on the other end spoke. To Razinkin it was clear the silence over there had been filled with a consultation; the man's voice was now firm and carried authority. "If the cold one is there, locate him and meet. Make him a gift. Determine his intentions. There's no point in trying to sway his allegiance, but perhaps his plan is to walk alone. After all, Thieves retire, eh?"

"And if not?"

"We will make a determination. The hook-nose relaxes in Europe, pursing the empty shadow of this Bone and similar others. For we here, this is a matter of some delicacy. We've made headway with many of the old ones; in turn they're able to control and channel the desires of the young ones. Imagine, my friend, a life of days without ancient intrigues, of harmonies that benefit all."

Razinkin, imagining instead a world littered with the bodies of dying Thieves, some dancing, some inflating, pursued his question. "And if not? If he has operations? What of it then?"

"We will see. How, my friend, is the snow? It is still summer there — are you seeing wolves?"

Razinkin thought of the children whooping in the swimming pool, thought of the clerical staff in the mornings in their bikinis on the deck. "It's horrible, my friend. Only this morning we found the scat of bears. Bears. Imagine their size, with snow to the chimney. Two of the children went out to play and we have rescuers seeking them in the banks of snow."

"A hard life, a hard life. But we must all persevere in this fuck of a life we've been given." There was silence, then: "Of the old fellow, use your judgment. You're very valuable to us: have protection for yourself but have wisdom, too. I kiss you."

"As I do you." Razinkin shut down the link. He stared at the wall across from him, sipping his drink, the whispering, howling voice of the old Tomahawk in his head: Kill him. Find the horrible fuck, the hook-nosed Solonik, and be done with it.

Instead he finished his drink and rang for Jam to fetch Little Novak and ready a car. He checked his watch and left the office by a rear door. Jam, his bruises purpling and yellowing, waited by a bone-white Mercedes, speaking through the window to Little Novak, who was sprawled across the rear seat, his favorite posture of leisure and reflection. The Mercedes passed through the gates of the mansion onto Baby Point Road, and Jam smiled as a station wagon, painted in the colors of the telephone company, with ladders racked to the roof, swung in behind them, a man and woman aboard wearing white hard hats.

"*Musor*. To dance with me again. Oh, the love." He adjusted the rearview mirror. "Shall I evade them, master?"

Razinkin turned on the radio and tuned it to a talk station. "No, we will go nowhere, but we will take the long way." When the Mercedes pulled out onto northbound Bayview Avenue, he positioned himself sideways. "You have heard the rumor, Jerzy, of the old *vor*, come?"

Jam nodded and shrugged, keeping the sedan at a sedate twenty miles. "Just the one rumor. He emerged from nowhere and got a donation from an old Jew. Lighter fluid and string. The old Jew told one of the Slavs, and the Slav told another and another, and it reached us. Is this the Bone we speak of?"

"A bum. You know of this one, then? A massacre in Moscow, then across the land of the slant-eyes, living by eating garbage, fucking whores in the ass in the weeds." He lit a cigarette and watched the enormous houses they passed, then he spoke bitterly: "These old ones. Kissing the dagger by firelight, singing old songs, and killing only to protect a code about which none care. Stealing garbage because they can; stealing one sock or one glove or half a pair of scissors. You know, at night they celebrate with poxed women, then fuck them like boys, just because they believe they've stolen another day from God."

"As you asked, master, we have people looking. Up and down the avenue, none have seen him. We're examining the park nearby, but he is called a ghost." Jam paused. "If he even exists. The old Jew might have had a bad dream about boxcars and thin soups."

"Head home now, Jerzy. If the slightest whisper comes, notify me. If a suggestion is hinted, come to me. This olden bum may cause many problems, or may cause none. In any case, we must locate him and decide if he dances or walks."

Dagg possessed no trust. After Cabbage reluctantly left the shop, she immediately backed the van up to the rear doors and, back in the basement, used a combination of balance and muscle to get Bone to the foot of the stairs. For such a small olden man, she thought, he is of tendon and his marrows are the weight of iron. He smelled of vomit, shit, and the most sour sweat. There were twelve steps up to the back door and she moved him one at a time, alternately rebalancing his body and tugging him under his slick armpits. It took her almost a half-hour to get him from the sofa into the rear of the van. Somehow she felt she was carrying history. With Bone secured by the duvet on a stack of cardboards in the bed of the van, she made her way out of the city, wondering if she was carrying a corpse.

Just before committing to the busy highway across the top of the city, she pulled the van into a strip plaza containing Middle Eastern fast-food outlets, a Korean tae kwon do studio, a real estate agency, and, at the farthest end, a small seedy storefront with Chinese, Korean, and Thai characters painted on the window. Inside that shop, she passed gaping bags of noodles and rice, tins of bamboo shoots and beans, and at the back, where wooden bins were arranged, she filled small paper bags with roots and herbs of a variety to entice poisons from the deepest middle. At the cash register she picked up a silver amulet of a man and woman entwined. Examined from one direction, there appeared to be two heads and a single body; from another, a single head and two bodies. The apothecary recognized her purchases and her lack of questions about her selections. He glowed his eyes at her and nodded, charging her for the paper bags — a combination, he recognized, of products for returning the dead to life — but not the amulet, pressing his fingertips together near his middle torso in an intricate circle.

Back in the van she reefed the duvet securely around the old man and drove to the highway, heading east. She didn't ask herself why she carried him. She didn't question her suspicion of Cabbage, who had allowed his master Ushki to be slain. She did, however, think about the briefest look of kinship in the eyes living in that bony, charismatic head, of the instant spell of her touch and poem, of how she once imagined putting a feverish boy child of her own to sleep.

And as Fairies carried within their souls a protected place where they hid while enduring the unendurable, Dagg kept a soul lair of which none knew, a place where her unrevealed self resided, secretly.

Cabbage returned to Dagg's shop at dark and found Avi, the shop boy, sweeping, the van long gone. Avi was confused but not concerned. "The evil one —" he made a three-horned sign of his top and middle fingers and his thumb "— appears and disappears. To ask where or why is to be bespelled. And spit upon, in addition — her mouth juice is a poison, it is well known. Ask not, and it will be revealed, she says."

Cabbage strangled on questions, but feared alerting the boy to the existence of the old man. Instead, he told him to check the basement, around the sofa to see if Dagg had left anything for him. The boy returned and shrugged. Cabbage too shrugged and nodded and left several numbers for Dagg to telephone upon her return.

Bone awoke: My God, the camp. He could hear water running into a tin basin, the singing of birds, and smell the rough unfinished slat walls of the room he was in. The scents of pine and earth through the unfilled gaps in the boarding. The ceiling beams were stout logs; he smelled wood cooking and recognized in the air the smoky light of early morning or evening. That donkey ride in the mountains of the slant-eyes, that party with Mikhailov, those creaking leaky boats of floating dead and that gouty fat man tripping in a thickening carpet of his own blood in the railway yards; were these but a gulag dream? A tale told me by my *zek*, he thought, but where was the warmth in that? The *zek* wouldn't speak of such things, only of beaches and a boiling sun close enough to touch; elsewise his miserable *zek* life would be forfeit. But no, upon me this sack of feathers, under me this pillow and a mattress of softness. I am elsewhere. He made to move but the duvet pinned him as a huge, fat lover; he felt himself naked. My chills, where are my chills? Am I in heaven with that woman's bag of vinegar, old God?

From an unseen room, he heard a voice muttering a high tune and the shuffle of soft slippers on a board floor. A pot banged, metal utensils danced. There was a smell now, of vegetables. The smoke of a cigarette, a sound like bracelets rattling.

He spoke but his words found little voice. He spoke in Russian, a croak: "One who is there?"

The sounds in the kitchen stopped briefly, the person wondering if there'd been a sound. Then the humming began again, the utensils rattled on, the sound of the soft slippers like someone slowly dancing.

Bone took a deep breath and formulated words into English. "Harken. One who is there?"

The slippers moved across the floor and a silhouette entered the doorway down past the foot of the bed. He could see a slim female child's shape in a dress, one hand holding a silver knife of size, the other a cloud of blue smoke. The shape stepped out of the shoes and crossed the room silently, put the knife in his reach on a table beside the bed, then stood back, smoking.

She spoke: "A bear peeked in the window yesterday, saw a sleeping Thief, and became a *zek*."

Bone reached out from under the duvet and wrapped his fingers around the knife; he could barely lift its weight. She put her hand upon his and he saw the angel with pincers: A parasite — I'm the prisoner of vengeful politicals. She watched his eyes and put the other hand, holding the cigarette, onto the knife, and he knew. The fingers of her hands were warm and familiar; he recalled being fed a liquid of bitter roots boiled in water, the seemingly endless singing of words on the highest of scales. Sweating and thrashing, the subsiding and dreaming.

"Where is this place? My park?"

"We are away. A friend from afar —" with her fingers she made Chinaman's eyes "— said a precious cargo required assistance and safety. One with a big head delivered you to me for safekeeping."

Bone recalled the aghast Cabbage looming above him, a bulge-eyed big man mewing concern. He recalled being gathered and lifted and carried from the park in a stumbling run. "The big-headed one, he is with us?"

"No. His new master is your enemy, the decayed spleen Razinkin." She shrugged and dropped her cigarette into a cup. "Love all, trust none."

"Am I a prisoner of Fairies?"

"Fairies do not take prisoners." She made a pretty but evil smile for him. "I am Dagg. There is a borscht of vegetables. And root tea."

"Root tea?" His throat, raw, closed; the roof of his mouth burned; his teeth were rank with residue of tree barks and powdery leaf. "No, not."

She made a less evil smile; his eyes were adjusting to the

shadowed hollows of her face and he recalled recently meeting a sadly smiling angel of the same features.

"You have emptied and filled many times, from many places. So, perhaps not tea, just borscht, eh?"

She left the room in a sway, taking the cup but leaving the knife. She returned with a flattened stack of clothing and put them at the foot of the bed. "When you want to leave the bed, harken me. I'll assist you to walk." She noticed the knife was gone from the table.

"I walk alone."

She laughed, and he thought of the chimes a gulag prisoner had made of unthreaded cloth and bits of glass and shards of metal that made music in the steady winter wind. "Perhaps . . . but maybe not today, eh, Thief?"

For the remainder of the morning, the room where Bone rested was silent as a cathedral. Twice she crept to the doorway in her bare feet and peered in, finding him asleep. She stood by the window over the sink eating borscht slowly, holding the bowl under her chin as she licked at the spoon, watching a moose wander up to the van, inspect it, and wander off. At the mouth of the bay, through a narrow break in the trees, she saw brightly colored canoes from an up-lake camp silently carry synchronized paddlers through to the portage by the collapsed bridge.

This was a Fairie's soul retreat, the refuge in which she didn't so much hide from the world, but prevented the world from bearing witness to her true self. Somehow, within, thought Dagg, there lives still a girl; if only I could remember her. Here she could sing and sew and expose her insides in the dark, crying if she wished, laughing if she wished, sitting mute or howling if she wished, while a reel of horror flickered through her memory. She could whirl barefoot dances in sunlight, bathe naked in the shallow bay, fish with one of the many rods racked above the fireplace, or dream of children she could never meet. At times she was reminded by the thick shadows of trees or the burning wood of camps and prisons; at others, somewhere in a locked-away gulag of her mind she remembered that girl and experienced a glimpse of the peace she'd long surrendered. The drive back to the city was five hours at least, and she always used the time to recreate herself into the devil of a Fairie, arranged her public smiles — bitter or hating or violent — into her persona. But one day, she dreamed — as much as Fairies were capable of this enticing act — of arriving and never leaving, of watching the beasts of the woods lick the shop van into rust, of watching the full cycle of seasons as the world washed itself, over and over until she died, an untold story, a secret history that would, too, be nibbled into oblivion by the teeth of bears and rodents.

In the late afternoon, Dagg crept silently into the bedroom and examined Bone. Sleep, she saw, was peaceful to him: his years of suffering horrors and committing horrors dropped away and he took on the innocent sleep of a placid child. She slipped her hand under the pillow and found the knife, drew it out, and lay it on the bedside table. I must be careful of this one, she thought. Thieves have a rat's radar that identifies and exploits weakness, softness. Tonight he will live or die; in the morning I will have a decision to make, or not.

As the sun began a sudden late-summer descent, she took a fishing rod from above the fireplace and found a tackle box by the door. Outside she lifted a straw mat and with quick, sure hands plucked writhing worms disturbed from the darkness and moisture of their loam, and dropped them loose into the tackle box.

She walked down a barely identifiable path toward a small dam where a railway trestle once stood. A small bear crossed ahead of her and she held her breath, walking backward gently, to within dashing distance of the cabin, then rattled her bracelets. Without looking at her, the bear became suddenly athletic, bounding back the way it had come. She continued on and fished until it became almost too dark to discern the path she'd taken and returned to the cabin with a pair of twitching bass dangling from her fingers.

She didn't realize she'd been singing until she stopped.

Dagg, damp and chilled from her daily baptism in the bay, chipped loose a drift of crusted flour in the bottom of a plastic canister and lightly dredged the fish in the day's first light. She'd never been a good sleeper — too many times she'd been awakened by sudden, unpleasant attention, her first instinct to fight quickly replaced by the Fairies' code of survival: acquiescence before all except death and in the face of death was required only one thing: focused insanity. The night before, she had scaled and cleaned the two fish, put them in the refrigerator, and fallen instantly to sleep on a lumpy sofa in the cabin's main room. Once in the night she'd awoken to Bone's turnings and tusslings with his relentless duvet; she had listened for the chattering of his teeth to change into measured breathing, and then returned to a sleep that contained a pleasant dream, forgotten upon awakening at dawn, but nevertheless in its residue she anticipated a day of song.

Outside the window above the stove top, she watched a spindly deer edge from the thinning pines. The deer tasted air currents as it edged toward the garden where few vegetables had survived. Dagg made a quick hand sign against the glass and the deer vanished in a sudden flex. She went out to the garden and salvaged some vegetables and roots. What didn't fit into her arms was for beasts and birds.

When she returned to the kitchen, Bone, swamped in the duvet, was sitting at the wooden table with the knife in his hand. His skull seemed tiny and his eyes larger and lurking deeper into his cheeks, but he had an alertness and beginning of vigor that came with restoration by the potions.

"Thief, you can choose fish and roots, or tea."

"If it is tea, I will bring your insides out." His voice was still rough as he watched her carefully. His eyes were narrowed and his mouth firm. He feared the foul tea he'd been forced to drink contained some spell that would shrink his penis away and dissolve the Code. He'd heard of women with certain gypsy powers who used their monthly blood as bitter ingredients and feared he'd fallen into a trap. And that he was alive and not butchered in his sleep might portend a scheme for a longer, more creative death.

"Fish, then, and roots." She moved widely past him and dropped the vegetables into the sink, pumping stubborn water with a rapid series of muscular motions. She washed each vegetable, then put them on the table by his side. "With the knife you can make these into smaller sizes for quicker cooking and sooner eating."

"As I could you." He studied her as though identifying a system of joints through which a blade would glide without nicking itself on bone. He rotated the knife to make it catch the light and gleam wickedly.

This was the humor of a Thief, and Dagg felt no fear. She smiled, swayed close, and made a Fairies' trick, one hand capturing the attention of his eyes and the other plucking the knife from the weakened clutch of his hand. "You may kill me later —" she put the knife back onto the tabletop and turned away "— but now it is just breakfast for an old man."

Impressed, he laughed and worked at the root vegetables. "Am I the prisoner of Fairies? Of a Fairie alone?"

"As I said: Fairies take no prisoners. Only lovers and corpses. And often the first becomes the other, so beware, olden man." She heated oil and began sizzling the filets. She retrieved the roots, chopped them herself, and sank them into boiling water. "It has been five days since you were brought to me for safekeeping. When you are able, you may stay or go, but in leaving I must blind you that no others may find this place."

"This is, then, a Fairies' soul lair."

"Ah. You know of these things?"

"Of Fairies, much. Submit to all and any, survive to sleep and awaken again to survive and sleep. A code of circles." He made a small bitter laugh and the face of a wicked clown. "I have met many Fairies, oh yes." He'd heard their screams and had made a few scream himself, not reluctantly by any means, but not with the voracious appetite of others in his *mir*. Not to take what was to be taken was a violation, as for Fairies it was a violation to refuse to be taken for any endeavor except death. And, it was said, his own mother was a Fairie who submitted to a *vor* and was captured by authorities and sent into the frontier where she died, or not. "Many Fairies, yes."

She gave him a smile. "So perhaps, then, one should not sleep as soundly as one does, eh?" But she made no judgment. Predators and prey: as the big ate the little, the little ate the tiny. The nature of a world far from this Fairies' soul lair, which was why there were such places. Who, after all, chose to be birthed, when and where and as which?

He put his hand on the knife on the tabletop and stared at her.

"There are many knives and many hours of sleep ahead

for you," she said, lifting the fish from the pan and spearing the roots from the water. "But there is no salt."

Bone had a gulag appetite. For three days, whatever Dagg prepared and put in front of him he devoured, his face close to his plate and the fork alternately cutting and stabbing his meal until the plastic plate was bare to its painted flowers, and then he looked around for more. The potions she'd fed him over the days had vacated everything in his system, and she was surprised at the power with which his strength returned. His sleep was erratic and he took it where he found it, some days arising for only an hour or two, sitting on the rocky sofa that was her bed, before falling asleep again.

He had dreams of deep peace, usually involving the rhythm of a mule, the endless quilt of smoky blue mountain ranges, indifferent Shan bandits, and dawns crisp enough to snap like a bone. What, his dreamy mind asked itself, what if I had dismounted my sick mule, then stepped no further? Would the Code still burn, even though for only a single Thief, sitting on a rocky hill?

But he also dreamed of tortured angst, the stretched grins of heads independent from bodies, gristle between joints, unimaginable slaughters of the brothers who had nurtured him into the *mir* and whose souls were the very tinder that fed the fire that was the Code that made him a Thief.

And he had sleeping illusions that were of neither, hearing the soft voice of his *zek*: "*. . . sharp salt fresh seaweed on the breeze . . . the sun is high and the heat falls in waves; there are no clouds to stop the burning rays; you can feel your body cooking slowly to brown; the sand is as fine as dust . . . it makes a perfect bed to the form of your back; it bakes you from beneath as the sun cooks you from above; the sounds of the water; the fading* *screeching of water birds, children laugh and whoop and kick a ball . . . it's hot, as an oven is hot, dry and relentless . . . You will never be cold; you're in hell and it will never be cold again.*" The *zek* and his good heart were, of course, gone up, where there were whooping children and swooping, fading birds, in a crowded heaven whispering his soft tendrils of poetry into God's ear. There would be a Thief or two lurking, just to keep the old cocksucker busy, but the *zek* would have his protection. Or, he asked himself within his dream, is my loved poet still under his cot, a puddle with hair and broken teeth, melting into the wooden planks?

In the end of his days of dreams, Dagg noticed he slept without the arm across the throat, the other arm across the vitals in his mid-body. One morning he came out in his clutched duvet, forgetting the knife under his pillow, and sat before his food.

"You said, in your sleep, Mikhail. Many times."

Bone stared at her. He remembered Mikhail, from Leningrad, who had been one of the few victims of the stronger of the *zeks*, set upon and strangled beside the logging trail. Ah, he thought, I loved that brother, and our vengeance was without limit. How many had lived and already died. He felt the sadness on his face and realized he was making himself naked before a Fairie. He laughed and said, "Ah, Mikhail. He was sentenced to three years, served five, and, because he was of good behavior, they freed him early after only eight."

She smiled gently at this Thieves' humor but noted the blink of sadness that tugged his face downward.

Chapter 10

For each of the days after Bone first arose, Dagg fished bass in the dim, chill of dawn and chill setting of the sun. On the evening of the fourth day, he walked with her to the sunken bridge and shivered in a stiff old oilskin coat she'd found in a closet. The rags he'd worn when Cabbage had lifted him from his trench in the park had been cleaned in the bay and dried on a branch, then folded and kept warm inside the stove. She'd cut his ragged hair with a pair of scissors, close to the skull. His beard became less vague and she took to calling him Babel in an increasingly friendly manner. She watched him closely when he was near and he noticed how she became a little less lithe, a little less trusting. There was still a kitchen knife unaccounted for, a factor she kept close to her heart; in fact, there was another knife missing and it lived under her own pillow at night.

At times he was silent, staring distantly with his lips moving over the Code, or having silent conversations with those she couldn't see. Other times he was garrulous, boasting of Thieves' adventures and glorious deaths. She said little, her own experiences having diminished the true of her self; for a Thief, the tales and blustering were part of the construction of the self.

At the sunken bridge, as she tore her worms in half, hooked them, and threw them accurately at a deep pool where the bass waited for food to float past, he suddenly began speaking, his voice quiet in the still air. He told her of hazy mountains where slant-eyed Shan roamed as bandits of times past. The poet within the Thief emerged and spoke of women dressed as butterflies, of the sinuous rhythms of mules, of watching a storm gather and explode on a faraway range, the color of the lightning and sparks and the blue smoke as it attacked trees growing impossibly out of the hard-rock skin of the earth. He spoke of camel-foot, the white flowers with dark centers that surfed like frozen waves between the gorges. She thought his words spoke of a religious conversion, that the lightning had indeed activated a hidden self. She closed her eyes as he spoke and realized he had likely never before been outside his precious *mir* of Moscow and prisons and camps, that he'd discovered the roundness of the world as a child discovered it: when the brightly colored ball just kept rolling away and didn't fall off the edge.

"Be alert, Fairie," he said at the very second a fish hit the line. "If we have no fish, I'll have to find other food." When she glanced at him, he lifted his eyebrows and made evil with a gnashing of teeth.

She smiled her lips into a beatific curve and became instantly calm and relaxed, for the first time since he'd become mobile. "I think not this one," she said, working the reel and the tip of the rod.

The fish left the water, a flashing, foaming black curve in the air, then took itself and the half-worm deep into the deep black water of the pool. She played it with a rhythm, twice more making the fish swim in the air; Bone laughed each time and like a bedazzled boy shouted: Ho! She fed out more line, then smoothly reeled the suddenly docile fish into the shallow waters. She captured it in her hands and turned its fat black body for him. "This one and I are old friends," she told Bone. "Many times we have met; many times he goes back."

"A good meal off one so large," he said.

"Ah." She freed the hook from the fish's inner mouth with her fingers, flicking the half-worm loose into the back of the fish's gullet. She kept the fish in her palms and looked at Bone. "Old ones such as this are only worth the catching, not the eating. Tough and of little flavor. He is a friend with a family and a name."

"Ah. This wet friend has a name?"

"Not by me." She held the fish in the water to reacclimatize it, then opened her hands to let it dart and dive. "But the other fish call him *dyed*."

After eating three small bass, he went to bed; a moment later he summoned her. She lay beside him under the duvet still in her sundress — none saw her without clothing — and in the dark thought his body was that of a lean boy, all long muscles, no excess fat, twisting and demanding and a little mean and greedy. She wouldn't let him take her as a *zek*, knowing if he demanded, she must. But he didn't and she engaged him while facing the beams of the ceiling. He grunted and pulled and bent, but didn't make her bleed or bruise; he chewed at her soft throat, but a moment later seemed to be inhaling the scent of lake water in her hair, tasting the strands of silver. She'd long been plundered of the mechanics and devices required for her own pleasure, but he stroked between engagements and she calmed under his hands. While he rested, she sang. When he returned, she made soundless songs, scales of hums and whispers.

There was a moon and, though they couldn't see it, its yellow light made the glass of the window glow, and she thought: It's a true love that doesn't kill me, that doesn't make blood run down my body or legs. He steals it as though it has a value; indeed, thus it does, as do I.

He lay beside her, his hand in the concave of her stomach under the bunched-up dress, thinking of the potions he'd been fed, the smiles he'd been given, some sinister, some of dreams. He realized that in their engagements he'd thought not of the Code, not of whether to walk alone, not of anything except the feeding of the senses. Is this the clouding of the gypsy's curse? He'd heard of the testicles shrinking into peanuts, losing their power, of the heart forgetting the true path, the eyes glazing with the look of an obedient, moon-eyed farm beast. Why else would a Fairie save a Thief, if not for mischief? He thought of strangling her, as he had his *zek* in the camp, a quiet going-up with but a moment of fear or pain. For this, he thought, I am a good man as well as a good Thief.

Instead, he asked, "Have you given the fuck to the authorities? For food? For position?"

"But never," she said, "for free or of free will."

"Have you given the fuck for money?"

"Only," she said, "with the soft place, but never the heart. The hands and knees were on the snow; the heart was in the stars."

"You have taken the heartbeat?"

"Yes," she admitted, she had killed. "But not for money, only for destiny."

He was satisfied; there might be no reason to send her up. And he would somehow have to leave this place; he'd never driven an automobile, and anyway had no idea where he was.

He might, he thought, even be back on the frontier. He murmured, "As is my mother of my blood, are you." He began, impossibly under such a thick duvet, shivering, and drew closer to her body.

"This chill — it is from the camps?"

He ignored her question; or maybe not. "Within: the wolf; without: the wolf."

"Inside the wire I dreamed of warmth, of heat. Now, out, I have much. Too much." She positioned herself around him. Indeed his flesh was cold and mobile, stuttering upon itself; indeed she had a surplus of warmth. He remained still, allowing her to cover him with the flesh of her body.

They slept, but before long even her copious heat receded and she, too, shivered.

The Fairies' soul lair was owned by a man, now long dead, who had deeded it to her by voice only. She had visited more than a dozen times and had never run into anyone, except for an inept canoeist who'd flipped into the water and waded to the shore of her bay. She'd hidden like a sprite in the trees until the canoeist had righted his canoe and passed on.

Each time Dagg left her lair, she had no assumption she'd ever return; the dead man, a lover of weakened heart who had negotiated her body for the good price of stolen wares and ultimately became a friend, may have had a family, someone to whom ownership belonged in law.

In any case, as she and Bone spent the last early morning gathering their belongings and cleaning away signs of their visit, she stopped often to sit on the shore where the old fish *dyed* came out to play. Under her light coat and thin sundress, her skin shivered, and she wondered if Bone would kill her after she'd returned him safely to the city. She experienced no fear, just a sense of loss that over these days she'd found one with whom she could spend a night in a bed without her arm bent across her throat to ward off the blade, or her body curled to protect her own vital places. His loving — for that's what it was: she didn't bleed nor die, and how much after all could a Fairie ask? — had been direct without being brutal, artless without being indifferent, and he had given no thought to her. But, she told the black old bass, I didn't bleed and I've seen him smile. She said: I'll be back, a promise Fairies never made, that recognition of a future and the assumption — the hope — of survival.

As she walked to the van, she began reinventing herself. Finding the silver amulet of the entwined couple in the pocket of her coat, she placed it on the dashboard in front of the passenger seat, then went into the cabin for the duvet. All knives but one were in the block of wood beside the stove; she took hers from under the sofa and slipped it into its slot.

She saw him standing by the rock where she'd sat earlier to speak her vow to her fish. Fragments of a persistent, cottony mist swayed behind him where the trees gave only a brief glimpse of the morning canoeists gliding to the portage at the dam. The water was black, a promise of a season of quick change; the sky was cloudless except for wisps of gauze laid across the farthest horizon to the east, where the sun was melting it away and offered a reluctant day of summer's heat. Bone looked strong and solid now, unlike the raggedy puppet Cabbage had delivered to her. She wondered if he too was reinventing himself, hiding away the face of a man and replacing it with the mask of a Thief.

An olden man — a Thief! — who, yes, did take but somehow did not diminish. Who conquered but did not plunder. Somewhere in her silver-threaded head, she recalled having known in her life the woman's pleasure, and wondered where it had gone and how that had come to pass. It would be difficult, she knew, to keep the days of this dream time alive in her mind: too many mornings had she awoken in nightmare, vigorously scrubbing her thoughts to blankness.

She called, her voice a song, to her old Thief: "Ba-bel," and heard him laugh as he turned to her, his mouth still moving in a silent mantra of his *mir*.

For the first five miles, until they were on a highway, she insisted he lie in the rear of the van, under the duvet. He agreed, aware that the Fairies' soul lair required the respect of deepest security, and it had, after all, saved a Thief. In his pants pocket was the amulet he'd found on the dashboard, a curious twisted thing of either one head on two bodies or two heads on one body. A gift could not be accepted. It could, however, be stolen.

At a gas station she filled the tank while he went inside and liberated snacks for the journey; as he emptied his pockets onto the console between them, she laughed, "Ah, treasures."

The day was heating up and traffic was swift. He ate a chocolate bar and began asking questions, questions of Razinkin and the Thieves, of Ushki, of the big-headed Cabbage, of the lines and shadows of the *mir* of the city.

Of Razinkin she said: When he had appeared, the Thieves in the city welcomed him as a savior, as one sent by the Circle in Moscow to bring prosperity, to bring harmony and calm and fair profit to a *mir* that flared in unknowable violence and anarchy. But in calming the noise, he weeded out the true Thieves and acolytes in ways spoken of with horror. From Zakon in New York came grim men who combed the city for wild Thieves and their followers; many of the *mir* vanished.

The survivors were given a monthly allowance and cautioned to steal quietly: Razinkin was fishing in deeper waters for the benefit of the Circle. Any who disobeyed were killed; some who did obey were also killed.

Of Ushki and the Thieves, she said: There had been several Thieves, but how many she didn't know. Ushki was the most respected and had the largest brigade, the most active. They would go on periodic rampages, smashing glass cases in jewelry stores and looting gold and watches; they would sweep through émigré neighborhoods collecting donations and washing windows with bullets. Children of the prosperous were taken on mysterious vacations and returned only upon payment of fabulous ransoms. Her own buy-for-little-and-sell-for-much business boomed as bands of burglars crept into houses and shops and brought her product. Desperate young women — chickens of no roost, she called them — were brought to the city to work in clubs for lap grinding, beaten and paid little and producing lucrative profits. Of Ushki she told of the plastic necktie, and Bone spat with horror and disdain.

Of the *mir* of the city, she said: There were many — Italians and blacks and the slant-eyed Chinese, there were the *hawala* men of India and gold men of Pakistan, there were Israelis; there were white-powder people of South America, and Africans with sloped huge foreheads and prominent scarring. With the most powerful, the Italians, Razinkin arranged for women to dance in the clubs of the *vor* Ricci, as well as for the repatriation to Europe of the profits of the Italian *mir*.

Of Cabbage, she said she was unsure; he might be a big-headed boy of a heart to match, but he'd allowed his master, the gone Dumpling, to dance and shit himself; although, she added, he ended the misery with gunfire and tears. "This

Cabbage, he is one who knows all, has been in the city's *mir* even before the swamp drained," she told Bone, swooping the van onto an entry ramp to the highway to the city. "When the one in Moscow —" here she tugged down her eye: the Chinaman "— said you were arriving, he'd been told by Ushki this Cabbage was of trust. He said you might walk alone, or you might blow upon the ember of the Code and make fire rage."

"How is it that you know of this one of the eyes?"

"He has a lady of whom I know."

"A lady Thief?" There were women of his *mir* who were as Thieves — tattooed, predatory, voracious, but never true Thieves of the stars, an unheard-of thing. There were wives of the *mir*, but not wives of documentation or of State sanction.

"A sister of my *mir*, of the black." As with the true Thieves, in the world before the whores of the new reality, the Fairies' *mir* was made up with no recognition of ethnicity, race, geography, or generation. All those of the vagina could join, all could assist, all could suffer, equally. There were, Bone knew, Fairies of Asian eyes, of blackened skin, of the Spanish and English and French tongues. There were Fairies of the world of picking pockets, of small money for the fast fuck, of stabbings during engagements, of selling a hole full of nothing for huge profit.

"This man —" Bone tugged his eye "— this brother has a Fairie? Like a second wife, for the bed only?"

She nodded. "Not only for the bed. For the companionship, the love. With the treachery, he used the only safe course. Thus, you were arrived and you were delivered."

He rode in silence and ate another chocolate bar. He sucked the peanuts from the caramel and spit them out the window, thinking and measuring her words. By the new Code, Razinkin was indeed a *vor v zakone*, a Thief within the Code. And it was forbidden for another *vor v zakone* to do harm to him without the fair judgment of a conclave. But if, as Bone believed, this new Code was damaged and he himself followed an old Code, one without the impurities, then did this nullify the new? As long as he and the diminishing olden Thieves lived to carry the true Code, could there be a new Code to replace it? If indeed there were two Codes, what was it to him, this second, lesser one?

He meditated on this, reflecting the information against the tenets of the Code within him, nurtured at long last by the fire of his passion.

In the end he was guided by the evidence: that he had crossed the world in the most difficult of journeys, that his steps had been guided by the Chinaman, that he had survived this twisting illness, and that he alone was alive, now with Ushki gone on up, and he was the only one of authority in the *mir* of the city. That he had survived the liquid curses of this silvery gypsy. In the face of this, was he meant to walk alone while Thieves were butchered and cowed?

He watched Dagg slyly from the corner of his eye. Wind from the open window was now warming and she smoked a half-cigarette she'd plucked from the ashtray. His passion had been great under the duvet, he recollected, and he believed she might have kissed at him within a passion of her own inner self. The only kisses he'd experienced were the greetings of brothers, and occasionally with the whores the guards were bribed to bring into the camps. Now, he saw, she was smiling secretly at the road in front of them, wondering what? It was fine that he hadn't killed her yet. Equally fine that she hadn't killed him.

As the van blended with midday traffic on the outskirts of the city, his decision was made and the Code within him was as a fed furnace.

"Tell me again," he told his Fairie, "of the *mir* of the city."

Avi the shop boy looked upon the gypsy bitch as his mother. And when she sometimes ran her jewelled fingers through his golden child's hair, he wondered if somewhere, in some delirium, she had birthed a boy inside the barbed wire and forgotten about it in the horrors before, during, and after, and just chewed the cord of flesh and left the red-streaked pink thing wailing in snow. She might have forgotten this if it were a Fairies' act of survival; certainly he couldn't remember being birthed out and clearly that had happened. Perhaps she too couldn't remember? He knew her saliva wasn't a poison in spite of his words of her witchery to the big-headed one who had returned and beaten him and then poured glasses of little water — vodka — and ordered platters of herring and small delights. He loved her as a mother — although she said he was the spawn of a syphilitic dancer and a deranged warden — and the big-headed one, he was certain, knew of a shop boy's lies. The shop boy entertained whether the big-headed Cabbage could indeed be his father.

Avi slept on the sofa that bore still the strong odor of sickness, shit, and sweat. There had clearly been an adventure, but Dagg's life was a serial of those, often followed by disappearances or depression that she showed only to him. He feared for her safety and prayed for her return. The plastic creaked when he moved, so in sleep he was absolutely motionless, covered by a fur coat a soft-footed Thief had brought in earlier in the week. He'd remained in the basement of the shop, listening to vehicles passing up the laneway, for the unique growl of the shop van. He'd slept when he was tired and ate only when he was very hungry, awaiting.

The scent of women's powders on the coat were giving him dreams of safety and longing when he heard the van grinding to a halt outside the window. Two doors squeaked open and then slammed shut. He was out from under the coat and halfway up the stairs when he recognized the footsteps of more than one person: hers a gliding sound as a dancer on polished wood, the other a shuffle of heaviness. Then a man's growling voice, and then hers, and then a key ring jangled and the slip of metal into the lock. Avi found a yellow-handled screwdriver and positioned himself behind the door: she never had men, although she had had the attentions of plenty.

Love first with the voice, with the whisper, she'd once said, then with the flesh and the juices. Avi, in his seventeen years, had never had nor been had by man, woman, or beast, nor even by himself except in thrashing sleep. He would love with the screwdriver and, if necessary, observe the flesh and its juices. He hoped it wasn't Cabbage, come to torture her into the secrets of her commerce; stabbing the large-headed one would be a weight on his heart, especially if he were indeed somehow his father.

But she came through the door first, laughing over her shoulder. Avi had heard the laughter when it was soaked in bitterness and drink, when it was derisive and authoritative, coquettish in bargains, and he had heard it as a laughter of pain when she slept and the moon and the shadows reminded her of dark things past.

The sweetness of this laugh, though, stayed the hand clutching the translucent yellow handle against his ear. His resolve faltered and he asked, "Mistress?" at the same time he saw an eye already peering at him through the edge of the door, near the hinges.

"Oooh," a hoarse voice said, "the wolfhound awaits." Below the twisting lips, he saw a beard and some dulled teeth arranged in a canine smile of their own.

Dagg, her hair matted and tangled from wind and seeming to have more veins of silver, put her hand on Avi's shoulder. "We're blessed: only friends here."

Jam wasn't a Thief, so Cabbage could lie in the face of his casual questions. He said old Ushki hadn't mentioned a *vor* was coming to the city and he hadn't heard of a bum of olden times lurking. He admitted he had heard the legend of Bone, as had all, for this was the making of a Thieves' fable to be told by firelight.

The men were sitting in a black Lexus, one of the Razinkin fleet, one that had never been followed by police, outside the garage entrance of a brokerage house off Bay Street, in the downtown core's financial district. They had begun the day at noon, picking up packages and bags; Jam had entered several buildings, including a nightclub run by the Italian *vor* Ricci, and returned to the Lexus where he sat stabbing numbers onto a piece of paper. After the final stop at a currency exchange, where an Iranian had stared with violent suspicion through the glass window at Cabbage, who always remained in the car, Jam had climbed behind the wheel and twisted in the seat so he could unload the packages and bags of money into a lawyer's accordion case.

As he pulled out into traffic, he told Cabbage, "The master provides a service to others of like mind and ways. The money is to be taken to a dirty man who will make it travel through many accounts in many countries and return as loans and investment. On this day, at this time, the collections should be complete." He punched a series of numbers into his cellphone, said the time he would arrive, and clicked off.

The day was warm but the steep sun portended the coming of autumn. Lunchtime, and the plazas of the commercial towers were full of workers soaking up the sun. When they weren't watching the mouth of the garage, both men ogled the secretaries and office workers in their short skirts and blouses, passing comments and evaluations.

Jam straightened quickly: "There."

"He comes?" Cabbage stared at the mouth of the garage for the man they were to follow. "Where?"

"No, not him. Across the street there — the three are gypsies."

Cabbage looked where Jam pointed and saw two dark, middle-aged, well-dressed men and a middle-aged woman in a pantsuit step from the revolving doors of a golden bank tower. They spoke briefly, then one man left the other couple and walked to the edge of the sidewalk. The couple stood thirty feet away. When a man in suit pants, shirt, and tie came out of the tower carrying a briefcase, the gypsies began moving. As the couple approached the man from the front, the lone gypsy closed him from behind; from his pocket he took a red plastic squirt bottle and launched a blob of ketchup onto the back of the businessman's shirt and kept moving, past him. The woman spoke to the businessman, who turned and tried to see the back of his shirt; the woman took a wad of tissues from her purse and began wiping off the ketchup. The businessman put down his briefcase and the gypsy man bumped it with his foot. The lone gypsy, the squirter, had meanwhile reversed his direction and, in passing the activity, scooped up the briefcase. The chattering woman tugged at the businessman's shirt while removing his wallet, her actions covered by her companion. The two quickly made to leave, each bumping into the businessman, disorienting him, and were gone.

"He comes." Jam broke off his examination of the street's activities and started the Lexus, watching for a gap in traffic. A black Mercedes SUV with smoked windows paused at the edge of the sidewalk and inched through the pedestrians before heading west. With Jam following, the vehicles stopped-and-started along the block.

"Ah, the gypsies. Of beauty, eh?"

Cabbage nodded. "In the south of the true America, in one of the countries, they have a school for such things. In my brigade I had an Argentine man who excelled at this kind of activity. He worked at the airport with another, a woman, and they came to me with many suitcases. One day they came with a suitcase containing packages of powders."

"Lucrative, that. These were powders for the nose?"

"Yes, but problems ensued and meetings were held between Razinkin and Ricci, who demanded the return, and the master agreed." Cabbage shrugged. "In this city there are many such interests."

Ahead the Mercedes turned left and Jam followed. It quickly turned right, and again the Lexus followed.

Cabbage said, "This one ahead, is this an adventure?"

"No, no. We will give him something and he will return to his company with it. We will follow him back to ensure safety, of both him and the gift. Investments, the master says. This one will take all currencies without documentation and will open a company for us." Jam indicated another turn. "I miss the days of a good loud adventure, when one could work hard like a man all day and relax like a man all night."

"Good days."

"Good days indeed. Sometimes it's like the tiger becomes a house cat, eh?"

Cabbage was careful. "This is how the master wants it. Quiet adventures, and no attention. Sometimes . . ."

"What?"

Cabbage forced a laugh. "Sometimes, sometimes I think the master is like a policeman, even more effective at keeping the order."

The Mercedes pulled over to the curb of a one-way side street. Jam stopped and Cabbage reached for the door.

"No, no. We wait; when each thinks it's safe, each turns on the emergency flashing lights." He adjusted the mirrors and glanced repeatedly at them. "With old Ushki, it was different times, eh? The master would get insane when he heard of adventures. This jewelry store, that explosion. Thieves, he would scream, oh those fucking Thieves. I'm surprised old Ushki didn't go on up sooner." He paused. "Bless a Thief."

Cabbage too said, "Bless a Thief."

The rear lights on the Mercedes began to intermit; Jam did a last examination of his mirrors and turned his own on.

"This one will be for you in future. I will explain the mechanics afterward, but you must always have one who is trusted with you, eh? If one steals, both pay, so select a companion who loves you, not one who owes you a large debt." He took the lawyer's case from behind the front seat, and he and Cabbage exited the Lexus. "It is well to be of ease and accidentally leave his vehicle without the briefcase. This man is always frightened, so one of you should stay in our vehicle to not alarm him, but should be of slow heartbeat and many eyes. Always on a one-way street. Any disturbance, and the street should be blocked with our vehicle; sound the horn and exit prepared to battle."

Cabbage rounded the front of the Lexus and climbed in behind the wheel. Jam went up the passenger's side of the Mercedes, knocking his knuckles against the rear quarter. He climbed in.

Cabbage thought about the missing old man and the treacherous Dagg. With one of his brigade he had, in frustration, revisited the shop and done the dance with the surprisingly tensile Avi, but to no avail. The wispy shop boy had absorbed several blows in silence: clearly his life had made most measures short of death a part of his diet. Afterward Cabbage — it was clear to him the boy was of marrow — and his companion had cleaned up the shop boy and took him out for cabbage rolls and cabbage soup. Avi outdrank both of us, Cabbage thought, pouring down little water as though it were dispensed from a mother's nipple. Cabbage also recalled the shop boy studying his face, one feature at a time, as though making a memory, and wondered if in the huge heart in the pale body there lurked a plan of revenge.

But where were they, that spitting gypsy and that wraith-like Thief? Had Dagg done the two X's and done what the Circle couldn't do? But why, then, not have someone of her milieu take him from the railway station directly to God's door? And why was the spittle Razinkin sending Jam and the rest of the brigade out sniffing, if the old man had already been betrayed? Or was Bone just another stolen fur coat, to be brushed up, cleaned and relabeled, and sold for profit in another season, taken by a Fairie who surely had some of the blood of Thieves within her?

Ahead Jam exited the Mercedes, still speaking to the driver; then, glancing both ways, he slammed the door. He came up the sidewalk without the briefcase and climbed into the passenger's side of the Lexus. "He wanted to have it counted before accepting it," he told Cabbage. "This is a squirrel, this one, and I had to make him piss his pants." He nodded. "Go ahead and follow as he goes."

"Did you count it?"

Jam laughed. "I counted his nose for him, is what I counted." He directed Cabbage to follow the SUV back to the mouth of the underground garage, after which the contents of the briefcase became a matter of indifference to him and were the responsibility of the sweating and soiled suited man. "May I take you to your home?"

Cabbage shook his head. Across the street a police car was parked where the gypsies had worked their red magic of distraction; the businessman was slapping his own head and pointing in many directions while the policemen wrote in their notebooks.

Cabbage climbed out from behind the wheel and came around as Jam left the passenger side. "No, my friend. I think I will do some shopping."

Jam slapped his shoulder. "A good day. Not a day of thievery, but still: a day of profit." He looked into Cabbage's eyes. "All who know you, love you, but please: if this bum of which we spoke appears, it would do you well to let us know. My master says his heart is a traitor and his blood is treachery."

"I will watch for him."

Jam reached into the Lexus' back seat and lifted over a white plastic grocery bag. "Lemons for your brigade. My master says there are four trees of lemons here, and you should distribute them as you wish, with a larger portion to yourself."

Cabbage took the bag. Four thousand dollars to be divided among his little brigade so they wouldn't make a disturbance, stealing big or noisy, for another week. "I thank you."

"Beware then, and have caution."

Cabbage walked along King Street chewing bile. Beware

and have caution. Bushels of lemons handed to him as though he were some kind of *shestiorka*, some bagman, some gopher. Where lives the thrill in that? Thrill — the expanding, bursting heart of raiding a jewelry store and smashing display cases. That was thrill, that was the work of a man. A shop boy could carry lemons for distribution; a shop boy could stop a car and watch for flashing lights. A shop boy could bust the nose of a citizen and hand him a case full of money.

Better, for a man, to steal copper pennies than be handed a gift of gold bars.

PART THREE

Chapter 11

On the fourth day after his return from the Fairies' soul lair, Bone made his way across the city on foot, refusing to pay to ride the streetcars, declining Avi's offer to ride in the worn shop van, an offer of protection that made Bone smile until he saw the depth of the boy's eyes. This Avi, he thought, when they cut his corpse they will find six hearts, all of them black as sea.

For directions he had a scrap of paper with traffic lights indicated on a scrawled map. Twenty traffic lights, then turn to the right. Nine traffic lights and turn to the left on the first street after the ninth light and then turn to the left again. At the end of the block, just before those traffic lights: on the left will be Ricci's club; on the right, a café with wide umbrellas and glass-topped tables made of spidery iron legs.

Bone kept an eye on the path of the sun. Thieves' measurement of time consisted of the period after the rise of the sun in the east, straight above the head, the sinking to the west, and the fullest of the moon, late night. Bone's meeting was for after the straight above the head but before the sinking to the west. The walk was long and he was amazed at the array of goods left in stands on sidewalks, of clothing racked in front of shops, of unloaders of trucks who left no one to protect the backs of the vehicles. He walked through a zone where the people all had China in their eyes; another where the skins were blackened; a third where men wore turbans and had massive beards; a fourth where young men and women all wore makeup and bangles in their skin, the men and a few of the women making him think of his *zek*.

He thought, as he approached the café across from Ricci's nightclub: Across the world I have clutched the Code to my breast as though it were a lit candle, the flame sometimes hesitant, at other times roaring. But it always warmed me and lit my path. To this café; wondrous can life be, of silvery gypsies, fish with names, a laughing boy across the table studying me as I drink soup that is hot and potato that is cold.

Cabbage was a morose lump slouched in a gaily upholstered chair. He wore a boxy suit of prosperity and was decorated with gold bracelets, gold rings, and a daring tie of yellow silk that matched the flag that spilled from the breast pocket of his jacket. Upon his face was a mask of frustration. For hours he'd sat for what, he knew not. Be at this place when the sun begins falling; you will be met by one whom you know. A voice unknown to him, perhaps a man or a boy, a woman or a girl, gave no further data; that the call came on one of his cellphones to a number known to only a few gave it weight. Perhaps, he thought, Razinkin with an apprentice's task to be done. Or perhaps the giddy Jam and his slab of a friend Novak to send me on up, dancing with my big melon even bigger and the shit in the back of my pants. Perhaps another of Razinkin's swine to be chauffeured about like royalty, his tastes and needs assuaged, his mysterious business to be concluded and then to be delivered to the airport.

Ah cocksucker, he thought. Ah licker of the ass. These are the jobs of a boy, not a man.

He missed his old dumpling Ushki and his trips around town to loot a little, drink a lot, and have a sporting afternoon in some whore's bleached apartment. Never did the old man treat Cabbage as a servant; there were always old Thieves' stories, Thieves' lessons, Thieves' work. When Ushki drank, Cabbage drank. When Ushki sported, Cabbage sported. Ushki, who could wander a vast store and identify potential adventures: racks of expensive clothing where a vacant-minded clerk had failed to alternate the direction of the coat hangers. A single grab would yield an armload of garments and then a quick dash to the door. A woman's purse hanging open; a man putting his wallet away carelessly; a clerk who turned away from the cash register just long enough to allow a successful till-tap. The shoulder surf, where bank-machine card codes were discovered and the pocket picked.

Ushki, he thought, wishing he had a drink to toast the old ghost.

A hand upon his shoulder awoke his mind. He looked up in shock at Bone's sudden, silent appearance on the patio. He half-rose awkwardly; Bone patted the air between them. "Sit, my son. One such as you should stand up for none. The honor is mine and I greet you."

"*Dyed*. Your death was feared."

"Ah, but I live, though." He sat in amusement at this, refusing to look around, staring into Cabbage's eyes. "And am I safe?"

"Always, always. One cannot endanger one's own mother once birthed."

A waitress wearing ballet slippers, a short skirt, and a flowery blouse came out of the café. She was as slight and narrow as Dagg but with no silver to be mined from her hair. Bone asked Cabbage for tea the old way; Cabbage asked the girl for tea in a glass with a cube of sugar, and for himself an Italian coffee. The tea came with a bag of sugar on the saucer. Bone poured the sugar into his mouth and sipped at the tea, his hands clutched around the glass, leaching heat.

Cabbage was amazed at this new Bone who he'd thought of as either road-weary at the railway station or sick unto death in his arms on the gypsy's sofa. The old man's face had color from the burn of the sun; his hair, though shaven almost to his skull, was glowing; his fingernails were clean; and the beard was short and soft, giving him the calm look of a monk. He wore a clean short-sleeved shirt buttoned to the throat, untucked over shapeless but clean suit pants with wide cuffs. On his feet he wore new blue canvas shoes with bright white laces tied securely into reef knots, and two pairs of socks of rough blue wool, both to warm his feet and to fill the too-large shoes. Someone was looking after this olden man, Cabbage deduced, suspecting the vicious Dagg.

Cabbage glanced across the street at Ricci's. "This may not be a place of safety. We should go elsewhere."

"Where friends abound, danger flees." Bone took from his pants pocket a tin lozenges box and opened it. Within were loose white cubes of sugar and large capsules of vitamin C Dagg had sworn would ease his chills; all they did was turn his urine a yellow that arced like a bright rainbow. There were loose coins in the box, as well as telephone numbers written on a slip of paper — hails for assistance if he somehow got lost — and a small bundle of herbs tied around a man-root for him to suck if his stomach told him it wanted to come out of either the entrance or the exit.

Bone put a cube of sugar behind his front teeth and sucked the hot tea through it. "I thank you for saving a poor Thief in sickness."

"I feared the Fairie's treachery."

"It was well. She hid me and played the nurse. She has returned me to a park where there are fish in the water and many places to sleep warm." Lies and truths. He looked at the club across the street.

"That place across is the *vor* Ricci's," Cabbage said. "He is of the Italian *mir* and does business with my master."

"You have a master? Have you a father?"

"Ushki," Cabbage said with true sadness that damped his eyes, "bless a Thief."

Bone touched his icy fingers to the big-headed one's wrist. "Everywhere, orphans. We must change this, eh?" He drained his tea and crunched the remainder of the sugar cube. "I'm told you may be trusted. That Ushki selected you to receive me. Is this true?"

Cabbage nodded. "Your safety was with me, but a witch . . . How did you escape?"

"Do not fear the witch — the witch is of powers that saved and talents that brought endurance. She fears you allowed Ushki to be sent on up; she now fears for my safety."

"No, no. It was a thing of the *vory*; could I have stopped it, I would have. All I could do was send him up faster."

Bone made a small smile. "Better to be killed by a friend than loved by an enemy, eh? Well, with the old cocksucker he sleeps, probably having angels fore and rear. Tell me of your state now."

"With Ushki's going, I and my brigade are with Razinkin. We are six, sometimes seven. We are forbidden to work, and he gives a weekly stipend that we may exist."

"And how many has Razinkin?"

"Here, perhaps fifteen who are the heart of his brigade. He has honest businessmen, he liaisons with the Italians, and it is said with some Asians. He is aligned with Zakon in America if he requires assistance. He is sometimes followed by *musor*, but he is protected by government spies to whom he gives information about businessmen from the city of spires in return for his own freedom."

Bone nodded and looked over his shoulder at Ricci's nightclub across the street. "And this Ricci is what? A partner?"

"Razinkin provides through an employment agency for girls to come here and dance on the laps. It's said that Ricci and he provide funds for bringing white powders here, that Razinkin cleans the profits of Ricci's *mir* and others who require service."

"Have you loyalty to this man, this abscess who steals the hearts of Thieves? Be truthful; I swear that if this is so, I may have to kill you later, but not here and not now."

"No, no, not."

The slim waitress came outside briefly and Cabbage ordered more beverages. The men sat in silence, Bone trying to suck the warmth of the sun into his body, Cabbage confused, feeling as if he were at a crossroads and this man of charisma was pulling at him wordlessly. He thought Bone still looked like a bum, some itinerant vagrant collecting bits of tin and string and glass to sell to second-hand stores. He wondered where Bone had slept these past days — in a shop basement, or had he truly disappeared into his kingdom of trees? Did the notorious dogs of the parks or the meat-ripping raccoons fear him? Had he empowered his will over their nocturnal nerves and trained them into pets, sending them out to steal for him, to drag bits of clothing and food across the wide avenue at dawn, down into the ravines to stock some buried larder? He was of the same bones as Ushki, but more so, enhanced. From a dead rag in his arms, how had the evil Dagg breathed into him this power? Cabbage felt strangled, full, that a small mistake would lead to another and another and another, until his life was in peril.

As Bone watched the anxiety within Cabbage grow, he found himself with many questions. The shop boy Avi — one who Bone often observed studying his face, detail by detail, over meals or talks or from silent corners — said this one and another had visited the shop and had beaten on his body. But afterward, Avi said, they'd taken him for meats and liquors, had even offered the boy a free fuck with the woman of his choice. Was it, Bone had asked, one of Razinkin's men who came with Cabbage? No, the boy had said, one of the big-headed one's brigade. Did they cut you? Break the bones? Make you play the woman? No, no, and no.

Avi, Bone had recognized instantly, was no *zek*, although he was of soft voice and slight stature. When the prison warden had brought Dagg to the north of the true America, she'd said she had a child, a boy, without whom she couldn't live. In fact, Avi was the son of all mothers and apparently no fathers, an obedient mascot of the Fairies' *mir* who the women dressed as a girl although some occasionally grabbed at his genitals in motherly fashion. "It was decided if any of us made our way out, the first would take Avi, this was a vow," Dagg had said. "That he wasn't born with the vagina is not his fault. Once west, he would be freed to go and live. But he stayed and persists."

And where, Bone asked, was the warden?

What warden? she said, her face a shadow of secrets.

The waitress delivered the drinks. Bone took another cube from the box and held it behind his teeth while he sipped from the glass.

Cabbage ignored his coffee. "I have seen the heartbeat taken, and worse. The strangling of Ushki was of evil. You know of the plastic bags, the lighter? Is this how men behave? Poisonings upon oneself, dancing with a big red head of blackening worms?"

Bone nodded. "You know of the Code? Of the true Code? Ushki's Code?"

"It is said you carry it."

"Will you follow it? You are my first friend in the forsaken place; you can never enter this life, you can never kiss the dagger. You know this?"

Cabbage nodded, despairing of his past life as a worker, his violations of a code he never knew existed. But this man, this man who drew him like a jewel, beckoned. How can one not recognize greatness, not recognize history?

"But," Bone continued, "you can keep alive a flame that will warm all who were, all who are, and all who will become. Many you've never known, many not yet born. The Code that refuses you requires your service. I wish it were another, but it is not. You will never be of the Code, but I would always count you as a friend and at your death would laugh."

"*Dyed*, to serve, to serve." Cabbage found his throat clogged with lumps. He searched himself: Oh, dripping orifice, unwind this life of mine as a film, backward, and choose my choice unto another path of sharp rocks to glory. He could only say: "To serve."

"Then," Bone said, leaning forward again and putting a hand on Cabbage's wrist, "we will make merry for the scabrous Razinkin."

"And we start when?"

Bone shifted his chair to better view Ricci's emporium, where the afternoon-shift strippers were leaving through the employees' entrance and others arrived. "We have begun already."

All the dancers carried canvas or leather bags of the type models used. Most of the women were white, several were black, and a few were Asian. They arrived and left singly in taxis or were picked up or delivered by tanned, athletic men in sports cars.

Bone watched with interest as a long-haired young man moved cars in and out of a makeshift parking lot beside the construction site next to the strip club, constantly inspecting the parade of young women. The young man had thin Slavic features and a manner Bone recognized from the labor camps: hunger, opportunity, and the furtive eyes of a food thief. He wore a gold chain at his throat, a ballooning white shirt tucked tightly into a pair of black pleated pants, black cowboy boots, and a pair of sleek sunglasses jammed into his swept-back hair. As motorists paid him a parking fee, the young man added the bills to a wad of cash he kept in his upper left shirt pocket. The drivers left the keys in their cars and he constantly jockeyed them around the lot as motorists returned for their vehicles, or said they would return a few hours later.

A rumbling in Bone's emotions came like the rumbling stomach of a hungry man who detects food nearby. He felt his pulse motivate and his senses sharpen into focus: "This one, with the cars, do we know him?"

Cabbage followed Bone's eyes across the road. "No."

"He works perhaps for the dance club?"

"I think only Italians from their *mir* work there."

"Read me, please, that sign."

"It says Ricci has fifty women, gorgeous ones. Gorgeous means beautiful of the type to fuck. There is a businessman's special, it says. And: new girls each week." Cabbage squinted, trying to read the smaller lettering. He was pleased at this duty from Bone; while the old man's spoken English was rough and archaic but serviceable, he had difficulty reading Roman script.

Bone nodded, his mouth moving as his eyes scanned the sign. "The car boy takes a lot of money, I think. Did he park your car?"

"Yes, he's from Odessa I think, a Jew. A curious accent."

"How much does one pay him?"

"For one hour three dollars, for two six, for three nine. I gave him ten more because of the keys staying with me because of a barking dog on the floor." Razinkin had banned guns in the brigade, fearing some might begin shooting and making disturbance. But Cabbage, visions of the dancing Ushki in his head, kept one always nearby, to shoot at the writhing worms inside his own skull of hot swollen blood if necessary.

"I think he parks more than one hundred automobiles each day there. At one time, there are, perhaps, twenty of them?"

"A lot of money." Cabbage rolled the muscles of his neck and looked at the parking attendant with a new interest. The attendant walked over to the side door of the strip club and spoke with the doorman. Both men looked up and down the street. The attendant turned his back to the road and, blocked by his shoulder, took some money from his shirt pocket; he gave it to the doorman. The pair slapped hands. The attendant accepted a cigarette from the doorman and went to smoke it on the sidewalk in front of his lot. The doorman went into the darkness of the club.

Cabbage wondered at Bone's interest: Is this to be our operation? Are we to rob this boy of, what, three hundred, four hundred dollars? And this adventure will enrage Razinkin? Perhaps Bone wants this boy's billowy white blouse or his metal-framed European sunglasses, to dress up and take the horrible Dagg dancing in some graveyard.

"I will visit and make a new friend," Bone said, getting to his feet, "while you notify the decayed testicle Razinkin that I am here."

"Here, now, at this place? Or in the *mir*?"

"You observed me and we spoke. I will be at this place for only one hour more and then: who's to say, eh?"

Cabbage was leaning against the driver's door of his black STS parked in the lot beside the strip club when he saw Razinkin and Jam approach the café on foot from the east. The passenger's door of the STS was open and Bone sat in the back with the parking-lot attendant. Bone had his right hand firmly in the attendant's crotch; periodically he twisted or yanked or patted. The attendant had tears in his eyes. With his left thumb, Bone brushed the tears away, then patted the young man's cheek.

"Every man must make his living, child. A good living, a bad living; no matter, he must live. To interfere with a man's right to make his living, it is an offense against God. You have these vehicles and I have you. So. I have the vehicles, do I not? It is as it is."

"But what of my life, my right?"

"Your right is the right of the cow — the right to perish and be eaten. Or to live and give milk. I have the right of the bear — I eschew milk, but I must have meat."

"But the Italians." The young man was crying openly, the tears absorbed by the fine cotton of his full white shirt. "They give me this right, to park them here."

"You're their slave, their whore. I offer you redemption. Salvation. As the Italians are, I am ten. As I must make a living, so must you. Tell me how this works, the parking of the cars. Who leaves which vehicle all day; who comes and goes quickly."

Cabbage watched Razinkin and Jam approach the café. Jam scanned the street, saw Cabbage standing near the STS, he began to change direction. Cabbage ran his pinkie finger across his top lip. Jam nodded vaguely, smoothly adjusted his course, and ushered Razinkin to the table beside the one Bone had vacated. Jam placed a Gap Kids bag beside his chair, checking that the contents weren't visible.

"They will serve us here, or must we go inside?"

Jam looked through the open windows of the café. "She is coming out. Coffee?"

"With the foam. The chocolate on the top, as in Europe."

Jam gave their orders to the waitress. She asked if they wanted menus; both men declined and looked across the street at the STS.

When the waitress was gone, Jam asked, "Do we know why he's here, this Bone?"

Razinkin shrugged as though he had not a care in the world. He sat, the boulevardier cloaked by his jacket, exhibiting himself imperially, relaxed, his long legs crossed elegantly, but within he was churning. To be summoned by a bum. "We are to evaluate and understand. You must be of many ears, Jerzy. There will be much said and seen and much to reflect upon. Make a better friend of the Cabbage. As you hear, so must I. This is your mission."

"So, he perhaps brings danger to us?"

"Over there, they don't know. Before he left there, he had a savagery."

"The head in the crystal bowl."

"The least of it. Until we know why he walks here, if he

walks alone or walks at the front, we must abide. We must be prepared for all and surprised by none." He steepled his fingers. "I know of this Bone. His father lost before '43, resisting the progress of the Code. Olden men in olden times, eh? I thought they were all dead, the Bones and the Irons and the Fedoras. Swept away by the new reality."

"This Code, it endures." Jam was careful to remain neutral. Through friends in the brigades, he knew that complaints had been transmitted back to Moscow, that the men here were unhappy with master Razinkin and his operations within this new reality, that the men couldn't live under Razinkin's edicts not to steal loudly. The extortions were quiet and, Jam knew, could make a fine living for a man. But when you had brigades of hundreds and a victim pool of only some few dozens, the men would have to take what they could. Jewelry stores, white powders, mostly. Public crimes with noise, or private crimes with high risk.

He wondered if Bone would kill Razinkin, or if he himself would have to kill Bone. Jam knew, as did all, how Razinkin had left the old way and joined the new order, aligning himself and offering his services for money. He'd moved outside the Code, forging a new career first as an assassin-for-hire, then as an extortionist-entrepreneur, and lately as a financial adviser and cleaner of dirty lemons. No longer was he referred to as Tomahawk, a name he'd earned after fatally scalping a Chechen clan leader with a meat ax. He'd aligned himself with the *biznesmen* who emerged as entrepreneurs and into a cartel of economic criminals that fed on the fruits of the Soviet years of blackmarketeering. Now he represented powerful financial interests, investing and laundering black money in the west, funding joint business ventures, creating a public image as a wealthy Russian businessman. It was in his interest that loud crime be suppressed, the better to operate his financial dealings without pressure from the police or tax authorities.

But, Jam had said many times over vodka and pepper to his friends who remained apprentices, Razinkin's betrayal of the Code wasn't the removal of a tattoo — after all, a Thief could leave the *mir* at any time, never to return — or the alliance with government agencies, although this was a violation of the old true Code. Razinkin had already exited the *mir* and declared himself an outsider so he was free to roam the moist Caribbean and the chocolate kingdoms of Switzerland, opening offshore banks and trusts, to plow oil and mineral profits through a dazzling maze of institutions and bank accounts. The greatest difference between Razinkin and those who adhered to the true Code was that Razinkin had killed for money. "It's like a whore who fucks for free," Cabbage had once said in intimate drunken confusion. "Except backward."

Across the street, Bone stepped out of the STS and solicitously assisted the young man in the white shirt. He put his hand on the young man's shoulder and massaged gently, speaking close to his face. At a distance, he appeared to be singing softly.

In spite of all, when Razinkin saw Bone, slight but solid, standing as one with the roots of his feet anchored into the center of the world, he felt in his breast the catch of a thrill. We each earned a spire together, he thought, recalling an affair of outrageous thievery that added up to a seven-year sentence. Within the wire was the same Bone as without: eyes looking at some far horizon, as one sits secured in an interrogator's wooden stool and absorbs blows and beatings and remembers either the happier past or anticipates a future when all is done and one is alone, survived or not. And always it was Bone to whom all looked. He was one voice and his knowledge of the Code was without peer. Never had he lost a decision. Razinkin remembered when a Jewish dissident was tossed into a car full of Thieves on a prison train by laughing guards and left to be dissected: at the destination the Jew was huddled in his corner, terrified but unharmed. Bone had adjudged that to punish the Jew for his political transgressions would be an act of assistance to the State: "We are not punishers for the fanged uniforms. To harm this person would be to carry out a sentence not imposed by us." And at a conclave, when it was debated whether Thieves would starve rather than submit to the authorities, someone said, "We can't be made to eat ourselves; we must adjust to this demand." Bone chewed at the little finger of his own hand. "Now," he said, dribbling blood, laughing and unbuttoning his prison trousers, "may I serve soup?" And they starved but didn't die.

If this man could be brought over, Razinkin thought, all would follow and the violence would cease. Perhaps the Circle was correct: ask and understand and then, if not, plant a tree over his grave.

Jam, too, in spite of his position with Razinkin, felt a vague thrill watching the slim older man standing erect in the yellow light of the western sun. As the smallest policeman in Moscow, he had met many Thieves but had seen none as able to project such a magnetic presence. He glanced at Razinkin, careful to maintain a bland face. Razinkin, he now saw, suffered the failure of comparison. Even at fifty feet, Jam recognized Bone as a point of power, a gatherer of loyalties and even love; at eighteen inches he recognized, smelled, and heard Razinkin's apprehension. Razinkin, he thought, was wealth. Bone was heritage.

Razinkin forced away his vague admiration. He was deeply aware that the prism of legend, no matter how thin the shadows, could eclipse the diamond light of reality. Like most of the old bums of the Code, this Bone was charismatic, able to lead wayward children whose heads were filled with olden stories of the romance of Thievery, of the passions of irresponsibility. Jam's head, Razinkin knew, was creating images of countrysides to be roamed in glorious sunrises. Festivals of fuckery without care of engorged, scabbed testicles. What did he know of the ticks that lived in the haystacks, that inhabited and scabbed the body, their bites festering and spreading purple lines of poison to the heart? The lice and leech and the rat? The teeth tapped out with steel hammers by thick dunces in uniforms? Scabbied whores with plagues known not to men? Ah, Romance, is that you? he called silently inside bitterness.

I must deal with the bum firmly and quickly, Razinkin thought. Reports from overseas constantly told of the thinning of these weeds — Palladin in a car bombing in Berlin, Scabber by the hook-nosed Solonik in Moscow, Tomay and Inchik together at a dacha outside Leningrad, both by Solonik's unblinking eye and frozen hands. The shooting victims hit cleanly through the heart with military rounds to leave their faces intact for viewing and grief, and for proof too; the bombing of Palladin a tactical error because rumors now abounded that he was alive and rallying his followers from a room under a brothel on Las Ramblas in Barcelona. In an underworld that ran on legends and shadows, living ghosts were far more dangerous than blood and flesh, rumor had more weight than fact.

These old ones owned their Code and their odd shoes and the rope that held their pants up; the new owned banks and industries and casinos. The old had bent and chipped daggers with birch bark rubber-banded around the hilt; the new had sleek machine pistols, brigades of Afghan War veterans, and smart bombs that exploded with precision. The old had an *obschak* of a few rubles in a welfare fund for feeding the families of imprisoned Thieves; the new owned offshore bank accounts with balances as fantastic as those of some small countries. The old had their fraternity of cold, tired men; the new had entire governments. Why were these children like Jam tempted by an unending world of nothing, measured by days of emptiness?

Why, he thought with a sudden frustration that made his blood surf and pound in his ears, am I sitting here waiting for an audience with a fucking bum?

Across the street, Bone spoke with Cabbage, then Cabbage spoke, then Bone stepped a little closer and Cabbage took something from under his jacket and, shielding his body, put it under the car seat. When Bone touched his shoulder and turned away, Cabbage made to follow. Again Bone spoke; a visibly reluctant Cabbage went to lean on the STS, alert and bursting inside his clothes.

"He comes." Jam didn't know whether to stand up when Bone arrived at the table, or to sit casually like Razinkin. The urge to rise was strong; the urge to apologize for the thick grease of greed he now wrapped himself within. What will I do, he thought, if my master directs me to pull my gun and give the old bum a bouquet of red carnations, popping six fast ones to the left of the buttons of the two-dollar shortsleeved shirt?

Bone solved the dilemma by passing close behind Jam, placing a hard hand lightly on his shoulder. "I greet you, my brother, with kisses from the mother. On the outside, the wolf is soft hair; inside, an iron of bone." He spoke Russian, his creased eyes looking unblinking down into Jam's, eating his will. "The inside is the world; the outer the dream. Live true, and may I die first."

He passed around the table to Razinkin and held out his arms. "My brother, I kiss you."

Razinkin got up slowly and accepted kisses. He held out his hand. Bone stared at it curiously, then melted his bones and gave a limp squeeze, allowing Razinkin to grind his knuckles in false, enthusiastic welcome.

"An honor for us, *dyed*. Please, a coffee? A sugar roll?" Razinkin nodded to the Gap Kids bag. "Within, a gift to warm you to this cold place. Your journey was fine?"

"Fine. And long."

"Your adventures were much spoken. The slant-eyed men, bedazzled. The whores of Bangkok, limping from pleasure. And, I understand, you took the health benefits of the sea air."

Bone shrugged. "An embarrassment. A luxury boat with a cabin of my own. Much fresh meat and unending array of dark women for fuckery. Temptations are the Thief's mosquitoes."

"And your needs now? Papers? A roof?"

"I have all. When friends are everywhere, needs fade."

At the curb, a white police car idled by and Jam watched it from the corner of his eye. The waitress came out, distributed menus, and went away.

"This place is strange and wonderful," Razinkin said, indicating the police car. "They must follow rules and procedures and cannot touch. They can be leased like milk cows and made to turn away for a clump of sod. Lawyers and advocates abound, greedy for cash. This isn't the mother, but it is a strange paradise for such as us."

"You are well, then?" Bone looked over Razinkin's suit, staring briefly at the left side of his chest. "The heart beats in harmony?"

"All is well. The sheep here are large and many, and shearing is complicated." He shrugged. "But a good meal for all, if none are greedy or loud."

Bone glanced at Cabbage and indicated he should join them. "The children behave and are allowed to play?"

Razinkin shrugged again. "Sometimes children don't realize their noise awakens the parents who must rise at dawn to work the fields. The children eat; their manners must abide to the table."

"There are things said over there, I'm told."

"Ah, good. You have friends, then, remaining among the spires?" Razinkin sipped at his chocolated coffee foam. "Our friend Mikhailov?"

"A true Thief, I think, my good friend Mikhailov. But when we last enjoyed company — we had a fine meal one night — I suspected he would leave this life in glory."

"And so he did, I'm told." Razinkin leaned across the table. "The children — complaints, always. My brother, here there are millions and billions to steal, but it can't all be stolen at once. My responsibility is to over there, as well as to over here. A balance must be found that allows me to serve my masters and maintain my children. One cannot suffer at the expense of the other, but success with my masters will soon bring success to my children. But they're impatient and rowdy and want to play all the time, making whoops to the sky that attract attention."

Bone shrugged and with his cold fingers plucked a partially smoked cigarette from his pocket. Cabbage, now settled at the next table, reached into his pocket for a lighter, but Bone lit the cigarette himself with a wooden match. "It is no concern of mine." As he slowly waved flame from the matchstick, he made an instant decision toward treachery. The pimp Razinkin was now outside the Code, unprotected by tenets toward a Thief's honesty, his truth. "You must be told: I'm here to walk alone."

"Alone? How is this?" Razinkin made a burlesque of disbelief. "A Thief is never alone, where Thieves abound."

"Perhaps tea? Hot tea."

Razinkin spoke to Jam. "Hot tea in a glass for *dyed*."

Jam looked from Cabbage to Bone to the Gap Kids bag. "But the —"

"All is fine. Friends know the face of love. When love grows, danger flees." Razinkin paused. "And a sweet roll with the sugar for *dyed*." He stood, rounded the table, swung his suit jacket from his shoulders, and placed it over Bone's shoulders. "The chill of your flesh is legendary; the warmth of your heart is a truth. Forgive me, *dyed*, for this meager welcome at this outside place."

"In the presence of a friend, the air warms itself. Perhaps the tea isn't necessary." Bone tugged the jacket closely around himself. "A fine cloth."

Razinkin watched him smoke, the cigarette cupped in the palm of his hand as he inhaled, the glowing coal warming his palm. And I was fearful of this cold bum, he thought. The rumors of his coming to enflame his Code, just that, the nattering of washerwomen. But, within the relief in his mind, a remnant of the old Tomahawk whispered in a wind: *You must kill him.*

Bone accepted the hot tea from Jam. He wrapped the sweet roll in a napkin and lay it beside his glass, took a sugar cube from the tin box in his pocket, and placed it behind his teeth. He sipped the thin tea through the cube. I will do this thing with the parking-lot boy, he thought, that I can do for these poor Thieves, being chewed by this pig. The Code demands the nurturing of Thieves; it demands a balance; it beseeches not revenge but redemption. I am powerless before its powers. Bone himself had killed many, friends and foe alike, always for the Code, for the harmony. But what Thief could worship a *pakhan* who stuffed the anus with plastic bags, melted them, and left the victim to inflate with the poisons and strangle on his own shit? Who tied the throat closed and danced about as a good Thief reeled to death?

Razinkin spoke: "And your needs?"

Bone shrugged inside the finely threaded jacket, inhaling cologne from the lapel. "Perhaps one to assist in the adjustment of this place."

"Jerzy will be yours," Razinkin said, glancing at Jam. "He knows all and is a fine driver."

Bone leaned in close and spoke softly. "Your man here, this one of the big head? An ox in the brain, a bull in the muscle. He would be of use to me in finding my way."

"At your pleasure."

While Razinkin directed Cabbage, Bone removed the coat and folded it onto a chair. Jam too stood and handed Bone the Gap Kids bag. He realized that although Bone was no taller than the shortest policeman in Moscow, he somehow loomed. "If I can be of service, *dyed*, please . . ."

"When a bird is needed, one always flies nearby; this is reassurance." Bone touched Jam's shoulder. "Had you chosen another path, you would be as I, and I would be in awe."

Cabbage escorted him to the STS, but Bone declined to get in. He had Cabbage reinterpret the map, backward, that would allow him to return to Dagg's shop on foot. "Tomorrow night, an adventure. Have you eight?"

"My brigade, plus perhaps a few others."

Bone handed him the Gap Kids bag. "Distribute this that honest Thieves may eat, and befriend the boy in the shirt. He is to be a friend, eh?"

Bone shuffled away, gnawing at his sweet roll, while Cabbage walked down the sidewalk to the parking kiosk. Razinkin and Jam were at the end of the block, their heads close together, strolling, the caped Razinkin speaking energetically.

Cabbage's head was full of a golden warmth. He daydreamed the STS up into the northern part of the city, where he parked, took the gun from under the seat, and put it into the Gap Kids bag, then wandered through a maze of apartment buildings, emerging in a small neighborhood of pink brick houses. At the door of one house, he was greeted by a sleepy fat man holding a sawed-off shotgun. Cabbage went through the house, hearing the slap of cards and the throw of dice coming from the upper floors; women laughed, low seductive sounds, in downstairs bedrooms. Cabbage went into the kitchen, opened a bottle of beer, and sat at a chrome table; on the floor beside the table were several envelopes bound by elastic bands. He popped out his contacts, put them into an oval case, and put on a pair of thick reading glasses, then began counting stacks of money from the envelopes, checking off the totals against a list on a clipboard.

Done, he went to the basement where he waited until a thick Hungarian finished his noisy business and left, then slipped into the bedroom where a tall blonde woman was wiping herself with a wad of tissues. He sat in an armchair while she silently disposed of the tissues and brushed her hair smooth.

When she kneeled in front of him, he thought about Bone and Razinkin and wondered if this new feeling of safety, of change, was an illusion like every other fucking thing on this earth where the landlord was a whore.

Chapter 12

BONE MADE his way back to Dagg's shop, looking into windows of parked automobiles and searching them for adventures. He looped around city blocks in the manner of one who knows that while God always observes, so do others. From the dashboard of a sleek BMW, he removed a pair of sunglasses through the open driver's window; from an idling delivery van left unattended, he removed two wrapped packages. In the Asian section he took two oranges from an outdoor fruit market and stood in a doorway eating his way through the thick skin. There was a motion, a shape, that caught his attention: a huge fatty man wearing a black tracksuit who walked with the flat-footed ponderance of a weightlifter, always well behind, always on the opposite side of the street, taking detailed interest in shop windows. An escort, Bone decided, provided by the rat's mother Razinkin, surely in fear of my safety. He stood in the doorway for an hour, his face toward the sun, then stepped out and walked quickly back the way he'd come, dragging the agitated shadow with him. After six blocks, the exhausted shadow fell further behind; Bone dumped him and reversed direction. A block from Dagg's, he found a chrome stepladder leaning against the front of a shop and balanced it across his shoulder. He ambled into an alleyway and stashed his shopping behind a Dumpster, circled the streets once more, and went to the rear of Dagg's shop. He made a series of knocks and she opened the door, checking the alley behind him.

She led him down the stairs. "I feared."

"My friend Razinkin? Where Thieves abound, danger flees." He laughed and sat on the plastic of the sofa. "Where's Avi?"

"Doing good work." She stood with her back to him at a hot plate and poured hot water from a kettle over loose tea leaves in a chipped crock pot. The silvery coal hair was decorated with a red ribbon at the back of her smooth neck; she wore another from her endless stock of sundresses, this one of red and yellow flowers; small marks from the urgency of his fingers, clutching, showed on her shoulders at the straps of the sundress. Her feet were bare. "May I put the mark?"

This was, Bone knew, a complicated affair. She couldn't offer but could only be taken. He could not ask. He had observed the look upon her face when she was desiring, an unblinking gaze. Once he engaged it, she dropped her face, victim-like, but kept the curving grin of a shy cat. These were games around the Codes, both hers and his.

He said, "We must talk. Put the mark."

She took a piece of blue chalk and went up the stairs quickly. Outside the back door she slashed a diagonal line to warn Avi that privacy was required: either she was involved in commerce of which he shouldn't know, or her mind was beset by self-torture and she required no sympathy or assistance — once she had screamed a dream during which she could hear Avi rubbing his palms at the back door and making the mewing sounds of heartbreak, forbidden to enter but unable to leave.

She locked the door and slowly went back down the stairs in a sway. Bone stood at the bottom and put his hands on first her calves and, as she descended, her thighs and then her hips, until the skirt of the dress covered his forearms; his hands continued to lift the sundress until it was bunched below her breasts. He wrapped her in his arms — she couldn't as yet welcome him with hers — gathering the scent of her flesh into his lungs. She stood, head down, and he loosened her hair, seeming to eat at it. She turned her face and collected an awkward kiss, her teeth softly into his lips, her arms at her sides. He used needless strength to urge her to the sofa and arranged himself beside her; marks of previous visits had purpled her skin in places, and these he gently stroked with his fingers.

She tasted the juice of oranges on his mouth, scented it on his breath. She imagined his shivers were of anticipation, as a boy's. She in turn stroked and massaged and licked. When it was time, she waited to be moved into a posture of acceptance, but he instead rearranged her above him.

"As the horse is ridden."

She mounted, and his hands began raising the sundress; at her breasts she stopped him with her hands but he persisted. She felt a wave like shame within as the dress passed over her head loosening the red ribbon, and fell behind her. Her breasts had always been as perfect as plums and remained thus. But about the nipples, where pleasures should reside, were the angry blemishes of cigarette coals, a pliers mark, an errant tooth scar, tracks of gouging fingernails.

She didn't look into his eyes when he said "Ahh" in a soft voice and touched there with his cold fingertips. He watched for tears from his Fairie, but none came. He pulled her weight forward to lick and blow on her breasts, as if to cool them. "Ahh."

He thought: As it is, it is. This one has had a life and, as a true Fairie, survived the living of it.

She thought: Perhaps this Thief won't kill me after all. What horse would murder its rider?

Avi was sitting under the chalk mark; he arose when he heard Dagg fumbling at the lock. It opened, and he looked past her suspiciously. Insane ravings, or a bargain with a fat Ukrainian? He had a hatred for the network of Ukrainian middlemen who stocked their ratty stores with goods acquired for free or bought for a little, and then sold for much. One, a brutal young man with the snout of a pig, had split Dagg's lip in passion and left the store in a pleased swagger with a case of brass faucets on his shoulder and his T-shirt decorated with a smear of her blood. You're young, he told Avi, to be a pimp. Have you other women, but younger? This one is as old as my mother and possibly with wet diseases. Avi had hung his head as the man passed, then followed him up the alley to where the man had parked his car. When the pig-faced Ukrainian bent to put the carton into the trunk, Avi was upon him, carving designs with his pocket knife, until the pig's face was hanging in flaps and, blinded, he could be given a new red mouth under his chin. Back in the basement, Dagg had made Avi change his clothing while she rinsed them of blood. She explained the emptiness of the body and the fullness of the soul, of the Fairies' value.

Now, as she opened the door, adjusting the straps of her sundress and beckoning him inside, he found no blood or bruising, just a well-pleased look on her face.

"*Dyed* is here?" He rubbed at the chalk mark. He knew one of his fathers was within; there was a glow upon her face, a smoothness and a wicked eye. "It is safe?"

"Yes. We had a meeting of secrecy."

Avi made a small smile; from his bed in the shop on the first floor he'd heard mooing and even laughter in nights.

In the basement, Bone was sipping at a glass of tea, meditating, peaceful. He looked up and told Avi where his shopping was hidden, behind the Dumpster. Avi left and Dagg accompanied him. They strolled, a mother and son, hand in hand.

"It was safe?"

Avi nodded. "The foul Razinkin and another man met with *dyed*. The big-headed one didn't betray him. They drank at the café and spoke; *dyed* left walking, big head in his car, and the others also walked, but in the other direction. One in a sports outfit followed *dyed* but got lost in the alleys."

"So, all is safe."

At the Dumpster, Avi balanced the ladder and Dagg carried the packages. At the shop, Bone made a present of the sunglasses to Avi. "You wear them up in the hair," he told the boy, arranging them. "We must get you a billowing white shirt like a sail. This is, I think, the appearance for attracting compliant girls and ladies in urgent need."

Dagg laughed and ran her fingers through Avi's fine hair. "Perhaps the big-headed one will find you such a woman," she said, glancing wickedly at Bone. "I know no other with this talent."

At dark, Dagg created plates of meats and spices wrapped in steaming cabbage and a rice dish containing small specks of meat and flecks of rough pepper. The three sat in the basement drinking icy vodka until Dagg staggered to the sofa, singing, and waited to sleep, listening as Bone and Avi held a competition of slamming glasses that neither won. Once, in the night, she awoke to the sound of Bone's voice softly whispering. She looked across the basement and saw the two with their heads together under a pool of lamplight, a man who was not a husband and a boy who was not a son. Bone was throwing hand signals at increasing speeds, laughing as Avi sought to mimic the motions. She heard Bone saying "*zakone*" — the Code — and a smile carried her back to sleep.

The boy in the billowing shirt — Taras — opened the parking kiosk beside Ricci's emporium at nine a.m., waving in and handing out tickets to short-hop breakfasters and Saturday-morning shoppers. He watched for the old man or his beefy friend; his mind was clouded with disbelief that this time next week he would be in Hollywood, California, U.S.A., doing valet parking at a restaurant frequented by starlets of great need. A Hollywood of his dreams: he loved the heat of the sun, loved cars, looked good in a Speedo bathing suit, and enjoyed resting his head between large soft breasts which, the great-headed one had promised, were prevalent. Since traveling from his home near Odessa, he'd emigrated to Israel long enough to apply for Canadian refugee status — complaining that he was being discriminated against because he was religious and from the Soviet — and to be brought to Winnipeg by a church organization of dupes that gave him some English with a Scots accent and a job washing dishes, and sympathetically paid his fine when he was caught shoplifting food. After three months he'd seduced the daughter of the family he boarded with, stole electronic equipment from their house, pawned it, and caught a bus to Toronto. There he'd connected with expat Russians and met a stripper from Moscow who danced at Ricci's and landed him a job bussing tables in the club. When the stripper dumped him for a city councillor in one of the city's Italian communities, the boy in the billowing shirt was given a job operating the car lot. He received five dollars an hour cash and stole an agreeable twenty per cent of the tickets; with the black bouncer, he operated a small but steady marketplace in steroids, weed, and rave drugs.

At exactly noon, Tony Ricci swung his black BMW 5-series off the one-way street, through the lot to a spot near the strippers' entrance, and climbed out, leaving the keys in the ignition. He waved to Taras and climbed three steps into the club. The boy didn't like the fat Italian — he called him, with his curious accent, a *wap* — while the Italian called him a white *niggerski*. Greasy fuck, the boy thought, taking money from a woman who wore a wide sunhat, carried a Gucci purse, and had perfect legs. She parked her Mercedes overlapping two spots, and when he indicated she should move it straight, she told him without looking at him to do it himself, she was in a hurry.

The black bouncer showed up at three and gave Taras a folded piece of newspaper containing various drugs; the boy gave him five twenty-dollar bills. At four-thirty, the girls began arriving, his Natash ignoring him as she poured her bare legs from the councillor's gold Dodge Intrepid. Taras vaguely hoped the councillor would leave the Intrepid in the lot while he popped into the club for a few shows, but the man gave him a negligent wave and the Intrepid squealed off. At five o'clock Taras changed the sign from hourly to flat rate. He took two squares of chocolate-flavored laxative from a foil package and chewed them, then waved to the bouncer and made eating gestures. The bouncer gave him a wide grin and went into the club, returning a few minutes later with a Greek busboy who struggled into a leather jacket and took Taras' place at the foot of the lot.

"Remember," Taras said, "the keys must be in, and collect the money right away. Park the beautiful cars near the front to make the club look prosperous. The candy is under the newspapers on the floor of the kiosk; there are fifteen of the white, fifteen of the red, and twenty of the ravers. Each they are five, five, and twenty. Can I bring you some food, my good friend?"

The busboy shook his head and took the booklet of parking chits. "No more than one hour, though, okay? The black woman dances at seven and —"

"The black one is a fine one, if you like the African. I myself like the Eastern girls."

"There are no Greek girls here, thank God," the busboy said, crossing himself and putting on a pair of silver-lensed sunglasses while examining himself in the smoked window of a silver Audi. "Lightning and fire would destroy this place." Over beers, the busboy had told of his love for the African, Aphrodite, and later over more beers, of the confusion of his love. At the end of the night he'd cried his shame: nowhere on earth could he and this black-skinned woman appear together before the eyes of people.

Taras walked toward Yonge Street, then south, as instructed, and into the next side street, where Cabbage and eight other men were drinking pitchers of beer on an outdoor patio, crowded around three tables pulled together. Cabbage smiled and waved him over, bum-jumping his chair to make room for Taras to sit beside him. The other men took no notice. They were dressed for work, wearing expensive knit sports outfits and running shoes. None wore watches or jewelry. Several had hand tattoos: Cyrillic numbers; small, elegantly etched stained-glass windows, serpents and spiders. These were Cabbage's crew, as well as a few others who kept to low thievery and robbery, attracting no attention from Razinkin but wishing upon him various cancers, bone diseases, and rotting at the roots of the mouth and the fork of the legs.

Cabbage patted Taras's wrist and poured him a glass of beer.

"Where is the old man?"

"*Dyed*?" Cabbage shrugged and waved his hand through the air. "He is with us always."

"My payment? The ticket for the airliner?"

"These I have. I will be in the final vehicle; you come away with me."

"The black BMW near the door should not be taken."

"A fine car."

"A fine car. And Ricci's."

Cabbage was expansive; he slapped the boy on the shoulder. "Ah. The worker bee has loyalty? You would make some lemons if I take the second-last car and you take this black gift."

"There will be many other cars as fine. Perhaps I will take another."

"If so, follow me closely and make no attention."

Taras nodded. "This California place. You've been there?"

"No. But the people there are of a tradition. You will be well taken care of."

The boy looked at Cabbage's eyes and took a deep breath. "If something . . . something should happen to me first?"

"The two X's? Us? No, no, no. This will not happen. You've been too long among the pigs to recognize the tiger. The *dyed* has spoken. We don't slit the throat for money. You're up to fine trickery tonight; like a man you'll be paid, not fucked like some girl. This tonight is a thing of beauty and means much to many people. It is the beginning of great things. You will travel safe, my assurance and his as well."

The boy nodded, embarrassed at his fear.

"Would you like a hamburger? You will begin a long journey very shortly."

Taras's stomach rumbled audibly, his bowels processing the laxative. A man beside Cabbage laughed and cringed comically. Three faint tattooed tears, obscured by makeup, ran from the outside corner of his left eye. He made a clown's smile. "Ah, within the fine shirt, a tiger growls."

Cabbage lightly punched his fist against Taras's shoulder. "You must eat. The hamburger meat sandwich?"

"Perhaps," the boy said, "with the fried potatoes."

Cabbage and Taras left the patio first, walking around the block. The boy went to relieve the busboy; Cabbage met Bone in front of the café across from Ricci's dance club. The old bum was dressed exactly as he'd been the night before, but he looked fresh and his eyes were bright. He scanned the streets for idlers and for opportunity, and watched the growing swell of Saturday-night vehicles clogging the side street. He wasn't shivering.

"*Dyed*. Greetings and wishes. I kiss you."

"Ah, to you also, the greetings and the kisses. Of the wishes, we have no need. This adventure is completed, except for the doing."

Cabbage steered him to a table at the back of the patio, then wandered inside to order tea and coffee and two sweet buns. He came out and the men sat watching the boy. Bone took a broken cigarette from his pocket and Cabbage lit it, then lit one of his own. The men sat back and smoked like well-fed generals until the beverages and buns came.

"You have arranged for this boy?"

Cabbage laughed. "He believes he might wear the red vest, the slitting of the throat, after: his Hollywood will be under the earth, surfing with the hungry worm."

"You assured him?"

"Yes. His stomach rumbled. He ate some bread and meat and potatoes and drank some beer."

Bone sipped his hot tea, inhaling the stale fragrance of the tea leaves. "The brigade are ready?"

"All. There's excitement tonight. Everywhere they talk of an engagement; even Razinkin's boys are laughing, but they wait for the door to splinter. Something wonderful or something ugly begins tonight."

"And the automobiles?"

"All to a location for shipment. Men from the east of Africa will take them and pay immediately. We've dealt with these Africans before; they're natural thieves and honorable. They are of a tribe with three scars on the cheeks, large penises, and fine laughter."

"It is done, then, except for the doing."

"*Dyed*. Have you a bed, a roof?"

Bone shook his head and smiled. "There is no need. Last night I dined well and slept with the sound of children. Can life offer more? I found an ocean with no salt to wash in and an automobile with bags of food inside." Truth and lies.

"Tonight," Cabbage looked around, "tonight the brigade would like to repay you."

Bone touched his hand to Cabbage's. "There's no need for Thieves to show gratitude. Their success is my crown."

"Still, with Razinkin's boot on their necks, they'd like to honor you after the fun here, with fuckery and feasting. It would be air to them, sunlight on their faces."

Bone thought about the Code: to train and teach and form Thieves. "It will be, then." He smiled, canine.

At eight-thirty, alone on the patio, Bone watched as a stocky man driving a panel truck stalled his engine ten yards east of the parking-lot entrance, effectively blocking the street; another, similar-looking man stood across the street from Ricci's ballroom, staring at the traffic lights at the corner of Yonge Street. He touched his right hand to his right cheekbone and men began walking up the parking lot and climbing into luxury cars, adjusting drivers' seats and turning keys in ignitions. The man across from the ballroom, eyes still on the traffic lights, counted off the seconds of the red signal, then ran his hands through his hair; a silver Porsche Carrera slipped out of the lot, followed closely by a second Porsche. Both cleanly made the green light. Several cars followed like a convoy.

Taras stood bent forward beside the open door of Ricci's black BMW 5-series and grunted and groaned, one hand on the door and the other on the headrest, his pants down around his knees, his nervous laughter impairing his ability to fully defecate onto the leather front seat. Cabbage stood in the doorway of an open Boxster. He counted as the cars slipped from the lot, and watched the signaller touch his hair with both hands: red light changing. Out of sight, behind the stalled panel truck, cars were honking their horns. The signaller walked quickly into the lot, his lips counting, and climbed into a silver Audi.

"Ten seconds, boy." Cabbage looked around, hearing Taras's grunting laughter, and began laughing himself. "Ah, now that would be a fine five-thousand-dollar shit."

The boy, close enough to being finished, wiped himself with a wad of paper towel, smeared the steering wheel with it, ignited the engine, turned the heat on full, and locked the doors, leaving the keys inside. He ran to the Boxster, pulling up his pants. Cabbage slipped the convertible along the driveway, last man out, muttering phrases that sent the boy into hysterics.

"The smelly salute, eh? The brown farewell? A little sauce for *vor* Ricci's *panatone*? Another serving, *padrone*? *Certainly*, my good man."

The boy howled and thought: A Thief! A Thief! This is truly life, even if I die.

The cars were taken to a warehouse west of Pearson International Airport. Half of the building was crammed with refuse: batteries, tires, buckets of toxic liquids. It was on a one-year lease signed by a company that removed rubbish from construction companies and auto wreckers, late at night, for thirty per cent less than any legitimate contractor. When the building was crammed full of deteriorating waste, the lessees would skate away, pocketing the rubbish removal fees and leaving the building's owner with a ticking time bomb.

An African man with tribal scars stood outside the building — the toxic chemical stench inside had become alarming — armed with a flashlight and a length of wood. Two tractor trailers were parked to the east of the building, three midsize Pontiacs and a dark green Mercedes sedan to the west, backed in. Beside each trailer was a forklift truck, a stack of rubberized tarpaulins, and power wheel-removers. The African heard the approach of the first car, which was the second Porsche off the lot, and pulled open the sliding doors. The Porsche flew past him into the building, screeching to a smoking stop at the far side of the unit. The other cars followed, with Cabbage and the boy in the Boxster cruising sedately at the rear. The boy appeared to be crying, his face damp. When all the engines had been switched off, the outside man closed the door from outside. Three African men dragged heavy, lead-lined duvets from a stack near the entrance and began draping them over the automobiles to thwart GPS signals.

Three very black-skinned African men in dark suits and white shirts, no ties, came noisily down from a glassed-in, air-conditioned office at the top of a flight of iron steps. The leather soles of their shoes rang in rhythm. A fourth man, wearing blue jeans and a gaily flowered pullover shirt, stood at the top holding a full-length shotgun just outside the office door.

Cabbage gathered his brigade around him. He knew these Africans were suspicious: Russians, the blacks knew, had their own busy market in Moscow or Ukraine or Dubai for the cars they stole. The complexities of the Code, of the new reality, were beyond the Africans: their own strifes were tribal and perhaps political.

Two Africans examined the cars, lifting the duvets and running their long black hands along the lines of the luxury automobiles, showing each other small scratches and wiping at them with dampened fingers. They shook their heads a lot and noisily sucked their upper lips against the ivory of their teeth. They knew there'd be no negotiation: the price they set would be the price paid. That Thieves were notorious for accepting the first offer was well known. Too low, and the Thieves might return to steal from them, or not return at all with other treasures. There were many car thieves, but few who could steal a parking lot. It was time for fair market value or, the Africans believed, something approximating fair.

"My friend Vlad E Meer," the tallest of the Africans said, flashing a wide white smile, squeezing a hug around Cabbage's shoulders. He had a squared head, square pure white teeth and a square torso. "A fine fleet. High milers, perhaps, but well kept."

"The lowest of mileages, and all driven by little women who carry groceries and babies. Perhaps the back seats are a little worn. A shoe scuff mark on the interior roof. Daytime fuckery." He shrugged. "As wives must do."

"For certain, I'm sure. The finest eight vehicles to come my way."

"Nine."

"Nine? My mistake. At the Christian school they only counted to three. The trinity: god the father, god the son, and the holy invisible person who scares the children at night." His voice was seductive, soft.

"That fellow would be the ghost. Count the trinity thrice. Making nine."

"Nine. Surely if I offered you fifty one-hundred-dollar bills for each you'd be amenable, my friend."

The offer hadn't technically been made, Cabbage recognized, so it could be adjusted without losing one's faith in the Code. In total, the cars were worth more than a half-million dollars, would claim more overseas. "These men have driven a long way at great risk. Some have fallen in love with these vehicles and could make papers to make them as legitimate as a married wife."

"I have at hand sixty times nine of hundred-dollar-bills. A fair price for an hour's work."

"Perhaps some smaller bills, for taxicabs to return my friends to their homes. Say, seventy hundred-dollar bills for each. My men would be happy and the next time they acquire a parking lot, they would give you their custom."

The African made a huge, friendly smile and turned to the man beside him. Speaking in a fast Yoruba dialect, he told him to bring sixty-three thousand in one-hundred-dollar bills — the good ones — from the office. He led Cabbage to the foot of the stairs, Cabbage maneuvering to keep the black suit between himself and the shotgun at the top of the stairs.

Behind the caution, the African noted Cabbage's enhanced thrill. Gunfire or money, this Cabbage of the big head would show his teeth in either case. The money man came down the stairs with a plain paper shopping bag with cord handles, and gave it to the African, who led Cabbage to the hood of the silver Audi, where he dumped bundles of currency secured by elastic bands.

"You may, if you prefer, count it. But my man is a master of the addition. Christian school, I assure you."

Cabbage picked up a thick bundle of bills and weighed it in his hand. He frowned. "This one's light, by two banknotes."

The African's laugh echoed loudly through the warehouse. He took a wad of bills from his pocket and peeled off two hundreds. Cabbage held out his palms, declining the money. "Not necessary; a small joke. But perhaps an examination of the quality? Unknown to you, someone may have given you currency that was meant to wipe the ass."

It took Cabbage and two of his brigade ten minutes to go through the notes, licking their thumbs and separating the obvious counterfeits located in the center of each bundle. "Ah, my friend, you see. This place, where even God fucks his children, is of dishonest thieves. Someone has deceived you by forty notes."

The African slapped his own head. "Dishonorable thievery everywhere. My apologies. This is very unseemly. These will be made correct by my man." He spoke again in dialect; the money man took a sheaf of notes from his inside pocket and counted out forty one-hundred-dollar bills. He gave them to the smiling African, who handed them to Cabbage, along with the forty bad bills. "Perhaps you can use them for your daily needs. My men will escort your men to a nearby hotel where there are taxicabs."

He led Cabbage and the drivers out to the Pontiacs, saw them away and returned into the warehouse where, unsmiling now, he ordered several men to begin work. A BMW was ramped up into the first trailer; its wheels were removed and marked with white chalk before being stowed in the back seat. The car was covered with a thick rubberized drop cloth. The next car, with its wheels removed and marked, was forklifted up a ramp onto the trailer and carefully set on top of the drop cloth on the BMW. Next a Porsche was ramped in, dewheeled, covered, and topped by drop cloth before the other Porsche was lifted onto it. When all the cars were aboard the trucks, two rows of packing cases stenciled "Machine Tools" were lifted into the trailers, effectively obscuring the vehicles from view.

The African inspected the security of the loads, gave last-minute instructions to the drivers and their passengers, and handed each driver a cloned cellphone and a clipboard of forged shipping documents.

The African finally smiled, signaling to the outside guard to roll back the doors.

Chapter 13

By saturday midnight, word of the Thieves' engagement had spread like pollen on a soft, secretive breeze, sparking sneezes of laughter and tears of admiration. The underworld passed the tale, inflated at every telling until the handful of luxury vehicles had become a fleet of hundreds, a speeding convoy snaking its way out of the city with a laughing tattooed Thief behind each wheel.

In the melt-down gold shops of Little India, the hard-faced *hawala* men giggled and spoke softly of their Russian friends breaking against Razinkin's notorious yoke; the Indians, Pakistanis, and Sri Lankans all felt an affinity for the true nature of the Thieves. The Israeli limousine drivers at the airport pinched cigarette filters and dourly spoke in clouds of smoke, their bracelets and rings flashing in the sodium lights, as one of them dictated into a cellphone the addresses of passengers they'd picked up that day — the addresses to be passed on to "break men" who'd work their way down the list looking for vacant houses. The Israelis, who had a circle of their own, spoke with a mixture of grim envy and fear, worrying how the engagement might affect them. In the obscure, bland restaurants on College Street, Somalians packaged *khat* and worried about the balance of power. At the Hell's Angels club on Eastern Avenue, the bikers stood out front, with their mouths turned away from the passing traffic, spoke of "those fucking Slavs," and laughed at how Ricci, the Italian they all despised, would be whining to his fading masters in Buffalo.

For Ricci, there was no recourse: had his club been wrecked by bikers, or his girls pirated to the airport strip clubs, he could have reached over the border to his American masters and demanded a sit-down and reparations. But the theft of cars from the lot was a fair turn at making a living for the Thieves, and even the dying old fucks in Buffalo couldn't argue with a man making his living. Under Dundas Street, in the Chinese gambling caverns, and in the pool halls of East Chinatown, the elderly Tongs and the youthful Vietnamese and Fujianese spoke with either fatalism or envy. The Jamaicans in the domino clubs on Vaughan Road and the bullet-riddled housing projects wondered if the cars were still in town and if they could trade them for their rattling Japanese Maximas.

Those in the know laughed at Razinkin and, while they couldn't fathom the change in the wind, were gleeful the tide was turning against him.

In his mansion on Baby Point Road, Razinkin felt himself burning from the inside out. He didn't have to hear the mean, pleased laughter of the city; he knew he was the oaf who'd bought a box of bricks. Cocksuck old bum, he thought, not realizing he'd said it aloud. Cocksuck and cunt. Is this a greeting card from the bum, this degenerate who swore he walked alone? Were there now to be reactions, campaigns that required military raids and intelligence? Would he have to hire guards to guard him against his guards? What is this mysterious power of an old derelict in twenty cents' worth of clothing and a dead history tattooed across his body like an engraving on a tombstone?

The Circle would give him no direction; they feared a failed attempt would swing the remaining undecided of the *mir* into Bone's sway. The fools still hoped to bring wild Thieves into a new reality where harmony would usurp mutiny and the truth of profit would be recognized by all. They could dream these dreams sitting in protected dachas and giving no consideration to the reality of his situation. They think I sit here in the snowbanks, he thought, counting gold bars and growing richer than they could ever hope to be.

There would be, he knew, no organization to Bone's campaign, not with the *mir* fragmented. To bring together a brigade created of several brigade*s* and complaining Thieves would take time — time to weave the web of fealty that was the bones of power. To eliminate the bum quickly and neutralize the magnet, that was the key, as when dealing with any insurrection.

Razinkin unlocked a filing cabinet, unwrapped a new cellphone, and dialed a series of numbers. He spoke, then dialed another number, spoke again, and finally reached his party.

"I require a service here. And in secrecy beyond the Circle. Can you act?" He listened, then told the voice he was indeed in the north of the true America. He listened again, frowned in mild confusion, and said, "Arizona, U.S.A.? It isn't far, my friend, and afterward, when matters are concluded, I'll send you there for a vacation."

He hung up and meticulously crushed the telephone into fragments with the heel of his shoe, then took another cellphone, unwrapped it, and made a short call of specific demands. That phone too was then demolished. He awoke his

Swiss secretary — Jam and Little Novak were out gathering intelligence on the whereabouts of the deceitful cocksucker — and had a car brought to the front of the mansion. He rode in the silence of volcanic rage through the city, to a converted warehouse owned by a business partner. A very large black man at the door recognized Razinkin and stepped aside with a small bow. Was that a shade of a smile on his lips?, Razinkin wondered.

He rode a rattling freight elevator to the top floor of the building and was greeted by another huge black man; Razinkin examined him for a trace of glee and found none. The man opened a door and said his guest would arrive in moments, that all was ready.

Razinkin smoked a cigarette in the corner of the loft, his heart pumping as he watched for a break in the scratch of light under the door. No more will I be able to do this without planning, he thought with regret. Now, each movement will require security and prechecking, reviews of those with whom I have contact, searches and much countersurveillance. Unless the bum is vanquished.

The light broke at the bottom of the door, then turned into an upright yellow wedge as a disoriented silhouette entered. She was as he always ordered: of small chest and narrow stature. This one had the crinkly, bushy hair of a tribe and the dark skin of the sub-equator. The hair, though, didn't matter one bit. She wore a short elastic skirt of a dark color and a drooping tank top; on her feet were unlaced running shoes. She crossed the room using furniture to keep her balance, until she was in front of him. He feared she might be too far gone to participate, to endure and enjoy. Of long habit, she fell to her knees at his anonymous lap. He could smell the residue of crack cocaine on her skin as he lifted her and took her to a chair, where he sat her in front of a mirror, patting her shoulder and speaking softly in Russian.

On the table was an electric razor. He activated it and began shaving her head blindly, watching her face in the mirror as clumps fell to her shoulders. When she was shorn to a dark dust and shaking her head in confusion or wonderment, he didn't attempt to use his erection, merely led her to the wide boards of the factory floor, turned her over, and, fully dressed and arranged, lay atop her, his smooth barbered face against the crown of her scratchy skull. He formed himself to her shape, whispered and laughed, remembering that same sandpaper sensation from many *zeks* in many places, she screaming into the mattress as he began biting. When he was ready, he sat up, turned her over, sat on her small chest and, grunting with effort, began meticulously breaking the bones of her face with his fists.

On Sunday morning, church bells tolled ten o'clock. Jam awoke on the floor of an apartment in the suburb of Richmond Hill, naked and covered with drying urine, liqueurs, blood, cigarette ashes, and, he suspected, semen. Glass shards, bottle tops, aluminum beer cans, and stubbed cigarettes littered the floor. Six heavy cardboard crates marked "Electronics: This Side Up" were stacked undisturbed against a wall; against the opposite wall, cartons containing microwave ovens were stacked five high. Cases of canned tomatoes, pears, beans, and assorted vegetables had spilled over.

Jam and Little Novak had discovered the Thieves' celebration the night before while visiting clubs, bath houses, and obscure delicatessens in the northern part of the city looking for the scent of Bone. Word of the adventure at the parking lot hadn't yet circulated, so they didn't hesitate to take their leisure. They were parked in front of a doughnut shop sipping coffee and discussing Bone's appearance and what would ensue in the *mir*, when a stolen taxi containing four screaming Thieves rocketed along Finch Avenue.

"Oh-ho. Something has been had." Jam started the ignition and pulled out behind the taxi. The four Thieves were the first sign of life in the *mir* that evening, and Jam had heard of a celebration someplace for some reason. Perhaps this was the welcoming for Bone; perhaps he could be found where the taxi parked. In any case, they had a night away from Razinkin's paranoid urges and instructions and Jam decided to make the best of it.

"We will invite ourselves," he said, watching the taxi — the driver clearly lost and disoriented — careen into a maze of side streets and back out again. "Always be welcome and never be a guest."

"Should we not find the bum?"

"Perhaps he is where we go. In the event, Thieves are scarce and we must investigate. Our sacred duty."

The taxi went north on Bathurst, clipping a parked car, then another.

"Perhaps our friends are returning from a party, and it's been had?"

"'Vak, 'Vak. Things may change. The appearance of the bum has our master showing a weakness. Perhaps we will find the old bum and report back. What ensues after, we must be sure we are not standing when all others are sitting, or the reverse." He sped around a bus and saw the taxi's lights flare through a red light. "Have you spoken to our friend Cabbage?"

Novak seized the dashboard with both hands. "No. Since the Dumpling . . . I have . . . difficulty. He cried as I gave him the barking dog."

"What love. He said, the Cabbage, that Razinkin did better work controlling the *mir* than the *musor*. If true, a terrible thing for such as us."

The taxi arced around a traffic island and vanished into a dark side street. Jam followed and they found the taxi still running, doors open, up on a lawn. Whoops could be heard from the yards beyond the houses, and Jam circled the block, spotting the silhouette of the final Thief disappearing into the side door of an apartment building. Jam and Little Novak followed, pausing at each floor to listen for the wild sound of merriment. On the eighth floor they found it.

Jam sat up, waiting for the echoes of the Sunday tolling to finish rumbling around in his head. The night returned to him in disjointed collages of exuberance, pain, and abandon. Oh, bless the Thief who has gone up, but fuck upon those who remain.

He had been on the door for most of the party, remaining alert until the sun had started to cut into the gray walls of the apartment. Throughout the night, Thieves arrived, some leaving to forage. Some didn't return, caught mauling the shelves of late-night stores. They would carouse in police station cells or holding tanks. Cellophane-wrapped pieces of meat had been stripped and stuffed into the electric oven throughout the night, barely heated through, and ripped apart by eager, bloody fingers; the refrigerator door was broken with the constant yanking to get at the beers and wines and liquors. Loaves of bread were scattered across the kitchen counters and doors had been torn off their hinges on the built-in cabinets. From the floor he could see holes punched into the walls, the crazed shattering of the screen of the television, the tufts of filling sprouting from the sofas.

He and Little Novak, ignorant of the cause of the funnery, had each been through a bottle of potato by the time Cabbage and his swaggering, laughing band — including a boy reeling in a billowing white shirt — showed up, whores and liquor in hand, looking for a campfire. An hour later, Jam was sipping vodka, a whore from the Urals bobbing for apples in his lap, another trying to break a coffee table with her forehead as she was fore-serviced. Jam recalled throwing up on a skinny, dark-skinned robber; the robber had laughed and tried to urinate on him.

Thieves came and Thieves went; whores came and whores went; a few Domari gypsies from Eastern Europe, led by their leader Luko from the notorious ghetto north of Sofia, who brought an eleven-year-old bride; a Colombian Roma who did magic tricks, making Thieves' jewelry vanish before they too vanished, leaving a wash of laughter behind. An apprentice had been given a shirt: mismatched buttons sewn through the skin of his stomach and chest, and a pair fastened in the skin at each wrist. A drunken Thief whose equipment failed him at the wet door was overpowered, held in a body scissors by one man while another shaved his groin and a third broke open ballpoint pens. A safety pin was used to tattoo "*Ne Rabotayet*" — not working — above his penis.

A bout of decoration began. The boy in the billowing white shirt — who would only give the name BMW — had the car's emblem tattooed on each shoulder. A dead-drunk Thief created a fierce, oaken erection — "one the dog can't bite and the cat can't scratch" — secured it tightly with an elastic band. Another Thief used a pin to tattoo "*Balanda*" — thin soup — on the top.

Several times Cabbage, who sat with an eye on the apartment's door, crossed the room to the prone Jam and poured a waterfall of vodka onto his face and into his mouth, once saying, "It starts tonight and you are welcome."

"What has been done?"

"An adventure. We are now led."

"Had you permission?"

"Thieves have no need of permission. Are you a cop or a brother?"

Jam glanced through an open doorway, where Little Novak was lost under a fat woman who outweighed him and seemed, she being sober and he being drunk, of even greater Olympic feats.

"Of my steroid brother there, and the dear Ushki?"

"All of the heart are welcome. In the café, when the old man danced, Novak could have made the dog bark at me while Ushki endured. He didn't, and I bless his charity."

Jam nodded. "We must speak." He opened his mouth for more little water.

Throughout the night the Thieves held ponderous private discussions, telling and retelling the theft of the parking lot, the warming presence of Bone, the boy in the ballooning shirt — the now famous Taras BMW — shitting into Ricci's car. There was much kissing and hugging, and Jam and the battered Little Novak looked at each other, envious of the conviviality.

Bone appeared very late with the gypsy woman and Avi in tow. Dagg was possessive and attentive and, when a brawl broke out in a bedroom, was into the fray with a sharp smile and curled talons. Bone stayed in a chair beside the window and exhibited humility as loving Thieves attended to him. Avi sat in a corner quietly observing, sipping at bottles of chilled potato shoved into his hands by Thieves who'd met him at the shop. Cabbage remained by Bone's side most of the night, leaving only when the gypsy woman was with his master, so he could stagger into the bedroom and sport with a slim black woman who spoke guttural Russian and howled like a hen as she feigned resistance and horror.

Cabbage brought Bone an envelope thick with currency. Bone protested; Cabbage, on behalf of his brigade, was insistent. "These are fresh lemons," he said, "fallen from the tree, destined for the one who brought the wind." Bone held the envelope in his hand, tapping it, weighing its significance and propriety through the prism of the Code. He shrugged, giving his wishes and thanks to Cabbage and his brigade, then handed the envelope to Dagg, who set it on the floor beside their couch. It remained there throughout the night and, after Bone and Dagg had left, was still there the following day.

Bone called Avi and the tattooist over and, with his hand on the shop boy's shoulder, spoke at length to the tattooist. The tattooist nodded, took the shop boy's hand, and began working. Avi didn't flinch and afterward admired the small skull engraved on the back of his knuckle — one who had killed, Bone said, even if it was only a Ukrainian.

Dagg had positioned herself as they chose, as Bone's lady, his protector, a fierce wraith that hovered in his sphere and emanated fearsome looks at those who approached. It was a role a Thief would discern and perhaps secretly appreciate, but it mattered not to her. That she would not be found by daylight, beaten and bruised and perhaps the subject of tales of community fuckery, was a blessing.

This strange Bone, she found, was a superior Thief, almost courtly, as though he perceived the purest of the human condition, unbiased by gender or history, but indeed conceived only the here and now, the resilience of the individual, not the presence or lack of cock and balls. None the rutting pig and all the prowling tiger. Yes, she was bruised and scratched in his passion; yes, her neck bore his bite marks, but they were delivered with sounds of urgency, not conquest; yes, her lips were bruised from devouring and her hair sore from tugs and urgings, but her lips weren't split for the mirth nor her hair uprooted for the glory of her screams of agony.

After the party they left together, leaving Avi and Taras BMW sitting together as children, conspiratorial new friends at play among the feet of the grown-ups.

Jam smiled, wondering why his lank hair wasn't hanging in his eyes. Oh, mischief, he thought, and went into the bathroom. In the mirror he found a monkish creature, hairless as a fish. He laughed. Little Novak with his fat whore on top of him slept in the tub, both snoring. The woman had a gulag tattoo of a long, hairy wrist and hand emerging from her anus and the words of Dante, in Russian: Abandon all hope all ye who enter. Around the couple lay empty bottles and food containers, used condoms, a tampon, and discarded clothing. Novak too had met a razor; he looked to Jam as a big, pouting, pink-headed baby, but a baby born with curiosity, one eyebrow gone and the lower beard in which his shrunken penis lived now as barren and bleached as a winter beach.

A richness of life, Jam thought, staggering out of the bathroom, looking for cold beer. A richness of life that the merchant Razinkin couldn't smother with his bags of lemons, sleek cars, and royal suits.

Cabbage arrived at Dagg's shop in the late afternoon after the Saturday-night celebration. Dagg answered the door, examining him suspiciously with her fierce eyes, and grudgingly indicated he should enter. Bone sat in the front room of the closed shop, positioned where the afternoon sun could angle through the windows and attempt to warm him as he sipped tea from a glass, a sugar cube clenched in his teeth. He wore a plaid short-sleeved shirt, shapeless dark trousers, and a pair of white running shoes — one Adidas and one Nike.

Dagg stood in the middle of the living room as Cabbage crossed to the old man and kissed him. How beautiful, Cabbage thought as he passed her motionless figure. How beautiful, and with all the money in my pocket I could take but never have. A thing of beauty once had by hundreds, if not thousands, this one of the unreadable smile and the threads of silver knitted into her hair.

It was a time for finding out more, determining where this one was positioned in the *mir*. He told Dagg, "Beer."

Now the intelligence, the information: should she go to the kitchen and return with a bottle, I could then take it and her, by the arm, into the bedroom. But if she's become a Thief's lady, a lady of this superior Thief, then elsewise would transpire and all would be known and accepted.

Dagg stood there, barefoot, the sunlight halfway up her perfect legs under the hem of a sundress of purple and yellow sunsets. She stared at Cabbage with a pleasant balance, as though she could love him or kill him, then made her decision: she looked to Bone, and this told Cabbage his answer.

"For myself, tea, the old way." Bone barely looked at her.

Cabbage nodded and sat, forcing himself to ignore the triumphant sway she exercised under the sundress. This one, I knew the day she visited me, was meant for one of stature, one who could walk his Code and find one of another code to walk a different but parallel path. This man, does he cease to amaze, to elevate us all? "*Dyed*, everywhere there is talk.

The plague Razinkin hears laughter and whisperings of beep-beep. He rages."

"No fear of them, for you or for I. Have you made romance with his men, the Novak and the little Jam one? Are they of marrow?"

Cabbage shrugged. "It seems so. Although they are not of fur." He laughed, remembering. "As bald now as convicts. Jam is the one of brains; the Novak is of heart. He follows where Jam leads."

Bone accepted tea and a bowl of sugar cubes from Dagg. She placed Cabbage's bottle within reach and smiled at him without the curl of the carnivore; as she passed behind his chair, she touched her hand to his shoulder. Ah, so she too knew not until now that all is in place, all valued and all measured, at least within these rooms. A superior Thief brings harmony, pleasures all. Dagg left the room and water began running in the kitchen.

"He will ask for a meeting, this boil Razinkin," Bone said. "He will give us blessing now for what's already done. He will be a friend and offer to be a mentor. This meeting will appear through the small Jam person or perhaps through the Novak one. At the meeting all will reveal themselves."

"He will give permission for us all to operate? Lift the sanctions against robbery and thievery?"

"Yes. He'll ask that it be kept small and the children behave quietly, but he will bless us all. This is not the Tomahawk of old who would take our scalps before the last car was out of the parking lot; this is the Razinkin of money transfers and investment."

"So we have won? With a single operation? A few cars?"

Bone leaned forward and clapped a hand on Cabbage's knee. "No, no. He will slowly kill us all. We are not his enemy

— his enemy is the Code. By killing me and all involved with me, he will kill the Code here. It will be in a way much talked about, that will be heard in Moscow and Mombassa and Berlin and London. He will have to be . . . This word? Means without a root?"

Cabbage thought for a moment, his mouth working the sounds. "Ruthless."

"Yes, that. You must engage the Jam and his friend. But you must be certain of them. I cannot evaluate, I cannot weigh. Only you will know. The moves our Razinkin must make will be small but noticeable, and they will require delicacies: planning, communication, and ultimately treachery. It isn't enough that I'm to be dead: he must show me to be dead or banners to a ghost will be ahoist and much legend will ensue."

"Ah. And what of us?"

"We will kill him."

"But the city of spires . . . ?"

"We may have to kill them, too, kill the living and fuck the dead." Bone sipped at his tea, sucking it through the cube into his mouth. Cabbage noticed he shivered no more. "A message must be sent to the decayed Razinkin. We must be first to call a meeting, elsewise he will have opportunity to arrange both the location and the surprise. Should I go on up with the Thief Ushki, it must never be known. No grieving of tears, no celebration of farewell. I must live even if I die, you see?"

Cabbage started, suddenly realizing the power of Bone's hand on his thigh. Dagg came out of the kitchen and glanced at them, then went to the window and turned her face to the sun, singing softly. A fine feline smile upon her lips as she listened.

There was surveillance on Razinkin's mansion. Atop an electrical pole opposite the entrance of the driveway, a small camera was mounted, its wide black eye watching cars entering and leaving. Its umbilical cord had been tangled by overnight winds and hung like a looped snake beside the pole. Jam smiled at it as he piloted a gray Jaguar Sovereign to the foot of the driveway and exited left. Jam could hear the breathing of Razinkin, who lay on the floor in the rear seat under a blanket. Jam turned on the radio to interfere with any electronics mounted in the car. "The eye watches. They will be at each end of the street."

"Be of caution, Jerzy. If they follow, return." Razinkin's voice was muffled. Oh, this shame, oh this lack of dignity, he thought. I must hide like the magician's frightened rabbit. This bum, oh fuck him aft. Was that a dimming of respect in Jerzy's voice? These shaven heads, that lost eyebrow: part, Jerzy said, of getting close to the old vagrant and his brigade, part of a bonding into treachery. Or perhaps not? Have they been bewitched by the rag-and-bones man of the *mir*? After the horrible hook-nose does his work, I must have Zakon send some of his brigade from New York City and have order restored. I will stuff the bags in some anuses and decorate some necks with plastic ties, and we will see which is the preferred way to go on up. Perhaps both.

The Jaguar rode in smooth silence. Jam said, "None follow yet, master. I will make a circuit and we will see." He made some sharp lefts and rights, mindful of discomfort to his master; once he ran up behind a bus and buried the brakes, apologizing but smiling.

After fifteen minutes he ran down an on-ramp to the highway and sped through a half-dozen exits, off-ramped and then ramped back on, counting cars, memorizing colors and makes, signaling left and going right. "Clear, master. None are behind."

At a shopping plaza, he pulled behind a big-box store and stopped beside a rented multi-passenger van, its engine running. Little Novak, with his pink dome and lonely eyebrow, sat behind the wheel. Jam got out of the Jaguar and assisted Razinkin with exaggerated solicitousness, affecting to wipe dust from the fine suit.

They drove back into the city, Razinkin regathering his dignity, repeatedly smoothing his lapels and recentering the knot of his silken tie. Little Novak drove with hands of ham and no expertise, ignoring his mirrors, his meaty head fixed squarely at the road in front of him.

In the back seat of the van, Razinkin could hear Jam operating pistols, checking and rechecking bullet clips and smooth action. This will be it then, Razinkin thought. If I see my brains and white bone on the windshield in front of me, in that brief second of noise and light, I'll know the old bum has worked his magic on these two.

But as Razinkin licked his lips and waited, nothing happened. Novak exited the highway at Avenue Road and made a ponderous turn south. He refused to change lanes and they followed a sleeping old woman for several blocks, made turns and stops, until the van pulled into a side street. Before the men alighted, Jam slipped a pistol between the seats to Little Novak. "Steroid whore, you know which end the little bees come out?"

"Might I try it on you, dwarf?" Little Novak smiled at his own rare wit.

Jam gave him a friendly smile. "Only try not to shoot off your penis. Many men will weep and have to return to women and sheep for fuckery."

They hid the guns under their jackets, and Jam led the way to a picnic bench outside an Italian grocery store. Novak went inside for cold drinks, while Razinkin arranged himself as on a throne, caped, preening in the sunlight.

"Why this place, Jerzy?" Razinkin looked around at ladies shopping from shop to shop. Strollers were pushed and straining little dogs bitched at the end of leashes. Babies were held up to absorb warmth from the increasingly faraway sun. Across the street, two young women studied the display in the window of a jewelry shop; an old woman rode an electric scooter up the sidewalk, a small-headed white dog in the front basket.

"I don't know, master. The big-headed one said here and now. The message said the olden cold one desired to meet to make amends."

"A trap?"

Jam shrugged. "There are many other ways, less public and more safe."

Little Novak came out of the Italian shop with small bottles of root soda. He and Jam arranged themselves as bodyguards, instinctively dividing the street into zones, one facing south, one facing north, one watching foot traffic, the other watching passing vehicles.

Razinkin said no more. He brooded visibly and smoked at a cigarette with a band of gold around the filter, ignoring his soda. He was toeing out the second cigarette and feeling himself inflate with dark frustration when Bone spoke at his elbow: "Greetings, my brother."

Jam and Little Novak were startled; they half-arose, each reaching into their waistbands. Razinkin masked the shock of his innards melting, merely turning his head and muttering indifferently, "And to you: love." He motioned his palm at

Jam and Novak. "Sit." He didn't arise to embrace Bone, but sat back and lit another cigarette, his face bleak.

The rag-and-bone Thief shuffled from the doorway in his odd running shoes, baggy pants, and stained shirt, rounded the table with a torn plastic shopping bag in his fist, and greeted Jam and Novak with a touch to their shoulders and a smile of acknowledgment at their exposed skulls. "With such as you, the success and safety of master Razinkin is known and is no secret."

Both men nodded uncertainly. Razinkin sent Novak into the Italian shop for more sodas. Jam rearranged himself to observe the whole street and the facing shops, as well as Bone.

Bone commented upon this security. "My friend, you have worries?"

Razinkin shrugged, small. "This, with the cars. It has made small problems."

Bone found a busted cigarette in his shirt pocket; Jam leaned to light it, earning a glare from his master. Novak came out with four drinks and Razinkin took two, directing the men to take theirs to a nearby table.

Bone drank from the miniature soda bottle. "My apologies. It was my fault, this with the cars. Some young Thieves came to me to greet, and I told them old tales of greatness and adventure. I fear I put into their heads ideas that aren't harmonious. An old man's olden tales make dreams for the new. When I heard of your displeasure, I petitioned them on your behalf." He put the plastic bag onto the table. "So, within, lemons. For your friend the *vor* Ricci, or for yourself. Apologies are also sent that blessing can be made."

Razinkin fingered the white bag, confused. Was it as such? Merely boisterous boys bedazzled by olden talk, dusty legends? This one was indeed walking alone and had spoken as an old soldier recalling glories of past war long concluded. The money within would calm the cold anger of the *vor* Ricci, a tribute that might make him smile with relief. Or to return the bag to the old man with a shrug and a small smile: what has been, has been. A sinister implication that what comes next must surely come.

Razinkin was aware of his men at the next table, surely absorbing all this. Casually, he picked up the bag and leaned toward their table.

"A gift from the *dyed*, that you may eat and grow strong." He tossed the bag as though it contained old lettuce. "Be calm — a misunderstanding has been solved."

Bone smiled. "This adventure, it is regretted. I must now return to my shelter."

Razinkin offered him a gold cigarette; Bone accepted and Razinkin activated his lighter. "This place is cold, with the coming seasons. Allow me to provide you, my friend, with a roof. You have had many years of the bitter, now you must have the sweet." In his mind he calculated the arrival of Solonik, the sweet sniper.

"I have no needs. My park is deep, with many places out of the wind. Of the snow, I have no fear. These vibrations within me will melt it, and I will swim in a bath of warm water."

"As you wish. Please bless me: if you find a need, allow me to fulfill it. I have much, and as a brother I must share." Solonik and his massive beak will surely end this foolishness, Razinkin thought, and I can get back to the real work. Whether he walks alone or walks in front is of no matter: this one in front of my eyes is dead in any case. I could ask these two scalped Jerzys to do it, but what if in their enthrallment they instead turn their pistols upon me? Oh dear God who fucks with his face: from where does this hobo's magic charm emit? "This gift of lemons shows your heart still beats with the rightness of the Code."

Bone shrugged and glanced modestly down at the table. "It is all I have, that old Code, and when I pass on up, a time will end." He stood and touched his right hand to his left temple, as though dislodging a flea irritating his iron hairline. A signal? A sign? Of what?

Jam and Little Novak too saw the motion. Their eyes had been glued to the power emanating from the old bum, remembering him as he was at the Saturday-night party, sitting modestly in his corner chair as penitent Thieves approached to touch his robe. Neither saw the heavyset man and slim woman with a huge bouffant of blonde hair holding hands as they entered the doorway of the jewelry store across the street. The man in a business suit and the woman in a blue pant suit and running shoes, they stood in the security anteroom waiting to be buzzed in.

Bone and Razinkin embraced. Bone touched each of Razinkin's men on the shoulder and bid them farewell with soft words: "All is a message. When the bird makes flight in the sky, there are words written for those who will read them."

His shuffling gait took him around the corner at the precise moment an alarm rang at the jewelry shop and the front windows were blasted out onto the street by a stutter of gunfire from within. Razinkin jerked for cover as Cabbage and Avi, holding a blonde wig to his head, walked quickly from the shop, clutching a stuffed cotton pillowcase. A blue Honda Accord sped up the street, a boy with sunglasses up into his hair at the wheel, and Cabbage and Avi piled into the back seat. Through the open window of the sedan, Cabbage waved a jaunty salute at the three men at the picnic table in front of the Italian shop.

The boiling Razinkin could hear their laughter.

Razinkin's brigade swept through the nest of apartment buildings in the north of the city. They bulled into the second-hand shops in the east end, throwing trumpets, rusted radios, and worn cameras from shelves. They crowded the Israeli limousine drivers with transparent bonhomie, stepping heavily on their toes while speaking softly and smiling into their eyes. Doughnut shops with small white-powder businesses in the kitchens were invaded by shouting men who frightened customers out onto the streets. There were beatings of varying degrees; doors were smashed and windows washed with bricks. At Dagg's, they pounded on the locked door, unmindful of the streak of blue chalk; inside, Bone and Dagg froze in embrace, Bone giggling into the smoothness of her neck: "The beginning of the end." When the banging stopped, he arranged her astride him.

Chapter 14

When cabbage went to meet the man who made music boxes, he invited Avi along. Bone had told Cabbage the shop clerk might indeed have the tiger within; Cabbage was to groom and observe, search for signs of the bones of a Thief.

But Avi wouldn't go without his new friend Taras. This new Avi decorated his head with chrome sunglasses, his narrow body swimming inside a white shirt with a large collar. In search of a father, the Fairies' child had found a brother. Cabbage recognized this and took both with him to an industrial plaza on the western edge of the city.

The man who made music boxes was a grossly fat Chinaman of the *dai huen jai* who operated a factory for reproducing very cheaply the finest names in computers and electronics parts. Cabbage told him of the dimensions and power of the music boxes he required; the Chinaman asked where his devices were to be played, as though concerned with acoustics. Cabbage made a sketch on a piece of notepaper and the Chinaman nodded, asked a few questions in Hong Kong English, and went to work. Taras and Avi played video games intently while they waited; Cabbage stared at a calendar of misty mountains and dreamed of the olden man riding through them on the back of a mule.

The Chinaman returned a half-hour later. This blue button was for tuning, this red for playing the music. He accepted a wad of cash, looking at both sides of each bill as he counted it, then counted it again and nodded. Cabbage and the children left the shop, carefully putting the music boxes on the floor behind the driver's seat.

Dagg made the mark and, like parents seizing moments in a frantic day of children, she and Bone had maintained themselves into the evening. Dagg had the sense, after Bone returned from his meeting with Razinkin, that he desired to be alone with her, to expose a little more of the man and not the Thief, although truly both were one. But perhaps at times . . .

Jam and Little Novak made sad eyes at the raid on the jewelry shop. They commiserated with Razinkin's rage, spitting curses and shaking their heads in disgust, but secretly they felt their hearts take flight. In the seconds after the robbery, they'd gone into their professional mode: no joking of minuscule penises now, of steroid whores or the smallest policeman in Moscow. With their hands on their guns, they spirited Razinkin from the café to the van, eyes out for a giggling Bone or any of his clan. Razinkin was stuffed into the back seat, catatonic with anger and with frozen bone joints as his muscles fought against exploding. His eyes were unblinking, and even Jam, who had no fear, shivered at the emergence of the old Tomahawk who had terrified all with his hatchet, plastic bags, and constricting plastic cords.

With metallic precision, Razinkin ordered the brigade out to find a trail, a trace, of the fucking derelict. None were to be spared — any with information would be paid, any who had none would be squeezed. They were to begin at the center of the *mir* then work their way outward, through the gypsies, journeyman burglars, pickpockets, pimps, and prostitutes. Parks were to be swept, railyards visited, bridges explored. If any — Cabbage or the boy in the white shirt from the Honda — were found, no questions would be put to them. Hammers were to be used from the toes on up until their teeth were tapped from their mouths and their foreheads had holes punched into them. When Bone was found, he was to be mummified in duct tape, allowed to breathe through a small hole, until an example to all could be made.

Business would continue, but security would be increased. Double the guard on the mansion, both inside and out, then get guards to guard the guards. The money pickups would require a crash car of no less than four armed escorts.

Jam nodded as he drove. He was reminded of when he was the smallest policeman in Moscow, when bribes weren't paid on time and it was necessary to poke thumbs deeply into eyes. The American police in movies had terms he loved: the heat is on, it is a dragnet, round up the usual suspects.

Razinkin was brought to a shopping plaza where he took a taxi to another taxi that would return him to the relative sanity of his mansion.

Little Novak wiped at his slick skull. "Woo."

"Indeed, woo, peanut penis." Jam began making his way in the downtown of the city. Jam loved the vacant stare, the thudding voice, the slow coupling of ideas inside the now-shaven skull, concepts that would, finally, interlock with loud clangs, like lazy boxcars on rusted railway tracks. He knew where Bone was likely squirreled away, remembered the lithe, silver-threaded woman, and knew her as a Fairie who ran a buy-cheap-sell-more shop. And he had recognized the driver of the getaway Honda that carried Cabbage as the Kiev boy with the funny accent from the Thieves' party. He had indeed taken with him from that party a wealth of intelligence as well as, he suspected from the persistent itch at his groin, little passengers of the pincers.

"A time of decision, my friend. Wealth or glory, but which?"

Novak was uncomfortable with direct questions that might require an answer. He pretended he hadn't heard. As Jam walked, so would he. While he knew he could easily pick up the little policeman and shot-put him a great distance, he had the sense that Jam could melt him off the ground with humor and sharp talk and make him disappear in a puddle of laughter.

"'Vak? Which?"

Little Novak chewed his lips, agonizing as though commanded to answer a crucial question in a complicated quiz. But he agonized in silence, seeing in his mind the dying Ushki, the weeping eyes of the Cabbage, the relief as he emptied the revolver into the old man's bursting brain, all happening as the psychotic Razinkin danced about the edge of the patio, caping with his coat.

At the devil gypsy's shop, Jam recognized the blue chalk mark as a signal. The door was secure; when Jam yanked at it, it didn't even rattle against the lock. Little Novak asked if he should open it with his foot, but Jam, who was familiar with sheet-steel doors and square lock bolts, shook his head. He pounded on the door, hearing the hollow booms of his fist echo inside and come back against the metal. He put his ear against the door; it was like listening to a rock.

"This mark," Jam said, stepping back, "means something to someone. Beware, stay away — something. We will wait."

They returned to the van, their pistols on the floor at their feet, and backed up the alleyway, out of sight of the shop's door, but at a vantage from which they could see anyone approaching.

"If they come," Novak asked, "what will be our plan?"

Jam shrugged. "It will become known as it unfolds." He made a miniature limp penis of his baby finger, rose it stiff, and then collapsed it. "Like all great things, eh, chemical man?"

They sat in silence, Jam smoking gold cigarettes Razinkin had left in the van. Novak lumbered around to the rear, climbed in, and went to sleep. Jam was pleased at the opportunity to think, to weigh: This Bone, I have met very few of his stature. None of the bluster and blowing of the average bandit or torpedo. In his chair there, with the smooth, pale princess alert at his side, accepting tribute from the parking-lot thieves, and then just placing it on the floor and forgetting about it. Jam had met many like the spittle Razinkin, both as a policeman and while pulling his time in the frontier. Brutish and without humor. Jam believed in humor in all things, whether as a policeman, convict, victim, or predator. Humor between men was a bond, especially when exhibited in the hardest of times in the most difficult of places. Based on that, Bone would surely be the choice. But on the other hand, the money Razinkin paid, the benefits and the power, also had a strong draw for him. And, in the long run, of course, the Bones of the world would ultimately lose. There was a relentlessness to those like Razinkin that went beyond brutality — it went to voracious survival. You could, Jam thought, kill all the Razinkins in the world and there would still be a Circle of brothers, an organization.

He weighed and balanced, but he didn't fret: the decision would be made in a single moment, a moment perhaps of a spoken word, a glance, an indefinable urge.

As the sun began to go down, he heard the door at the rear of the shop open briefly; when a moment later he crept up for a view, he saw the blue mark was gone and the door was again closed. Five minutes later he heard feet in the grit at the mouth of the alleyway, and laughter.

"'Vak, quickly." Jam took the guns from the floor of the van and both men climbed out and caught Cabbage, Avi, and Taras clustered at the rear of the shop, the boys laughing as Cabbage clowned — "Oops" — pretending he was going to drop the music boxes as he tapped a tune on the heavy door.

When Dagg opened and peeked out, she saw only the precarious, addle-faced Cabbage and the laughing boys. When she pulled the door open fully, Jam and Little Novak had their guns focused and all entered the shop together.

Bone was in the basement, his shirt tucked into his trousers and his collar button fastened, sitting in a chrome chair at a card table where he idly spun a silver amulet. He recognized the vast number of feet on the wooden steps. First, Dagg. Then the children no longer smiling, then Cabbage with his body inflating in shame or anger before Bone's very eyes. Finally the little Jam and the looming Novak, each with a shiny skull and a gun, and one eyebrow between them both.

"Good, good," Bone said, bestowing a smile. "Now we are seven. And you brought barking dogs. Please, little water? Tea?"

Dagg moved quickly to stand between Bone and the guns, facing them; her fierceness radiated as heat from an iron stove and momentarily ceased Bone's cold shivers. Jam spoke, and the boys moved to the farthest wall; Jam spoke again and poked Cabbage in the kidney with the gun, hard, sending him stumbling, trying to protect the music boxes.

Bone eased Dagg from in front of him and moved to the center of the room.

Jam rounded the pistol on him. "Sit, old man. Witch, you as well. You boys sit on the floor there, assist your better."

Neither Bone nor Dagg moved; the boys went to the wall where Cabbage had rolled himself and sat beside him, not knowing what to do but touching him gently.

"I will see to the big-head," Dagg said, moving in a wide arc around the gunmen, a lithe journey that took her close to the worktable where Avi kept his screwdrivers. Jam turned his head to follow her, and she made a gypsy charm trick, flipping her hair prettily with one hand, the tension on the sundress forming the cloth to her breast.

"No, no. Sit, witch." Jam's eye was drawn to the glow of her face and the stretch of her fabric. Little Novak didn't know where to look except at Cabbage, who writhed. Jam shouted in the largest voice of Moscow's smallest policeman, "All, sit! Sit now, all!" He stepped back, away from them all and aimed his pistol up.

When only Little Novak sat with a thud, all in the room except writhing Cabbage laughed.

"Oh, oh my Jesus," Jam said. "Steroid whore —"

As a sly dancer inside veils, Dagg spun low and rising, the yellow plastic handle of the screwdriver clutched in her white fist. She grunted, her bracelets jangling, as the slot head of the screwdriver took Jam through the forearm when he moved to protect his lower vital innards; Dagg didn't pause as he pulled away, the jerking motion twisting the screwdriver from her hand. She was upon him immediately with teeth, unmindful of the gun as it wagged in the air for a target; then it slammed against her skull, then skipped off and out of Jam's grip. The boys went for the gun. Bone went for Dagg's dented head, where the silver and black hair absorbed blood.

Little Novak fired and all froze, as noise and blue smoke filled the basement.

"Jerzy, Jerzy?" He was confused; being in charge of anything was alien to him. To be the only one with a gun in a room brought with it huge pressures. What to do? What to say? Had Jam made the decision and told him and he forgot in his chemical mind, in this ringing in his ears? Was he to shoot, and if so, who first? He pointed the pistol around the room but found nowhere comfortable to settle the aim.

"Steroid whore, step away from them. To the back wall. This witch, she has . . ." Jam thought of his words to come and began laughing ". . . she has screwed me."

This was too idiomatic for Bone, who merely stared. Cabbage, huddled on the floor, began laughing, then groaned as his kidney resisted.

Jam slid the screwdriver out of his arm and picked up his gun in his left hand. "My master wishes to meet again with this legendary Bone."

"Your master is a master of whores." Bone had moved beside Dagg, his tattooed fingers combing lightly through her hair. The boys and Cabbage sat with their backs to the far wall.

"Perhaps so. But he is my master."

"Who offers you what?"

Jam shrugged and looked at the still frozen Novak. "Novak, can you kill these others?"

Novak jerked as though in a daze. He looked in turn at the boys, Bone, Dagg, and finally Cabbage. "For the boys, yes, to save them the harshness of life to come. Not this big-headed one or the gypsy. He has heart and she will leave the stain of curse upon me."

"Too late for the curse of the shriveled penis, eh? Or the falling out of the hair." Jam tucked his bleeding forearm under his opposite armpit. He walked sideways to the music boxes and nudged one with his foot. He examined the buttons on the top. "Oh-ho. Adventures to come."

He smiled, but inside he still hadn't made any decision. It will be sudden, he recalled thinking, a look, a word, a mood. Stabbed through the arm by a Fairie, standing in a cellar of diminishing blue smoke with powerful music boxes at his feet, the much-admired Cabbage with a future soon of pissing blood. None moved him from his balance of indecision until he looked at the beautiful bleeding witch and the olden man now staring up at him at her side, and it was into the magic yellow eyes of Bone that he found his decision.

Am I to be, he wondered, the man who murders the last tiger, the man who plucks the final eagle from the skies?

Alexsandr Solonik watched the road signs for directions to Arizona, U.S.A., but found none. The limousine driver, a silent, hunched Israeli, piloted the pine-scented white Cadillac out of the airport, down the 427, and across the Gardiner Expressway into Toronto's downtown core. Solonik believed he had never seen a city so bland, so un-European, so lacking in distinction or excitement. Outside an anonymous hotel, the driver popped the trunk without exiting and watched in the mirror as Solonik took his own carryall and another, longer one from the car. After Solonik slammed the trunk shut and went inside to register, the taciturn Israeli dialed a number on his cellphone.

"He of the nose arrives and is delivered."

Razinkin breathed a sound of relief. "And his tools?"

"He has," the Israeli said with a dour laugh. "The magic pipe, eh?"

Razinkin too made a laugh. "Let the music begin." He hung up.

The Israeli hated them all, the new reality and those who walked the old path. He hated the gypsies who looted the airport, he hated his own senseless love for the Fairie who bought his stolen goods and paid little, refusing to bargain in the bed because, he was sure, he was a Jew with only a numerical tattoo on his arm. But of all, he most hated the grimy Razinkin, a come-lately who swaggered and wore his coat like a matador.

He dialed another number. "The filthy one has a friend from overseas." He gave the name of the hotel and the address.

"It is good that you called." The woman's voice was musical and friendly in a way he'd never heard before. "A favor from a friend is a blessing from God."

"A bargain is better."

"I will tell Avi. Of this friend, you know what?"

"He is a master piper and he has acquired a pipe." He didn't mention it was he who provided the pipe. He listened to her breathing as she sorted this out. The Israeli pictured her haunted face, that willowy waist and those long pale feet, the silver-painted hair and the endless supply of sundresses. "He makes his music and vanishes, you see?"

Alexsandr Solonik met Dmitri Razinkin late that evening in a corner of the seedy hotel bar. They'd spoken several times in the months before Bone had fled Moscow, but had never met. Razinkin tried not to stare at the ungainly nose in front of him, tried not to laugh or show sympathy. This blond one, he thought, chewing back a grin, and hiding it behind his snifter of brandy, carries his own rifle, there, under his eyes, a double-barreled scattergun. Above it, those eyes, though, those eyes are what I'm buying, those and that finely sandpapered fingertip. But, oh, observe that mouth below: the saw-blade underbite of a cannibalistic fish.

Solonik ordered a rum and cola. The waitress was of fine ass and legs, but chickenlike in the bosom. This place, he thought, this place of women of either too much meat or none at all, or, as with this birdlike creature, an unappetizing combination of both. In Arizona, U.S.A., there must be fine women; elsewise why would the gentleman Mr. Bananas, even at almost a century old and likely in possession of his manly powers, settle in a place populated with these ungainly flat storks?

Razinkin briefed him: Bone was to be located — he himself would use his own brigade to find the old bum, to set him up for the piping — and Razinkin had specific instructions for Solonik, instructions that would exact a revenge and eliminate the possibility that Bone had survived, that a legend could be created of a vengeful Bone ghosting his way through the *mir*, haunting those of the new reality, commanding from invisibility legions of new and young Thieves to do his imagined bidding.

"That he shouldn't hide inside a painless shock, I bid you to use careful choice, use little bees of the type to hunt little beasts," Razinkin said. "The toes of the feet perhaps, perhaps the joints of the arms and legs. Then the penis and testicles must be found to gather his further attention. Then —" he shrugged "— as you like. I will, of course, require the head, which should have no damage, no disfigurement. Is this too exact for you, my friend?"

"I have had much reaction to firing into the cup of the hip. Full of nerves, the pain excruciates. Then: play at leisure as long as there are bees." He too shrugged. "But the collecting of the head, it is above and beyond my duties. Perhaps you have torpedoes who can assist in the gathering?"

A cellphone went off under Razinkin's jacket. He listened a moment, excused himself, and went out into the lobby, then outside the restaurant entirely. Solonik watched him walk a short distance from where his white Mercedes awaited. A slim man with a shaven head dusted at the fenders with a handkerchief, and another man, also shaven, a huge hulk in a sports outfit, loitered on the edge of the sidewalk. A liveried doorman with gold rope at his shoulders and on his peaked cap stood a distance away, a true urban worker who knew what he saw when he saw it; he knew the time to study the sky and let the pavement take care of itself. Solonik watched Razinkin nod and nod into the cellphone, then clench a fist in victory. He returned with a jaunty step, calling something to the shaven-headed men.

Back at the table, Razinkin wore a wide smile. "By tomorrow, my friend, I believe we will have your target. Immediately after, I will reimburse you, privately. Is this satisfactory?"

"Then, then Arizona, U.S.A.? I must find the home of a Mr. Joseph Bananas."

"A restful holiday, much heat, and the friends in Tucson or Phoenix will be made available to you, to find this person, to pipe him, if you wish, and assist you to make away."

"Pipe Mr. Joseph Bananas?"

Tony Ricci wasn't concerned about the cars swiped from his parking lot, but he was livid at the smelly mess cooked up by the powerful heater of his BMW. When word came back to him that the raid was carried out by Russians, he'd called Razinkin to make a fierce complaint. A few days later, Razinkin had appeared with a key to a new BMW, black and leather and chrome, and waiting in the parking lot. Explaining that renegade Thieves had appeared in the *mir*, Razinkin assured Ricci that the miscreants would be rooted out and punished. Ricci was important to Razinkin: one of his duties in the north of the true America was to forge allegiances for the profit of all.

Ricci, of mainland Italian descent although locally born and raised, instinctively felt the twang of insecurity in Razinkin's tightly wired network. He feigned a continuing, although abating, anger at the adventure and monitored Razinkin closely. He detected a faint unbalance and explored how to exploit it. The money-laundering service the Russian provided was lucrative: Ricci, with this channel of finance, was able to gather others of various *mirs* with money to clean and profited himself by adding on a surcharge for Razinkin's good works. Thus a new component was added to Ricci's underworld initiatives of vice and extortion, enhancing his status both here and with his masters in Buffalo. Privately he used these extra profits to fund a channel of white powder, which in turn brought more profits; thus the continued need for Razinkin's money service. This joint enterprise had the completeness of a snake eating its own tail.

Ricci recognized what was happening in Razinkin's *mir* as similar to what happened every ten years or so in his own: a struggle for recognition, a washing of generations as new criminal initiatives emerged, confusion among friends and enemies as allegiances changed and new players appeared. Some bombings for attention, some kidnappings for profit and terror, a few murders for ascension. Merely housekeeping, decade by decade, of dusty, mysterious corners, dust balls that grew, forgotten, under the bed and had to be swept out by a new broom.

When Razinkin tried to explain the split in his *mir*, Ricci's eyes glazed over. Codes and olden men and new realities and gulags — all were a matter of indifference to him. Crusting shit on the leather of his BMW, though, this he understood with clarity. "Can you get the little fuck that shit in my car, Dmitri, that's all I care about, and break his fucking fingers?"

Razinkin assured him the problem with the renegades would be resolved quickly. He offered to bring the hand that had wiped the ass that had violated the BMW. Ricci, thinking he was joking, laughed, then remembered Razinkin's preference for girl-like women whose faces he could pulverize. "No, just slap him in the head. And should we hang back on the money for a while? I'd hate to see it backing up while this thing gets fixed. You want to take a week off?"

No, Razinkin said. All would be well.

Now, when the box made its music in the hallway between the dancers' room and the entrance to the bar, Ricci wasn't thinking at all about Razinkin, Russians, or money: he was dozing in his office, spent and sticky from an audition with a new Thai girl who wanted to be a runway star. The narrow corridor acted as a gun barrel, focusing and channeling the power of the bomb's debris straight out into the street where the club's window sharded and glass hit the facade of the café across the road, breaking its windows. There were, he could tell from the screams that pierced the smoke, injuries both inside the club and out.

After the firefighters had left, the ambulances had sped off with wounded, and detectives had pretended belief in his arguments that he knew nothing, had no enemies, Ricci went out to the back of the lot where he found his sleek new BMW with its engine running, the doors locked, and the unhappy sight of crusted excrement on the padded steering wheel and across the beautiful dashboard.

Ten minutes after Jam picked up banded currency from the Iranian trader — the second-last stop on the money route — the second music box demolished the front of the building, shredding the proprietor who glared through his front window at the passing world of ignorant infidel bastards.

Now twenty blocks away, again driving the Lexus, Jam stopped near the mouth of the underground cavern, watching both the entrance and the security car, a rented red Buick, behind him. All four in the security car were smoking and blue smoke poured from the windows, as though the Buick was smoldering within. The four had arrived from New York the previous evening, loaners from Zakon.

The black Mercedes SUV slipped to the edge of the sidewalk and rolled out, left. Jam followed. At the drop point, Jam stopped the Lexus in the middle of the one-way street behind the Mercedes and waited for the intermittent emergency lights. When they came on, he activated his own and got out, waving at the security car. Carrying the bag of money, he came up on the passenger side of the Mercedes and passed the bag inside, then climbed aboard. Taras sat behind the wheel in another billowing shirt. In the back seat, Avi, in an identical shirt, sat with the slumped, well-dressed body of a businessman who had a clear plastic bag sealed with tape over his head and beneath it appeared to be wearing a red ascot, but wasn't. Two machine pistols lay on the floor under a towel.

"We will have a pause while I count these lemons," Jam

said, lighting a cigarette and ignoring the bag. He twisted in the seat, backward. "Are you prepared for this thing?"

Avi nodded, speechless within the experience of a hyperreality.

Jam said, "It will go as planned. Remember to not close the vehicle's doors, to keep the finger moving — blip blip blip — and change the aim often. This is easy as long as each of you keep the side mirrors beside you; if one moves ahead, the other will surely shoot him. Always be beside each other, facing away. Think of the shape of a triangle and do not be stingy with the bullets; afterward, time will become very slow. And even then, only one approaches to finish it. The other will wash this Mercedes, but only after removing this case, and then he will wash the security car. You have decided?"

"I will finish," Avi said.

"I will put my barking dog on the hood of the Buick and retrieve the bag and wash this Mercedes and then the car," Taras said.

Jam nodded and opened his door. He moved to the Lexus and heard the Mercedes drive away. He held up five fingers to the security car; none of the men inside nodded or acknowledged him: they were thick, bored shapes, dozing already and hating this city. Jam leaned on his car and smoked his cigarette.

Behind the security car, the Mercedes SUV crept up the block. Taras and Avi stepped out, each with a machine pistol bulked with a fat, perforated tube silencer, and came up behind the crash car, already aiming at the silhouettes in the rear seat. As they came to the trunk of the car, both fired into the rear window — blip blip blip, as instructed — then moved quickly forward, making another triangle, and poured bullets, endlessly, into the driver and passenger.

Taras put his gun on the hood of the Buick and walked back to the Mercedes SUV. He took out the bag of currency and a red tin can. He washed the vehicle's insides with gasoline, stepped back, lit a book of matches, and tossed it in. Avi walked to Jam and the Lexus, backward.

"No," Jam said. "The gun — get it, and finish."

Avi's mind was deaf in shock. He said, "Yes, mother," and climbed into the back seat of the Lexus. The SUV was billowing black smoke, and flames danced out the open doors. Taras skipped away from the flames, backward, his flowing white shirt glowing, the handle of the red tin can in one hand, the money case in the other. He looked at Jam.

Jam held up a finger, reached into the back seat of the Lexus, took the front-heavy machine pistol from Avi's hand, and went to the red Buick. He picked up the other gun from the hood. There was no motion inside, a soaking of blood throughout. He leaned in and identified heads; he fired one careful round into each of the four skulls, then did it again in rotation, until he ran out of bullets. He threw the machine pistols inside.

He told Taras, "Wash it."

Chapter 15

BONE MOVED BACK into his precious park. He made a bed in the culvert and meditated upon the birds, who seemed to remember him and calmly perched in their trees and bushes. Thinking as he rarely did of the concept of time, he clutched at handfuls of dirt and let them idle through his fingers. He meditated upon his gypsy bitch and the boys who had become his own lineage. It is as a family, he thought, and was it a true violation of the Code? Is this the seduction that weakened the Code? But no devotions had been said, no covenant with the State had blessed it. He would, if the Code demanded it, kill both the boys and the enchantress; this he knew without question, and if he had regrets, it mattered not.

He noticed now the discomfort of the ground, how it gathered and held the cold of the night; he thought of thick duvets, of the scent of cabbage and peppercorns in his nostrils, of the crinkle of warm, moist curls; heard the sounds of the boys laughing at their adventures, how Taras and Avi had a bond he had once felt with his brothers of the *mir*.

This Jam. It was unthinkable that he'd been the smallest policeman in Moscow. Of what mind had he been when he applied, trained, and donned the uniform? He could kiss or kill with the true heart of a Thief: in joy and laughter. And the oafish but hearted Little Novak, a servant of the State, allowing it to capture his self and inflate him into some popular hero, dumbly accepting accolades of his own greatness, when in reality his greatness, his heart, would exist without the adulators. Had Bone had these two, and the two young ones: what a brigade, what a brigade. And that fierce Fairie alurk, her destiny of survival as a mother of all, to bewitch and scheme and foretell treachery before it was even birthed. None of the Circle would have lived to flee that dacha; all would be skulls in ice water in silver bowls, smiling at each other in the wake of that sorceress.

When Bone had left the shop to return to his park, he'd refused Dagg's casual offer of comforts, food, and the duvet that held her essence and scents within its weaves. She wanted, he knew, to play the mother role, to send him off with foods and medicines and coins and scrawled numbers to call if she were needed. But she also knew it was impossible for a true Thief to become the husband, the lover, the father. When he returned to his dense paradise of tiny biting bugs, screeching birds, of damp and cold, all he had that he hadn't possessed the first time was a man-woman amulet of silver and a tin of yellow pills that made him piss sunrises.

It was cold in the night; he hugged himself in the same coat he'd been swaddled in the night he'd been assailed by the sicknesses within. This is true life, he thought, smiling. How can a Thief have comfort, a woman who awaited, these giggling children always around to fetch another bowl of soup, to carry a piece of bread? A roof above and a woman below — although sometimes both above, he allowed himself to imagine with another smile. Had it been otherwise, then it would have been such and so. But it wasn't.

In the night, as Bone slept with his little animals and bugs, Dagg wrapped herself in the duvet she knew would carry his scents and essences. Unless so instructed for the enhanced pleasures of the predator, a Fairie never truly cried; on demand she could moan and thrash her head convincingly, could beg and scream, but within herself there were neither tears nor true sobs. Upon that faraway sky, upon the shard of moon at night or the round sun in clear days, or upon the gray mysterious swirl of overcast, the Fairie would meditate outside her body, a bird far above watching this grunting joke below, this theft of pleasures in which something was taken but in fact couldn't be.

But, she thought, this man. Below her, gazing upward and grunting the sadness of orgasm, the only time a Thief truly gave. Then eating at her hair with a greedy mouth. Blowing lightly upon the tragedy of her breasts: no sadness or rage, merely acceptance that all that has been, was. Naked in the cabin as she washed him while he slept inside his malignant sickness; did he feel the fingers tracing the washed-out lines of ink that carried his history, exploring the scars and dents? Is the time passed for Thieves and Fairies? No, not yet. Ultimately, like a hungry wolf he would have to choose whether to kill her or let the Code die and wither; and he wouldn't be the *vor* he was if he chose other than the Code. And of her code? Survival above all, as the frozen watching stars often told her, as her hands and knees froze in the barbed-wire world of iced snow.

The boys sat silently inside her gaze but unseen. The comedic Jam and the slab of rock Little Novak were out creating mischief. There would be adventures anew. All were speaking now of the raid on the jewelry store as Razinkin watched, of the bombing at the Iranian terrorist's store, of the turning inside-out of Ricci's club, of the fiery massacre of Zakon's torpedoes in the side street. Razinkin had made a bounty for the actual head of the beloved Bone, but his rich enticements were met with hollow assurances of eager cooperation but no action or intelligence. The Israeli limousine driver had determined the sniper had met with Razinkin, that evil was afoot. A time for decision, for choice, had come. What protection, what survival, from a spitting sniper who could strike from afar? What, to a Fairie, is the death of a wild Thief?

Dagg reflected and then decided. She stirred and stood, her body tiny within the folds of the duvet. The boys looked up expectantly with large eyes, like young dogs awakening to a master's sound. Avi spoke: "Mother?"

"We must betray him," she said in infinite sadness.

Bone heard them coming, the clank of a wine bottle against glasses, the murmur of their voices in quiet urging, and he climbed a tree. The lovers stopped below, a balding man with a beard and a woman of flaming hair. They were only yards from the singed skin and bones of feasting. But they were away, those two, lovers in a paradise of their own.

It will all happen without me; this hook-nosed sniper the gypsy divined was in the city. Rest and hide, she said, burrow deep and enjoy the smell of the earth, a scent not likely to be enjoyed when dead. You are the Code, you walk the way of the Code, you breathe the scent of the joy of life. Burrow deep and let come what is to come. But she sent him off reluctantly; for a moment he thought he would witness an impossibility: a Fairie's tears, as rare as a Thief's pity.

Below, the man penetrated the woman; rather, she impaled herself. Her neck, thought Bone, it strains with cords like those of the gnashing Dagg; he moos like a pained bull, startling my friends the birds — they're away. Another track, if not the way of the Code, this is the path I'd walk. Can there be anything but an earthly happiness such as this, pinned by a woman? But I have been chosen this path, and that gypsy of the silver-ruined hair cannot walk alongside me with her temptings and beckonings.

Still, he thought with the smallest of smiles, I'm glad I haven't killed her yet. A sad day yet, there ahead of me.

Razinkin had no driver. It was clear to him after the funeral pyre and the revelry in the side street that Jam and Little Novak had been entranced and bequeathed themselves unto the fucking old bum. Razinkin had seen this before: daydreaming boys engaged as he himself had engaged many, many and more. Only a Thief could sprinkle shit as though it were stardust. In places far away, in times long past, that would have been the life. But not now, not in this world of countries to steal and entire financial systems to loot. That old man, Razinkin thought, I should have given him a calendar.

The slim Swiss was pressed into service as a driver. No bodyguard he, resisting this duty, imagining perhaps the hosing down of the Jeep by automatic gunfire, blowing him out from under the imagined sophistication of his cheap yellow toupee. The outrageous adventures had been related by all; even Razinkin's wife had lifted her head from her tedious bridge games, frowning with puzzlement. Instead of the slim brown girls, perhaps this Swiss is the one I should have made play the *zek*, he thought.

He had the slim Swiss take evasive turns, looping back and coming upon themselves in the rearview mirror, it seemed. There was a police vehicle for a while, but, operating under his master's precise and sudden directions, the slim, damp-faced Swiss girlishly made hesitant turns and somehow the *musor* were lost, unaccustomed to such amateurism.

At the trade office, Razinkin told the Swiss where to wait and made his way inside. It seemed the men in the office stared at him as though seeing a dead man arise and walk. Wordlessly Razinkin walked through doors and down hallways until he was in the white light of a humming electric womb, operating his secure telephone.

First he contacted Zakon at his mistress's apartment near Coney Island. He waited, strangely calm, as Zakon affixed devices to his telephone.

Zakon said he had heard of the adventure of fire and bullets. "So, four gone up, eh? I will send eight. Then I will send sixteen. Don't worry, my friend. Ask, and it will be."

"No, no. I have one here who will solve all this, and soon. I just want to advise you there will be an event and after this event all will be as it was."

"You must send a proof." Zakon was quiet a moment. "A proof must be sent over there. This old one must not only be gone on up, he must be known to have gone on up, without question. Can you do this alone?"

"It will be done. I must notify the Circle."

"After this, your position will be assured, known to all."

Razinkin waited a beat. "If I deliver the proof to you, can you assure its safe delivery?"

"How large will this . . . proof be?"

"Of the size of a bowling ball. You know bowling?"

Zakon laughed. "A smiling bowling ball, I suspect."

Razinkin made his own laugh. "Smiling? Yes, perhaps. But, in any event, there will be many holes for the fingers."

"Yes, yes. Best if it arrives packed and ready for shipment. We have a friend among the fools at the United Nations who sends many things back and brings many things forth."

"I thank you and I kiss you."

"As I do you. Great times make great men; great men make great times."

Next Razinkin dialed the endless numbers required to reach Moscow. His neck tightened in tension, he leaned back in the swivel chair, counting the tiny holes in the ceiling tiles that sucked sound and devoured it. I must find another of the dark children, he thought, must have Ricci enable me somehow. But after the explosion of his club, Ricci had lost his friendliness, had become instead as demanding as a wife. That old bum knew what he was doing, that Bone the scum: loss of the control of one's *mir* was worse than being cuckolded by a wandering gypsy with his cheap flute and doglike, baggy eyes on an afternoon when the husband was culling morels from the forest. A BMW was no longer an option.

"A friend from afar."

Razinkin stirred and sat upright. "Events here are murderous and without mercy."

"As I would hope you yourself are capable."

"The old cold one has made events, has made adventures. I must act."

The voice was indifferent. "As you must."

"I have permission? A blessing?"

"An old friend has gone on up. A crab acquired an appetite and had a banquet."

"Our friend with the eyes?"

"Bless a Thief."

"Indeed. All is now possible?"

"If not the comforting and welcome for that wandering one, then it must be the resolution. If you tell me the sun cannot rise in the east, then I must beg you to find the hand that holds it hidden. Can you find this hand that prevents the light to lead us from darkness?"

"I will have him soon."

"Do you require assistance? Our friend in the true America?"

"I have one of a nose."

The voice essayed mild but unconvincing surprise. "Already?"

"I anticipated."

"In failure, anticipation will be seen as treachery. In success, as wisdom."

"I will send a gift."

"It will be received. Over here the anarchy continues, and it must end. Already they talk of music boxes, of barking dogs. There is a stirring, a rumbling. New slogans appear on the walls daily, telling of the adventures of that old fuck. He lives. He prevails. We can have no heroes."

"Except us."

"Of course, and none other."

"I have a blessing?"

"And of course a kiss." The voice made incomprehensible sounds of pondering. "A failed attempt is worse than doing nothing. Measure twice, cut once."

"Be careful and precise."

"As a craftsman."

"As a brother in destiny."

Chapter 16

CABBAGE DIDN'T QUESTION Dagg's instructions. She sent him to fetch the old man from his park and take him into the neighborhoods, to prowl and plan a new attack on the nerves of Razinkin.

After watching him leave in the Cadillac, and allowing time for a pickup, Dagg — with Avi and Taras — visited Bone's park in the van and wandered on foot. It was a vast place that reminded her of her Fairies' soul lair where the olden bass swam and teased. There was an unhealthy pond with rivulets of water running from it in several directions. There were trees beginning to shed their leaves, although it was only late summer — the leaves sensed they would die in the smog of the city and the bitter earth below; better to now become mulch that through nature's rebirthing others might live.

Dagg found the old man's den, counted the skeletons and pelts of little rodents. A wine bottle and a broken crystal glass, a used condom: has my good Thief had himself a party? The remains of a gulag fire, a busted shopping cart. A trough where a body shuddered the naked earth; she could see where his drumming heels had dug deeper at the southern end of the living man's grave.

It will be here, she determined, leaving Avi and Taras to caper while she foraged with the mind of a sniper in the surrounding hills and bushes. She found the only spot that allowed a view that would please a hook-nose. She called the boys and sent Avi to the shop's van to bring a shovel. While Avi dug a coffin-sized hole, Taras ogled Dagg's body; she tilted herself to his pleasure. The confused Avi, pleased at having a chore, dug without question.

At the shop, waiting for the big-headed one to return with the olden man, Dagg telephoned the hungering Jew prick who drove the limousine. He'd demanded payment in swag for calling Razinkin with the intelligence that Bone would be located within a day and would be available for piping.

Now she spoke in enticements, her gypsy charm stirring his greedy desire. He assented and demanded his payment early for the work later. She agreed and walked in trepidation twenty blocks to his apartment. He surprised her with his demand: that he could call her Ruth, that she whisper his name, Ariel, into his ear as he beseeched her in Hebrew. She did thus and was again surprised when his lovemaking was civilized and courtly, with soft murmurings and much stroking of her shot tresses. He gazed past her in the bed throughout their encounter; afterward she turned her head and realized he'd been staring at a silver-framed photograph of himself as a much younger man standing beside a young woman under a wide tree. The woman had premature silver veins in her thick black hair and a heart-shaped girl's face not unlike her own, although life hadn't been scrubbed from it.

Later, he treated her as a lady, both of them dressed, drinking white wine and eating little cookies on a couch, listening to piano music that played in the air as soft as butterflies. For an hour she listened to the story of his Ruth, of a Palestinian outrage, of activity that struck a stake through the heart. He had the pig face, she'd always thought, of a prison guard; behind that face was a broken heart, unfixable.

She instructed him as he looked at her with tired, tormented eyes.

"The blemish Razinkin will be ruthless if this fails," the old Jew told her. "I require perhaps more than this one visit to compensate for the danger."

She looked upon him as a friend. "How many?"

"One day of the month," he said, nodding his head at the bedroom behind. "But not for that, in there. I thought that you as you are would make me as I was, and we would become as we were. But it wasn't so. One day a month you come and we'll sit here and listen to music. I require only to look."

Dagg nodded and arose. She skirted the coffee table and kissed his cheek. "How many diamonds have I stepped upon believing they were glass beads?"

There were flights daily to Phoenix, many of them, an array of choice, seating, and price that confused Alexsandr Solonik. He could, he discovered, purchase a ticket at the last minute, as long as cost was no object, which it wasn't, and from Phoenix take a shuttle to the holy site of Tucson. He was between calls and sanding idly at his fingertip when Razinkin called.

"I have heard from a friend. Tomorrow at dawn. Are you able, my friend, to reconnoiter today, before darkness?"

"Yes, yes. This is certain?"

"He sleeps in a forest like a sick old bear, awaiting you. In the dark tonight he will return there to make his bed. At first light you will play your music and I will arrive to take my proof."

"I cannot wait, after. I must be away."

"The car with the same driver will take you today for an examination, and tomorrow will await nearby for your bidding." Razinkin sounded positively ebullient. "Your payment will be with the driver. He is trustworthy. A bitter old Jew cocksucker who has no love except for money."

At midnight Bone kissed all and whispered poems. The detritus of a Thieves' party was scattered about: broken bottles, platters of chewed-upon food, some of the inside projected out with velocity. Avi and Taras and Jam and Little Novak had been medallioned by the drunken, vomiting Cabbage: beer-bottle caps had been aligned upside down on a tabletop and Cabbage had smashed each of their heads down, leaving blood-encrusted decorations in the centers of their foreheads. Cabbage had arm-wrestled the still-powerful Novak and lost, even when he used both hands; Jam had shown complex Japanese finger locks needed for survival when you were the smallest policeman in Moscow. Dagg had been the mother, sitting placidly off to the side as her doomed icon sat at his chrome chair observing all with pleasure, beaming upon his tribe. For his brigade the day had been both interesting and profitable, all at the expense of the pig's entrails Razinkin. There had been robberies of shops under his protection, a needlessly violent holdup of security guards at a shopping plaza, the extorting of prostitutes who were used thoroughly and creatively and told to suck upon the tiny soft root of Razinkin for their payment. An attempt had been made to penetrate the overseas trading office, but Jam and Little Novak were rebuffed by a security squad: they settled for vandalizing the cars in the underground garage, setting several ablaze. They went by the ruins of Ricci's club, but two carloads of his cheese boys were parked in the lot alongside and they left, looking for mischief to undertake before returning to the shop.

An hour before midnight, Dagg and Bone had vanished upstairs to the back room of the shop, where a window ledge served as a bed. Dagg had her forehead against the cool glass, trying to find stars or a moon to witness her. Even backward she was urgent and desperate. Bone kissed at her neck for nourishment. His fingers felt her skin aglow as his hands prowled beneath the sundress of purples and golds and read the markings around her nipples. If I live through this week, he thought, I will send her on up to await me. Surely in heaven a Thief could have a lady. Surely, after all, God is a wild Thief at heart.

In the basement of the shop, as they returned, Cabbage was nursing a broken finger. The boys were on their hands and knees banging their beer caps against each other like young bulls. Jam had Little Novak in a one-handed jujitsu hold and was demanding a kiss upon his ass from the steroid whore.

It was important, Bone knew, that all events were believed to be directed by him. Slowly Thieves would come under the sway of his Code, the more so as the vampire Razinkin lost his grip upon the city. Already there was a buzz that, from his secret den, the glorious Bone was waging war, wrestling the *mir* back to its former glory, and had repelled a battalion of torpedoes from New York. When a man cannot be found, a legend must lead. He knew it wasn't enough that Razinkin kill him; it was the very idea of Bone that would have to be eradicated.

Piping powerful bullets across vast spaces, imagining the rotation of the bullet, the piercing of the still air with the sound of detonation traveling in hastening waves in its wake, and watching blossoms of red appear where a millisecond before there was none — this was the joy and magic of the secret sniper. Once, in Latvia, he'd met a NATO bomber who had drunkenly and seriously said he didn't bomb *people*, he bombed *down*. If Solonik shot off, for example, a nose for sport, it was a nose that wasn't a real nose: it was a nose in a round picture window split by one verticle hair and one horizontal hair. He'd had his sport, no doubt, fun and games with gasoline or wood alcohol, and he'd heard the screams and watched the amusing dances of fatal confusion that ensued, but that wasn't the sniper's business, it was the soldier's. For Solonik the true violence wasn't the sniping — sniping was the end of the violence.

He thought of those happy, successful times as he moved through the darkness on the rim of a rise above the olden one's earthen bed, cautiously following the steps he'd made the night before, in light, as the greedy, mean Jew awaited in his white limousine. He'd determined where noise of transit was possible and took pains to prepare a silent path. There would be a moon, he'd determined, and its glow would be helpful; however, he had no trust in the promised lack of clouds, and as a sniper assumed he would be operating in darkness. Stones and small rocks were securely placed to allow him to feel his way with his feet if needed. He'd computed the degree of slope and, even with the puny rifle supplied by the Jew, believed he could successfully insert bullets in the manner demanded by Razinkin. The rifle fired .22 caliber bullets from a clip, and a second clip had been delivered by the grumpy Jew this morning on the ride across the city. He had no silencer but made do with a bulky device made from electrical tape, a hotel hand towel, and a roll of toilet paper. It would suffice for a half-dozen shots, and, if necessary, he could retape a second towel over the end of the rifle's barrel. He didn't question the demands of the client Razinkin, but wished to finish quickly and looked forward to worshipping at the shrine of the greatest hook-nose of all, Mr. Joseph Bananas. How great it would be, he thought, if this legend has heard of me, of another hook-nose afoot in the *mir*. I shall offer my services; surely so great a man has many, many enemies to be piped away?

As dawn hesitated its bluish way between the trees to the east, he made out the old *vor* lying in his trench, wrapped in a coat or blanket. The white soles on Bone's running shoes faced the sniper's post, and Solonik thought of firing the first nasty little bee past the running shoes and up the leg into the groin, a ringing of the old man's rusty bells to awaken the placid shape and get him into a motion of agony, to present more tasty targets.

Below, Bone shifted in his sleep, rotating his body to evade the cold and dampness emanating from the earth. He rearranged the coat and appeared to be speaking to himself.

There, Solonik thought, the precious hip, the cup of nerves and pain and, for me, the observance of frolic. Hunching his torso over the mechanicals of the gun to mask the sound, he quietly slid the bolt of the rifle.

Bone shifted again, then sat up, looking about.

Oh, those old man's ears, Solonik thought, sighting the desirous cup of the hip in his amateur's scope.

At the distance, Bone didn't recognize the nose; the rise around his grave was a bluish haze. He did recognize danger, his Thief's instinct alighting his nerves and processing data into conclusions. Above him, partly screened by a bush, a hunchback and a long stick with a white bulb on the end. The hunchback was a darker shape than the blue dawn, but lighter than the greenery. But even as alit as Bone's nerves were, his old man's body contained creaking muscles and joints, dull coldness in his bones. He moved, but his motions were slow, far too slow for what was to come to him.

Betrayal, he thought. One has led this one to me. Sacrificed, and by my gypsy bitch, one I should have sent on up, the better to prepare for me a bed and a hot meal when I arise. Her urgencies the night before were on a plane above even the most passionate of their other nights; it felt like a final goodbye, a kiss to remember. It was her code, her survival, and even the power of his own Code must fall before it.

He smiled and was in the midst of beginning a laugh when the hunchback straightened and fired a puff of blue smoke — he no longer hunchbacked but instead a frozen rock of a man, elbows down, concentrating.

And up there on the rise, at the feet of that rock man, the bush and the ground in front of him erupted in an explosion.

The ground, Bone thought in wonder and sudden pain, it just erupted up and a white demon from the middle of earth was embracing that rock man.

When the shape materialized in front of him, Alexsandr Solonik was instantly confused. Not by the naked, soiled shape, which was womanly and toothy and had wide eyes and a rag of black hair streaked with pewter, but by the sheer *immediacy* of it, right there in front of him. There was disorientation in the scope, an out-of-focus mass of fluid grays and blacks, and the old man sitting staring up was gone. He knew he'd fired — he could inhale the burning powders — and knew he'd struck.

Solonik's head jerked back from the scope — this intrusion had occurred many times before; for example, when a target at two hundred yards was interrupted by a cow passing the line of fire, perhaps fifty yards out — but now his throat was full of shock too thick for him to swallow.

She's kissing me, he thought, this black-haired woman of Palermo, shorter than me, nibbling and gnawing up at the skin of my throat and chest. The sounds were the same here as at the Hotel Dante; snarling love and wet urgency to completion. I thought then she was hurrying me to permit a new beginning of it all, of her joy, but truly I knew she was making me squirt so she could demand payment again. No matter: the Circle has stuffed my bank accounts, so let the little whore play her game. I would have her a hundred times, each time demanding more: the mouth, the ass, blood and bruises, the tying with neckties, the baying of a dog at my feet. Invite in the barman, invite in the deskman, invite in the moronic boy who carries bags up the coffin-shaped elevator.

But how did this one find me, from the Hotel Dante? Is she too going to Arizona, U.S.A., to meet the man of fine nose, Mr. Bananas?

The rifle was gone, spun away. Solonik's arms went around her, responding to this sudden love. Holding the woman, cuddling him in her desire, the top of her head where the hair was soft against his clenched, ugly teeth. Ah, this rough joy, he thought as he fell back onto the ground. Where did you come from, *cara mia*? And, God Jesus, this erection, sucking the blood from my body, such a swelling: it weakens me with its purple need.

Dagg, filthy with soil from her trench, raised her face. She knew that that which needed to be opened was opened, that that which was meant to flow, flowed. Such a handsome man inside those blue eyes, she thought. But that ratchet of a mouth, that curse of a nose. He looks at the wet red mask of my cheekbones and mouth and wonders. Look, the confusion in his eyes. I know you, she said, blond guard; barbed wire, your happy dog, your spittle, and your scorn. O Fairie, you said, be a Fairie and dance on the head of my pin. And all the pins I can bring to you.

This now that is in your pants, Dagg thought, feeling his erection recede against her. This now in your pants is all you take with you, pale man, bleaching white. Do you love me now? Have you a smile now for me, a smile and a piece of bread to eat from your dog's bowl? Let your heart beat it out of you. Sleep and dream of these red teeth, smiling, this body of the earth, warming.

Inside the mansion they set upon Razinkin with a fury of joy and loud humor he vaguely remembered from his own efforts as a young Tomahawk.

It was well before dawn, and he'd packed a toothy saw and green garbage bags, had taken some blue ice packs from the freezer, and located and filled a sturdy liquor carton with newspapers. He'd asked the slim Swiss to purchase plastic gloves the night before but couldn't find them; he would drive himself to the park and had no need to awaken the Swiss. Fine, he thought. Without the gloves I will then feel the wet essence. It isn't, he smiled to himself, as though I haven't washed my hands with the insides.

In just minutes the hook-nose will have eliminated the cold Bone — perhaps he lay dead already, his perfectly criminal face still and his pointed ears being gnawed by small carnivores, suckling at the inside now out.

Jam and Little Novak, now with strange metal symbols

hammered into their foreheads, were suddenly in the kitchen. That they'd had a few bodyguards on their way in was apparent: they were laughing and their long boning knives were already wet and red. I hope they've killed my Swiss, Razinkin thought. He was stealing the silverware and selling it, I know, in the rag-and-bone shops.

Did I expect other? Truly at heart I'm still a Thief, he wanted to say, although in these past years that feel like mere moments I've strayed, but I've returned now to the Code, like a lapsed Catholic who finds his true God on the bed of his death. How could I be bedazzled by all that is gold, all that is sweet, all that, ultimately, is transient? Did I need a wife, did I need children? Did I need, or even want, this pink ice-cream mansion, larger, it seems, than the entire village where a whore shit me out alive?

He tried to say the oath of the Code — "O Brothers, I . . ." — not to save his life, but to make a redemption. But they stabbed him so much and so often he became bored waiting for death. The throat, you fools, he commanded silently, is this a game? Of course not, of course not. He watched his essence splash onto their faces, onto their clothing, onto the clothing he'd paid for. Not as fine as my own, but my own aren't stopping those plunging blades, no matter how much I paid the tailor or the shirt maker. I wish I could bring this back to the city of spires, to the Circle, this sudden knowledge. To convince them that the Code lives in the air, not in the blood of men. That finery and wealth is like steam from a tea kettle: there, then gone. But it's the heat under the kettle that endures, not the steam or the kettle itself. As does the heat of that old Code.

He was able to say to these, his sweet brothers: "Agh, agh . . ." And Little Novak, with his single eyebrow wriggling like a curiosity, laughed above him and made buggy eyes and mocked him — "Agh agh agh" — and the littlest policeman in Moscow stabbed him in his eyes, careful not to break the skin of his forehead or cheeks, then began the process of slowly killing him.

Epilogue

Cabbage sat out the evening with Dagg, waiting for her to speak, to instruct or inform. Throughout the day they'd sat across the room from each other, watching programs on the television set.

That morning, when she'd returned from her mission, Cabbage had heard the limousine door click shut, heard voices, and heard the car creep up the alley, away. At the rear door he'd carefully peeked out; clearly she was naked under a woolen blanket. Blood and earth matted in her hair and stained the smooth flesh above her breasts. Her eyes, he noted with an urge to thrust, were those of a horse in a storm he'd seen as a boy and never forgotten, its hooves skidding in the frozen rutted mud of a treeless plain — inside its broken balance, he'd had at its throat and quickly learned the art of butchery.

As had that horse's, Dagg's chest heaved. She had, he noted, the breasts of a girl, even with the dreadful scarring and burns. She passed him with an erect glowing pride that dazzled him, beckoning at his heart. Shortly after, water ran through the pipes in the basement. He descended and saw thick steam leaking out from under the bathroom door. After, she'd emerged naked and pink and folded herself into the duvet, seeming, Cabbage thought, to inhale its fibers and weaves into her body. Throughout the day she was asleep or awake; the only difference was that her eyes were open or shut; there was no motion. Taras and Avi arrived from a day of mischief; Avi wanted to sit the day at her feet. Cabbage ordered them to his stash house to count money and watch television.

At the end of day, Cabbage made a broth, feeling like a man with a noble purpose, and silently urged her to drink.

Now she spoke. "He is gone."

Cabbage, who had known this in his heart, nodded. "Bless a Thief." He waited.

She told him of the adventure. How in the middle of the night she had driven the boys to the park, arriving before Bone, and how the boys had loosely buried her body in the most likely place for a sniper to pipe, how only her face was aboveground, covered by a loose bush. How she waited hours for the sound of a piper's approach and his breathing and then the snick of the flute's mechanics. How she'd been too late, that a single note was played and she arose cramped into a cloud of burning blue air and feasted, too late, but a feast as vengeful as that of an insect nonetheless.

She told him the corpse had been made to vanish, but she wouldn't even whisper to him how or to where. "Because he must live, eh?"

Cabbage looked at her. "Live?"

"In legends. That this hook-nose missed and was defeated and now the olden one directs and commands from secret, followers will follow, adventures will be had, the Code will burn and live."

"And Razinkin?" He recalled Jam and Little Novak slipping out in the night, laughing and tapping their medallions. "Has he been gotten?"

"Oh, yes." She smiled. "Yes."

Dmitri Razinkin's head made its way, in a diplomatic bag of the Russian embassy in Ottawa, to the Kremlin, and, undisturbed in a ball of tinfoil, cotton, and clear plastic, was delivered by chauffeured car to a dacha north of Moscow where the head of Bone was expected to arrive, although through the service of the United Nations. When the *vor* Wrecker opened it, he stared at the shriveling head of old Tomahawk and sighed. Then he laughed and turned to his companion *vor*, an unblooded young man whose claim to fame was his willingness to please his betters. "Oh-ho. Interesting times indeed." He handed the young man the head, watching for his reaction; there was none. The horrors of the *mir* had frozen the man's emotions and nothing rattled his calm except, perhaps, finding the vodka supply diminishing.

"And," the young man said, "of the hook-nose?"

"For certain: dead," Wrecker told him. "It is said he was set upon by a wolf and eaten, so perhaps that." Wrecker then spoke to the bodyless Tomahawk. "It was, it seems, as you said, my friend. A land of wolves and savages and an altogether dangerous *mir*."

"And now?"

"Now?" Wrecker mused. "Now that the cold old one lives, we must root out a ghost, eh?"

Dyed, the old bass recognized how the worm had been threaded onto the hook, how it squirmed in the cold water ahead under a sheath of the thinnest ice. None else shopped here in his waters; above the crust of ice, a pale face floated like a shimmering silver moon. The face was placid and still and perhaps even happy, although that might have been a rippling distortion. He took the worm and hook in a muscular flexing rush; quickly he was going up and was out of the water. He made a smart sharp twist in the air, for form, really, showing off — and then was caught. There were murmuring sounds and perhaps a smile; warm hands and a brief holding underwater to reacclimatize. Then: freedom, and like a good Thief, he took the worm away with him.

Fishless, the woman, wearing a short leather coat with a fur collar, a flowered sundress over thick black woolen leggings and scuffed brown ankle boots, gathered her rod and tackle box, following her own footsteps through a dusting of snow up an almost invisible path toward a cabin with a gray flag of smoke waving thick at the top of a chimney.

Within, the rooms were warm; cabbage softened in a simmering broth. The walls of main room had been covered with sheet insulation and thick clear plastic was tacked over the windows. Outside, a blurry stack of blue insulation waited. Two wooden sawhorses were set up, a piece of plywood across them, a saw upon it, and a ghosting of snow over all.

In the bedroom an old man snored. The woman went in silently, raised the duvet, and lifted a flap of gauze. Ariel the old Jew had ministered him well after driving the shivering one from the park back to his home to await her visit. I cannot, she told Ariel, make payment as promised, the visits would have pleased me. I must vanish now and beg your secrecy. He said: I know of these old ones such as this. He will kill you.

She laughed and said: Yes, but not today.

She examined the purpling hole in his left ribs a few inches below the eight-pointed star that was his compass through life. She blew upon the wound lightly, whispering gypsy words, then covered it with fresh tape and gauze. She tucked him as if a baby and unwrapped his tight fist, removing a silver amulet that was either two bodies and one head, or two heads and one body.

She licked her tongue across the warm amulet, put it under his pillow, and went into the kitchen to sniff her soup.

Author's Note

There is a man very much like Bone and I met him once, briefly, on the cold sidewalk in front of the home of a murder victim. He was a raggy, spare man who stood in tired, worn clothes, muttering incomprehensibly. Like Bone, the man had a washed-out bluebird tattooed on his hand. And like Bone, this man was a charismatic with the look of an aesthete, both characteristics rare enough to make him unforgettable. It was only years later, during an interview with a Russian bandit — the model for Cabbage — that I understood the secret history of raggy, spare old men on cold sidewalks.

There was also a real Alexsandr Solonik, a legendary killer who often targeted *vory v zakone* in the Russian underworld. He was not a sniper in war, as I've presented him, but an ex-policeman who became a mercenary assassin. Because he was found murdered a few years ago in Greece and no longer needs the name, I decided to keep it.

There are Fairies in the underworld, although they're not as organized as I present; many are indeed gypsies and lady Thieves and prostitutes and pickpockets. They live small — almost invisible — criminal lives and, like Dagg, are ferocious, though few are as beautiful. Several years ago, in Sao

Paolo, I spoke to one of these women, and, as in many things in life, once is enough and I had my character.

There are men very much like Dmitri Razinkin. They follow the new reality of profit and maintain a hatred of the old Thieves. Even today, long after the war against the wild Thieves began, the decimation continues.

There was a Bitches War in the gulags in the 1940s in which the Code of the Thieves was altered; thousands — perhaps tens of thousands — died in the bloodshed, and the Thieves who believed in the old Code lost.

Anyone who has visited Palermo knows there's no line of sniper fire, as I describe, onto the Grand Hotel et des Palmes; however, I love the hotel, and when I first visited there in the 1980s while covering the Excellent Cadavers assassinations, I memorized the place, knowing it would be a fine scene for something. The Hotel Dante is based on the Hotel Ponte, where I stayed on a later trip, when money was tight. There indeed was a German shepherd barking through the night in the shipping compound outside the window; I fantasized sniping him.

Some of the dialogue in this book is taken from wiretaps, some from informal talks with people who live in or on the edge of the Russian underworld. The rhythms are a little archaic, a result of criminals learning their English from books.

Although I'd like to take credit for conceiving the events in the book, very few required much use of my imagination. The grounding of the "pig train" — the boat carrying Bone from Kenya to America — is based on the fatal voyage of the *Golden Venture* that grounded near New York City in the 1990s. Razinkin's "plastic bag" method of murder is based on a technique used by a notorious *vor v zakone* from Vladivostok. The theft of the jewelry by Ushki is based on an event that occurred in Toronto. And on and on.

But *The Last Thief* is still a work of fiction. Subtle changes to the tenets of the Thieves' Code and alterations to timelines of actual events were necessary to tailor the characters to the plot and the plot to the characters. Naturally I take any responsibility for inaccuracies beyond those parameters.

* * *

Thanks to Janine White, for the oil painting "The Last Thief"; David Ross for research assistance; Stuart Ross for the crafty editing and strong coffee; and Don Loney. And of course to the crew at ECW Press.

Lee Lamothe
May 2003